M000046054

The

Intercepted

Heart

Lyn Ellenbe
I Cor. 13:7

By Lyn Ellerbe

The Intercepted Heart
Chef Charming
There Will Be Dancing
Love Beyond Repair

The Intercepted Heart

LYN ELLERBE

The Intercepted Heart
by Lyn Ellerbe

Copyright © 2021 Lyn Ellerbe Books

ISBN 978-0-9892464-6-0

Lyn Ellerbe Books
www.facebook.com/lyn.ellerbe

All rights reserved. This book or any portion thereof may not be reproduced or used in any manner whatsoever without the express written permission of the publisher except for the use of brief quotations in a book review.

This is a work of fiction. Names, characters, businesses, places, events and incidents either are the products of the author's imagination or used in a fictitious manner. Any resemblance to actual persons, living or dead, or actual events is purely coincidental.

Dedication

In memory of my wonderful parents

Thanks to my family for their patience as mom fulfills a passion, and to my good friend Kathy for her continuous encouragement. This story was inspired by my love for pro football. It was a love passed on to both my sister and me from our parents. Our mother became a true football fan through sharing the interests of our dad who was the love of her life. My father took me to my first professional football game when I was in college, ensuring that I, too, would become a lifelong fan.

It is my prayer that this story encourages Christian men and women who have perhaps given up hope on finding someone to share in their journey. God is indeed a God of love, and we need to trust Him as He brings people, even unlikely ones, into our lives.

1
The Pregame

Holiday decorations had transformed the gymnasium into a festive dining hall. Delicious aromas greeted the two handsome men as soon as they entered. Sloan Mackenzie was acquainted with most of the partygoers, but his tall, dark-haired companion was not. As expected, heads turned as they recognized the newcomer. He appeared to ignore the attention. Sloan nodded to several people as he led his friend, the local sports star, to an open table.

"Sit." Sloan pushed his friend toward a table close enough to the buffet table for their large appetites but far enough away the kitchen. He didn't want the attractive young woman helping set up the buffet to overhear their conversation.

"So, when do I get to meet the famous Julia Fitzgerald?" Richard Adams settled his tall form into a folding metal chair across the table from Sloan. When the two friends walked into the Monday-after-Thanksgiving party, Rick saw the petite young woman with long light brown curls behind the counter. He knew who she was immediately based on Sloan's description of his childhood friend.

"I know you've been hoping to introduce your two favorite people for weeks. I'm glad the team schedule and your duties at the hospital coincided finally."

Sloan's schedule as anesthesiologist left little time for socializing. This had been frustrating over the last few months since Rick had bought a house on this side of town. The two men had met in college and had remained friends despite having had few chances to see each other over the last few years.

"Well, Julia is definitely a favorite," Sloan said. "Jury is still out on you."

"Ouch!" Rick clutched his chest.

Sloan ignored Rick's theatrics. He knew that people rarely said "no" to Rick Adams. Being the star quarterback of a professional football team meant he usually got his way.

"Like I said, Julia is a good friend of mine."

"And I'm not?" Rick raised an eyebrow.

"Yes, you are, but pursuing her is not a good idea." Sloan tried to find a specific reason that wouldn't sound too harsh. "She's had a rough last couple of years and honestly, I can't see her being a part of your glitzy life."

"My glitzy life, as you call it," Rick pointedly reminded his friend, "is my absolute least favorite part of my job. You may remember that I was complaining about it last night, correct?"

Sloan conceded the point but still hesitated. His college friend could be disarmingly charming when he chose to be, and Sloan didn't want the well-known athlete to play with Julia's affections.

"I guess it's inevitable that you would meet once she moved out here."

Rick drummed his fingers on the table, still waiting for the real reason for Sloan's hesitation. Instead, Sloan leveled his own question.

"Why the sudden interest in dating?"

Rick shrugged. "Just ready, I guess."

Sloan met Rick's steady gaze, then turned toward Julia as she finished setting out the plates and utensils. "I don't think she'd go out with you, anyway."

"Why not?" Rick asked. "Is she already dating someone?"

"No." Sloan was enjoying his friend's discomfort, having recognized the hint of arrogance in Rick's tone. It was a fault he saw in himself, and one that Julia reminded him of regularly. Sloan could also see that the idea that someone would shun his attentions surprised the mighty Rick Adams. The star athlete usually had the opposite problem.

"Well, she can't be married, or she wouldn't be here." The Singles Sunday school class was a good mix of those in their twenties and thirties, along with a few older men and women. Most were career-minded singles who had never been married.

"Not married. Not engaged." Sloan hesitated. "Widowed." As Sloan carefully laid out the situation, Rick glanced at the lady in question.

"Her husband died in a car wreck just over three years ago," Sloan explained. "They'd only been married four years."

"Oh, Lord, why?" Rick's prayerful plea echoed the same question Sloan himself had often asked their Heavenly Father. He glanced at the normally self-assured athlete as he watched Julia in the kitchen. Most people had no idea that the tough quarterback had a soft heart. At college, his closest friends nicknamed him Teddy—short for "Teddy Bear." Of course, few people other than Sloan had enough courage to ever use the term to his face.

"Now you see why I don't want to introduce you," Sloan said. "You will want to hop on your white stallion and save the damsel in distress."

"Maybe she needs saving. Why are you warning me off?"

Sloan and Julia were childhood friends and treated each other more like siblings than anything else. Being single and successful like Rick meant Sloan attracted a lot of unwelcome feminine attention at work and on the social scene. Since she had moved to the area Julia had provided the perfect foil, by attending work parties as his date.

Sloan was already in a committed relationship with Julia's cousin, Jocelyn, a senior at a college a couple of hours away. Sloan kept their relationship extremely quiet, since they were waiting until she graduated in December to announce their engagement. Sloan had shared the information with Rick months ago.

"She's off-limits. Let's leave it at that."

"At least introduce me," Rick said. "There can't be any real harm in that, right? We have you in common, so it's natural that she and I will cross paths. I promise not to push a relationship without your permission. I'm still hesitant about this "dating" thing, anyway, so she should be safe."

"Not very reassuring, Rick. I'm serious. Julia is important to me."

"Understood." Rick leaned back, stretched his legs out, and folded his arms. "At least tell me a little more about her. What if she meets all the qualities on my list?"

Sloan knew exactly where Rick's thoughts were heading. He mirrored his friend's stance. "Remind me again what's on your list." During a campus ministry retreat in college, the speaker encouraged the young men to pray for their future wives. Both Rick and Sloan had taken the suggestions of the speaker seriously. At the time, Rick knew he was on the way to the professional leagues and had listened intently to the minister's admonition to set his values firmly and stick to them. The friends promised to pray for these unknown ladies regularly. Rick hadn't dropped the habit, even ten years later.

During one of the last sessions, the retreat speaker had also suggested making a list of attributes that they would like in a spouse. He did make it clear that God would meet those desires, but not always in the way you expected.

Rick ticked off his list. "Loves God. Loves me." He grinned. "That's the easy one."

"Of course." Sloan shook his head. "Continue, please."

"Smart," Rick continued ticking off his wish list, "likes kids."

"Check and check." Sloan nodded. Rick missed the slight smile on his friend's face.

"Willing to open our home to ministry groups—Bible studies and stuff—and be actively involved in her local church." Rick had memorized the list. "And funny."

"Check, again." Sloan saw the advantage shifting. He realized he'd have to give in and introduce his two friends.

"On everything?" Rick had a hard time concealing his excitement.

"Well, except for the 'Loves me' part," Sloan said. "Don't hold your breath on that one."

"Funny. She puts up with you, right?"

"Touché," Sloan said. "And I wouldn't exactly say she's funny, but she has a wicked sense of humor." Sloan remembered the verbal battles he had witnessed between Julia and her family during holiday gatherings. "Not in the evil sense—more like extremely dry, but quiet. A lot of times no one hears her comments except those of us sitting right next to her." He paused and smiled. "Come to think of it, though, I'd put her up against you in a battle of wits."

"Oh, really?" Rick asked sarcastically, traces of his former habit resurfacing.

Rick was known for his sense of humor, which in high school and the first couple of years of college was quite vicious. He could cut even the most confident person to shreds with his funny but harsh wit. When he had started attending church with Sloan and turned his life around, his tongue was the first thing he had to give over to God.

"I'll take that challenge, thank you very much. Does this mean you'll introduce me?"

"Not yet, brother." Sloan was rapidly losing control of the conversation.

Even if Rick was interested in Julia, Sloan was sure she wouldn't be interested in him. But it was only fair for Rick to have an accurate picture of her situation. Unsure how Rick would take the rest of Julia's story, he bought some time. "You haven't finished your list yet."

"I didn't mention blonde, blue-eyed, tall, and athletic. But those have become less and less important over the years. Oh, and loves, or at least tolerates, football."

"Well…" Sloan hesitated.

"What?!" Rick looked as though his hopes were fading. "She hates football? Please don't tell me she's a soccer fan!"

Sloan laughed at the thought of the famous quarterback falling for a soccer fan. "Her husband James played soccer, but Julia only watches sports, doesn't play them." Sloan glanced at Julia. "And you can't tell from here, since she's behind the table, but Julia is maybe five-two, on her tiptoes."

"Five-two?" Rick turned in his chair to get a better look at Julia. "No problem. She'll be easier to carry over the threshold when we get married."

"Slow down, buddy!" Sloan's raised voice caught Julia's attention. She smiled and waved.

"Let's go." Rick started to stand, seeing that the young lady in question had spotted them.

"Wait!" Sloan pulled him back into the chair. "There's something else you need to know."

Rick tried to drag his gaze from the petite form moving in and out of the kitchen making final preparations for their meal.

Sloan delivered the news. "She has kids."

2
The Draft

"Kids?" Rick whipped back toward Sloan.

"Yes." Sloan watched his friend's reaction. "An active boy who just turned five, and an adorable two-and-a-half-year-old little girl." He watched the ramifications hit Rick as he did the math in his head.

"She was pregnant when he died?" Richard couldn't keep the anguish from his voice.

"Yes, and had a two-year-old at home."

Rick stared unseeing at the cheerful decorations in the middle of the table. "Why?" He repeated his earlier appeal.

"Listen, Teddy. She is doing well, though." Despite his own concerns about Julia, Sloan knew Rick needed reassurance. Otherwise, he would continue to press for details. Details Sloan wasn't ready to give. "She's dealt with those same questions and has grown remarkably strong in her faith. Most people who meet her would say she's amazingly joyful and content."

"'Joyful'? 'Content'?" Rick's frown proof he doubted Sloan's assessment.

"Yes," his friend explained. "She'll tell you that God's love has continued to fill in all those places that felt like gaping holes when James died."

The two men fell silent, both so lost in their thoughts that they didn't hear Julia's approach.

"Wow, you two look serious." She sank into a chair next to Sloan, pinching him playfully. "Solving the world's problems?"

"Something like that, imp." Sloan hugged her. He knew he'd have to grant Rick's wish for an introduction.

"I'm sure you recognize this big lug." Sloan pointed to Rick, who had pinned a warm smile to his handsome face. Sloan knew him well enough to see the lingering concern.

"Rick Adams." The quarterback reached across the table to shake Julia's hand. His huge paw seemed to swallow the delicate one he now held.

"Nice to meet you, Rick. I'm glad you were able to join us tonight. I know you two have been friends for a long time"— Julia patted the quarterback's hand— "I'm so sorry. How did you two meet?" The humor Sloan mentioned was peeking out.

"College fraternity," Rick said. "I lost a bet."

"Hey!" Sloan protested. "No ganging up on the poor helpless soul here!"

"Poor? Helpless?" Rick and Julia's synchronized retort drew looks from the nearby table.

"That's it! I'm outta here." Sloan abandoned the table for the now-open buffet.

"After you." Rick held Julia's chair and they followed Sloan to the sumptuous array of food laid out for the party guests.

They returned to their seats with their plates, both men's dishes spilling over, Julia's helping a more reasonable size. While Sloan was getting their drinks, Rick used the time to get to know Julia.

"So how do you know—or should I say tolerate—Sloan?" he asked. "We should share strategies. I know I could use all the help I can get."

"We grew up together," she said. "Our parents are best friends. They're so close that most people thought we were related. He and his family always attended our family reunions and holidays. That's how he met…" She stopped mid-sentence.

"Jocelyn?" Rick caught the slip.

9

"You know?" She looked around making sure no one was listening. Most of the members of their church group thought Sloan and Julia were a couple, a misconception neither made any effort to dissuade. "Keep his secret, okay?"

"Will do." Rick let the matter drop as Sloan returned to the table.

"So, Julia, tell me what Sloan was like as a kid." Rick downed a deviled egg in two bites."

"Do you want the good, the bad, or the goofy?" Julia asked.

Sloan groaned.

"Oh, the goofy, definitely." Rick rubbed his hands in delighted anticipation.

"Sorry." Julia sighed. "That would take too long."

"What did I do to earn this abuse?" Sloan pretended to be offended. "I could tell some stories about you, young lady, so you better behave!"

"You wouldn't dare." Julia wagged her fork at him.

"Watch me." Sloan raised his fork back, meeting her challenge.

Rick cleared his throat, reminding his companions of his presence.

"Oh, and you," Sloan said, eyeing Rick. "I'm sure you don't want me to tell about that time you got locked out of the dorm."

"You wouldn't dare!" Rick said, echoing Julia's previous admonition. Sloan turned to Julia, ready to tell the embarrassing tale, Rick threw up his hands. "Uncle!"

The trio's laughter caught the attention of several more in the room. Julia was new to the group but already had made many friends. They were happy to see the young widow having a good time.

After dinner, the emcee invited the diners to share their favorite Thanksgiving, Christmas, and other holiday memories. The funny stories were interspersed with poignant memories.

Their Sunday school teacher ended the evening with a gentle reminder to be thankful for God's love, and to remember those less fortunate. He went on to explain he didn't only mean those materially less fortunate. He encouraged them to look for opportunities to show God's love to the hurting people that needed emotional healing, the lonely people that needed social interaction, and those simply seeking answers to the tough questions of life.

After Julia batted her dark blue eyes and sweet-talked Sloan and Rick into helping with the kitchen cleanup, they walked her to her car.

"Ask her," Rick insisted as they walked behind her.

"Julia…" Sloan's voice held a touch of reluctance, "Rick wants us to go to his party next weekend."

"Party?" Julia turned to face her two handsome escorts. Sloan knew she accompanied him to parties solely out of her commitment to their friendship. She wasn't particularly comfortable meeting new people, and she definitely didn't like being the center of attention. He knew this would be the case at the party.

"Please," Rick said. "Since making the playoffs seems to be a distinct possibility, this may be my only week off. It'll extend the season, which would normally be ending around Christmas."

"I know." Julia's incredulous tone let Sloan knew she was a little offended that Rick thought she didn't understand the ins and outs of the football season. She didn't know that Sloan had earlier implied she wasn't a fan.

"Have mercy on me, please," Rick said. His appeal appeared genuine. "I don't ever get to socialize with anyone but the lugs I work with."

"I don't know if Terry is free." Julia said. Terry Hampton, Julia's neighbor and on-call babysitter, lived with her aunt and uncle while finishing her graduate degree in education. She stayed with the kids whenever Julia needed her and was more a family member than a babysitter.

Sloan was surprised that Julia seemed to be considering the party. He'd have to think through the implications. Surely, she hadn't fallen under Rick's charm in one evening.

"We'll let you know, Rick." Sloan opened her door, effectively blocking Rick's access to her.

"Nice to meet you, Julia." Rick leaned around Sloan. "Hope to see you next weekend." Realizing Sloan wanted to talk to Julia alone, he moved away.

"You don't have to go if you don't want," Sloan told Julia. "I know it's way out of your comfort zone."

"Maybe so." Julia shrugged. "But he's right. You guys are friends, and you haven't gotten to spend much time with him this season. You've wasted a lot of time taking care of me and the kids."

"Well, it helps that he moved to this side of town." Sloan admitted. "At least we're going to the same church now."

"Tell you what," Julia said. "If Terry's free, I'll go with you, but you have to promise we won't stay late."

"Deal."

3
The Play Clock

Sloan's phone rang, as he expected, early Tuesday morning.

"Hello, Rick," the sleepy doctor answered without even checking the caller identification. "How are you this early morning?" Rick didn't know that after the party, Sloan had been called in to the emergency room. He had been out until almost four in the morning. He looked at the clock on his nightstand; it read five till eight.

"Am I that transparent?"

"Yes," Sloan answered grumpily. "Are you on the way to practice?"

"No, sitting in the parking lot," Rick said. "I've got ten minutes. Give me everything you've got." The quarterback had been reviewing film for a couple hours and had returned to his car to call Sloan.

Still irritated from lack of sleep, but sympathetic to his friend's plight, Sloan teased, "About what?"

"C'mon, Sloan," Rick said. "Please. Tell me about Julia and the kids." Sloan sat up and rubbed his face to gain some lucidity. The great Richard Adams almost never begged.

It would be difficult to communicate everything he knew and loved about Julia Fitzgerald and her kids in a short time, so he wanted to be fully awake. He'd have to be careful, also, to not reveal too much.

"Are you sure you want all the gory details this early in the morning?" Sloan knew Julia's story would be tough for Rick to hear, surprised by Rick's insistence.

"Nine minutes and counting, Sloan."

"Okay, but if none of this makes any sense, it's your fault for calling before most sane people are awake."

Sloan spent the next few minutes giving Rick an abbreviated version of Julia Pearson Fitzgerald's recent biography. He explained that having grown up as neighbors, with parents that were good friends, he and Julia were closer than many siblings. Sloan introduced her to her late husband. James who was a graduate engineering student at the university where Sloan got his medical degree.

"I met James on an intramural soccer team," Sloan said. He knew the emphasis wouldn't be lost on Rick.

"I'll ignore that dig, thank you very much," Rick muttered.

"Julia was at the undergrad school, majoring in education. She and James got married in between her junior and senior year. Their firstborn, Curtis James, or C.J., arrived a year after graduation. They moved several hours away from family when James got a job at a large engineering firm." Sloan paused. "But you could call that both a blessing and a trial,"

"What do you mean?"

"They missed being close to Julia's parents," Sloan took a deep breath, knowing it would be difficult to keep the bitterness out of his voice. "His parents, not so much."

"What? Did they not have a good relationship with his family?" Sloan heard the concern in Rick's voice. Both men had grown up in families that were free of 'in-law' difficulties. He also knew Rick remembered that the retreat speaker in college had emphasized the importance of family support in a relationship.

"James grew up with money," Sloan explained. "Lots of it. When he chose not to take over the family business, his parents were not pleased. Add that to falling in love with a girl from a middle-class family and you have a perfect recipe for getting cut off from the mighty Fitzgerald family."

"They cut him off because of Julia?" Sloan could almost picture Rick saddling the white horse as Julia's plight unfolded.

"Yes, although they did go to the wedding," Sloan said. "For show, mostly. Then when he died, they blamed Julia."

"What?"

"Yeah, like she had anything to do with it." Sloan made no effort to hide his true feelings for James's parents.

"So, they don't have any contact with the kids?"

"As far as I know, they set up some sort of college fund, but I'm not sure Julia will ever touch it. James' death devastated her, and although her parents were supportive, they were hours away."

Sloan was privy to the issues Julia had to face after James died. Not sure how much he should share, he continued carefully.

"She had to handle all the financial responsibilities and decisions, along with dealing with the children. His parents could have easily helped her, but they chose instead to spend a year of mourning on a European vacation."

"They sound like splendid people," Rick said, his voice dripping with sarcasm. "I've only got a couple minutes, Sloan, so give me the important parts for now. How did she end up here?"

"Well, like I told you last night, when James died, Julia was six months pregnant with a little girl. When Elizabeth Ann, now nicknamed 'Bethany', made her appearance..." Sloan hesitated at this point in his story, obviously hiding something.

"Hey, wake up!" Rick voice snapped Sloan back to present day. "Finish the story."

"Okay, okay." Sloan continued, thankful that the unhappy story had been interrupted with a happy memory. Sloan filled in the gaps.

By the time Bethany arrived, Sloan had already accepted his current position, but hadn't moved yet. A year or so after James's death, Sloan started suggesting that Julia and the kids move out this way. The job market here matched her unconventional teaching style, and it put her closer to her parents, who live a couple hours away. She and the kids moved early last summer.

"Sloan, I've got to go. The rest of the team is heading into the locker room. But I'd like to talk more about Julia before my party, if that's okay."

"Listen, Rick," Sloan warned his friend. Concerns Julia's parents had raised resurfaced. "Be careful. As much as I love you, friend, Julia and the kids are my priority, you understand?"

"I understand," Rick said quietly.

Two days later, Sloan stood at the kitchen sink, washing dishes after his weekly dinner with Julia and the kids. He had waited until after their meal to bring up his concerns.

"Julia, are you sure you still want to go?" Sloan asked her as dried the dishes from their dinner at her house later that night. "I'm glad you're willing to go out of your comfort zone, but I don't want you to feel pressured."

"No, really," Julia said. "I don't know why, but I feel fine about going. Not that I want to meet a bunch of new people, but I know Rick is a good friend of yours. Besides, it's not like I'm going to fall in love with him." She shuddered playfully. "He's definitely not my type."

"Do you mean if I find somebody that *is* your type, you'll think about going out with him?"

Thinking about the call he had received from her parents last week, he broached an issue she continued to avoid. They wanted their daughter to get out and around some eligible, godly men, and prayed that God would start changing her mind.

"Don't go there, Sloan." Julia placed the last of the plates in the cabinet and turned to face him, arms crossed. "I am not looking for a relationship and won't be for a long time. If ever."

"I'll let this go for now, but it's time," Sloan said, "and you know it."

"Whatever," she said, throwing a dishtowel at him.

"I'll pick you up at five on Friday." Sloan gave her a quick hug and called good night to the kids.

On his way home, Sloan shook his head when he thought of the irony of Rick's interest so close on the heels of her parents' concerns. Julia wouldn't see the humor in the situation, though.

We'll see how this goes, he thought as he drove to Rick's house that weekend, a festive and relaxed Julia next to him. She actually seemed to be looking forward to tonight. *This might turn out better than expected.*

4
Team Spirit

"Sloan! Julia!" Rick greeted them at the door. He had seen Sloan's sports car pull in the long driveway.

He took their coats and opened the closet. Sloan reached around him and grabbed two hangers. Julia laughed as the two men tried to delicately hang up her wool coat. It was an expensive brand, if not quite fashionable. Only Terry knew its marvelous thrift store price.

Still smiling at their antics when Rick turned back to her, Julia saw a smirk break across his face as he glanced up. Following his line of sight, she saw the sprig of mistletoe.

"Milady?" He took her hand. She would later wonder at her own response as Rick hesitated. Her nod was encouraging, but he chose to make sure. "Rules are rules?" She nodded again.

He bent and kissed her lightly on the lips.

"Wow," Rick said. Too stunned to move, Julia saw surprise in his gray blue eyes.

"Let's meet the crew." Sloan grabbed her hand. He had missed the whole interchange while he found room for their coats in the closet.

Rick's closest friends included some of his fellow teammates and their wives. They were all scattered around the comfortably furnished living room. They were playing a rowdy game of charades, apparently. It was hard to tell between the friendly insults and crazy guesses.

"We'll heat up the grill in about an hour," Rick explained to the two after he introduced everyone. "Stephen won't be here until later."

Stephen Schmidt was the placekicker for the Wolves. Many would be surprised to find the young man in the inner circle of Rick's friends. Kickers weren't given a lot of respect by some fans, and they even had a rough time in some of the league's locker rooms. Rick had liked the Stephen immediately and brought him into his group, acting as mentor and friend.

"Will he be alone?" Garrett Stahl, an offensive lineman, asked. His wife elbowed him. "Sorry," he muttered.

Julia saw the look on Rick's face and guessed correctly that he wouldn't answer Garrett's puzzling question.

The party guests made room on the sectional for the two newcomers, but before they could navigate the path to their spots, Sloan's phone rang.

"Sorry," he apologized, "it's work." Julia followed him into the hallway.

When she heard him say, "On my way." Julia headed to the closet to get their coats. *It must be a huge emergency,* she thought. She knew he wasn't on call tonight.

"Here are my keys," Sloan said to Rick as she appeared with their coats. "The hospital has already ordered a taxi for me." Rick turned to her and relieved her of Sloan's leather jacket.

"Keep us posted, okay?" Rick handed Sloan his coat. Julia stood speechless as Sloan closed the door on his way out. Rick took her coat and reopened the closet.

"Going somewhere?" He replaced her coat on its original hanger.

"Home?"

"No," Rick stated simply. "Doctor's orders."

"But I don't know anybody here." She reached for the closet door.

"You know me," he said, "and it's my house, so everyone will be nice to you." Grabbing her hand, he pulled her back into the living room. "They're all scared of me, you know."

"Hilarious." She tugged her hand free. At least his playfulness made her feel a little better.

Rick squeezed her between Garrett and Monica Stahl. The linebacker was as tall as Rick but outweighed him by close to a hundred pounds. Monica was only slightly taller than Julia, and ironically, that brought comfort to the reluctant guest.

Charades was one of Julia's favorite party games, although she wasn't naturally competitive. It usually made her teammates mad when she felt sorry for the opposing team, and started helping them, too. By the end of several rounds, Julia found herself joining in the antics of the close-knit group.

During Rick's next turn, he attempted to act out some unrecognizable movie title, gesturing wildly, and hopping around like a madman. As a quarterback, one of the frequent criticisms he received was a lack of agility. For some reason, Julia felt comfortable enough with her new acquaintances that she let her wit accidently slip out.

"Wow! Who knew he could move like that? Certainly no one watching him on Sunday," she said to Monica. Unfortunately, the commotion had died down, so the comment reached the ears of everyone in the room.

Julia looked around at the shocked faces. Finally, Tyson Michaels, the oldest lineman and one of the few willing to stand up to Rick, started chuckling. Within seconds, everyone, except for Rick, was rolling with laughter.

"Wow!" Ezekiel "Zeke" Burns, the center, said. "Rick, you've finally met your match!"

Julia panicked as she saw the anger on Rick's face, not sure it was phony, although she had also seen the involuntary grin when her words had first registered. Garrett also saw the look on and acted quickly.

"You'd better get out of here pronto, little lady." He stood and lifted her over the back of the leather sectional so she could make her escape.

"But I don't know where I'm going!" Julia scrambled, slipping in her stocking feet on the tile floor. One downside of wearing slip-ons meant her shoes had fallen off as Garrett lifted her over the back of the couch.

"Run!" Monica said, pointing down the hall.

As if to disprove Julia's original point, Rick leapt over the large, square designer coffee table. Excusing himself, he stepped between Monica and Garrett and over the back of the couch, close on Julia's heels.

Laughter followed them down the hall. Julia desperately searched for an open door but suddenly found herself in midair. Rick caught up to her in short order and slung her over his shoulder. With one hand, he opened the closest door, and a laughing Julia found herself unceremoniously plopped onto a stool that flanked a tall game table.

As she looked around, she saw they were in a small but well-stocked library. She remembered vaguely reading that Rick had majored in English Communications, which would explain the floor-to-ceiling bookshelves.

"So," Rick said, his arms folded as he stood in front of her. "I don't move so well, huh?"

"I'm simply repeating what I had heard." Julia avoided his gaze. She wasn't sure if he really was mad or was pretending. When she finally braved a glance up at him, he was staring at her.

"Your eyes," she said. "Did you know..."

"Yes, I know," he interrupted her.

"Oh. Sorry."

Rick hung his head. "No, I'm sorry. I shouldn't have interrupted you. Continue, please. Tell me about my eyes."

"No, that's okay. Obviously, it's something you already know and don't want to hear again."

"Actually," he said, tugging one of Julia's long curls, "I'd like to hear you say it. For some reason, I think it will mean more coming from you."

"You are impossible. You know exactly what I was going to say."

"Ah, but maybe you have new insights," he said, answering her smile with another tug on her hair. "Sorry for the pun."

"Your eyes appear to change color depending on what you're wearing," she said, leaning back from his playful touch. "There. See? Exactly what I'm sure hundreds of other," she hesitated and saw one of his eyebrows rise slightly, "people have observed."

"Yup. You ought to see them when I wear my red plaid jacket," Rick said, as he ran a finger down her jaw. "I was right. It did sound different when you said it. Different from all the other people, or at least from all the other women."

"The many, many women, I'm sure."

"Jealous?"

"Absolutely not," Julia said.

"I'm glad you decided to come tonight," he said. "We'll have to do some damage control for Sloan's reputation, though."

"What do you mean?" she asked as she hopped off the stool and began to explore the library.

"I heard a couple of the guys comment that they couldn't believe someone would abandon a date like that," Rick explained. "I know Sloan well, and that the call meant a real emergency, or he wouldn't have left. It may take both of us to make them understand, though."

"Sloan was not my date. You know that." Julia turned back to face Rick, who had followed her across the room.

"Yes, I know all about Jocelyn, but I'm still curious about your relationship with Sloan."

"It's not so unusual." Julia made her way around the room, Rick following closely behind her. "He gets so much unwanted attention that I often attend his work-related social events to help him out. It gets me out of the house, and it provides him with a buffer."

Not knowing how much of her story Sloan had told Rick, she didn't divulge that she wouldn't have made it through the weeks and months following the death of her husband without Sloan's support. Now he provided her children with much-needed male bonding time. They called him 'Uncle Sloan' and considered him their personal jungle gym.

"Gotcha." Rick said, reaching around her to re-shelve a book that had been sitting on a side table.

"I know Sloan implied I'm a bit of a hermit, but that's not completely true. The main reason I agreed to come tonight, though, is that he's like a brother to me and I know your friendship is important to him." She wandered to another section of the library, looking at the eclectic mix of book selections.

"I'm glad you decided to stay," Rick joined her in front of a shelf full of framed photographs.

"Not that I had any choice," Julia grumbled.

"True," Rick said. "Are you ready to get back to the crazies? If we're away any longer, I'll never live it down in the locker room tomorrow."

Julia attempted to cover her blush by turning toward the array of family photographs. As Rick approached and stopped behind her, she gasped.

"Oh my." She held a picture of two young children. One was a blond-hair, blue-eyed boy.

"What's wrong?" Rick reached around her and took the picture from her hand. "That tow-headed young man is me. It took me several years to achieve the striking dark color I have now. I think I was three and a half in that picture. The cute one next to me is my sister Miriam."

Julia remained silent.

"Are you okay?" He took the picture from her hand and set it back down on the table. He turned her to face him and took her hands in his. "You look like you've seen a ghost."

She stared at him, in a daze.

"You look like my son, C.J."

5
The Huddle

The phone rang, breaking the stunned silence. One of the team members wisely grabbed the phone, not wanting to interrupt whatever might be happening in the library.

"It's Stephen, Rick," Zeke called down the hall. When Rick stuck his head out of the library door, the center tossed him the phone.

"Hey, man." Rick's voice showing he had recovered sufficiently from Julia's pronouncement to resume his hosting duties. "Yeah, we could use some ice, if you don't mind. The ice maker decided to go on strike this afternoon."

Rick paused as Stephen responded and then apparently delivered some not-so-good news, if his clenched fist was any indication.

"Thanks for the warning, buddy. I owe you."

"Are you okay?" It was Julia's turn to be concerned.

"Yup," Rick said, as he grabbed her hand and ushered her back into the living room. The nervous fingers run through his hair convinced her he was hiding something. "We'll talk later, okay?" She nodded, happy to pretend as if nothing had happened.

"Stephen's bringing ice," Rick announced.

Instead of dropping into his favorite chair, which had been strategically vacated by the unidentified trespasser, Rick moved to the large fish tank at the end of the room. The fish responded to the familiar presence as he ran his finger along the glass.

"Melissa's with him."

Groans came from every corner of the room. Julia had resumed her previous spot and looked to Garrett and his wife for clarification. Monica offered the explanation.

"Melissa is Stephen's cousin who thinks she's going to be the one to finally 'catch' Rick."

"Oh." Julia frowned slightly. "Obviously, she's not a favorite, I see. Rick looks like a hunted fugitive." Monica and Garrett laughed at Julia's astute observation.

"She's an ambitious, selfish, money-grabbing—" Garrett began.

"Honey, watch your language," Monica said. "She's not the nicest person in the world and we don't think she has Rick's best interest at heart. Personally, I think she needs someone who can get her to see that looks and money are not what bring happiness."

Julia thought Monica's last statement was ironic, especially coming from the wife of a highly-paid professional football player, but she let it go. Her life experiences had tainted her view of the wealthy, to a depth that few people even knew. This evening was beginning to show her that these people, even with their wealth, were still just people.

What she didn't know was that the four couples sitting here were unusual. All of them had come to realize that the money and fame were fleeting. They worked hard at their marriages, knowing that this phase of their lives would pass soon, and they needed firm foundations for the long haul. These characteristics were what drew them to Rick. He shared the same values.

"It's a shame you don't have a real girlfriend to show her," Evan Roberts, the second-string safety, said. "I know Melissa never believed those false press reports."

Julia remembered vaguely having heard reports about Rick and a secret girlfriend. Her questioning look brought an explanation from Evan.

"His publicist invented a fake girlfriend to keep all the lovely ladies away," he said. "Too bad she couldn't be here tonight. Not sure how many more times Melissa will believe she is 'out of town' or 'not real keen on crowds.'" These were Rick's normal excuses for the fictional young lady's absence.

Julia noticed that Rick was ignoring their conversation. She didn't see the looks passing over her head between Garrett and Monica. Ezekiel and his wife Carolyn joined the secret looks. Monica glanced at her husband in silent communication, and Garrett shrugged his reluctant approval.

"Julia could pretend to be her," Monica said, mentally crossing her fingers as she made her suggestion.

Unfortunately, the lady in question had just taken a drink of her diet soda and almost choked. Garrett pounded her back as gently as he could manage.

"No!" Rick's voice cut across the room as he turned back toward the group. "I will not allow Julia to *pretend* to be my girlfriend!"

"Dude, calm down!" Zeke popped up off the couch and pulled the irate team captain out of the room. Julia was afraid the harshness of the linebacker's command would anger Rick, but it had the opposite effect. The relationship between these teammates was fascinating.

Monica quietly filled Julia in on the details after Rick stomped into the kitchen. Melissa had been thrilled when Rick was traded to the expansion team a year ago. She set her sights on the famous bachelor, convinced she'd be the one to get him to the altar. Stephen did all he could to keep his money-hungry, fame-seeking cousin away from his new mentor, but Melissa played the family card cunningly.

"She's tried several times to trap him alone in a compromising situation. The fake girlfriend was Rick's last hope," Monica concluded.

"He looked worried," Julia said quietly to Monica. "I don't want to lie to Melissa, but I'm willing to help."

"Are you sure?" Monica asked excitedly. At Julia's nod, she turned to Garrett. "Get Rick and meet us in the library."

Garrett pushed Rick into the library as Julia settled into the stool she had recently vacated. The quarterback leaned against the table, arms folded.

"We don't have much time," Garrett and Monica explained to Julia. "They'll be here in ten minutes. You two need to decide if this is going to happen or not and what we need to do to back you up."

"I'm not thrilled with lying to Melissa, but I see you guys are desperate." Julia turned to Rick who was glaring at Garrett and Monica. "I'm the one that's agreed to do this. My one condition is that no one else adds to the lie."

"What do you mean?" Monica asked.

"If she asks for details about me, tell her that you just met me tonight, and leave it at that. No other details. Don't make up anything to fill in the blanks. Deal?"

The couple agreed and returned to explain the plan to the others, leaving Rick and Julia alone.

"Why are you doing this?" Rick pulled the stool around to face him. "Sloan is not going to be happy that I've dragged you into this charade."

"Sloan is not the boss of me," Julia said.

"You sound like a pouting five-year-old," Rick brushed a curl off her shoulder. "Does C.J. throw that one out a lot?"

"No, Sloan does."

Rick laughed but crossed his arms again. "I'm still not sure I'm going to agree to this." Julia ventured a light touch on his forearm. She felt him tense.

"I had a friend like Melissa in high school." Julia thought back ten years to her friend Candice. "She was gorgeous, at least on the outside. She had a domineering mother and emotionally absent father. She went from boyfriend to boyfriend trying to find love."

"That's supposed to make me feel better about involving you in this?"

"Hold on, let me finish." Julia held up a hand. "She was in a bad car wreck our senior year. Although she had to spend a couple months away from school, the only visual reminder of the wreck was a small scar on the side of her face. It was hardly noticeable, but it devastated her."

"Again, this is not making me feel any better." Rick had left her side and wandered around the room, stopping in front of the picture that had caused Julia's shock earlier.

"There was a boy at school that had always seen past her exterior, even past the harshness of her personality and he liked her despite her faults. He visited her almost daily in the hospital and at home during her rehab, and he stuck by her when she returned to school. Having someone that accepted her and loved her for who she was on the inside made all the difference. She was a different person."

"And you're hoping Melissa can find that?" He rejoined her, leaning one arm on the high game tabletop behind her.

"Yes, eventually," Julia said. Changing the tone of their conference, she playfully punched him in the arm. "But for now, I want to protect you from her. You look terrified!"

"Ow!" He rubbed his arm. "Terrified, huh? You should be the one terrified." He paused once again. "You don't have to do this, you know."

"You've said that already." Julia said. "So, what's our plan?"

"I have no idea!" Rick paced back and forth in front of Julia. "We need to convince her somehow that we are a couple. Short of her catching us in a passionate embrace, I'm clueless." He stopped in front of her once again.

"As fun as that sounds," Julia said as she patted his cheek, "I think if we overdo it, we won't be believable."

"'As fun as that sounds,' huh?" Rick grabbed her hand and lifted it to his lips.

"I do have one other condition," Julia said, ignoring Rick's comment as she pulled her hand away. "I want the freedom to tell Melissa the truth—even tonight—if I need to."

"Deal," Rick said.

Carolyn appeared at the door. "They're here," she said, then disappeared back down the hallway.

Julia took a deep breath, ready to face the lioness.

"Thank you, Julia." He pulled her into a quick hug, precisely as they heard Melissa's voice floating down the hall.

"Where's my boy?" Melissa trilled.

"In the library, but…" Garrett's voice ended abruptly as Monica stomped on his foot.

"I'll go let him know I'm here!"

Rick's expression was pure panic. Julia took his face in both of her hands.

"It will be okay, I promise," she whispered.

Without thinking, he leaned toward her and kissed her tenderly on the lips. At least the kiss started out tender, but a spark flared immediately. Rick slid his arms around her waist.

"What are you doing?!" Melissa's screech caused the couple to jump apart guiltily. Their genuine embarrassment lent validity to their pretense. No acting was required to convince Melissa that she had interrupted an intimate scene.

"Melissa!" Rick kept an arm safely around Julia's waist as he introduced her.

"Julia, this is Stephen's cousin, Melissa." Julia recognized the mischievous hint in his smile. She realized he was greeting his nemesis from a position of confidence for the first time.

"Melissa, this is Julia." Rick kissed his newly acquired girlfriend soundly on the cheek.

"Stop it, sweetie! You'll embarrass Melissa." Julia pushed against his chest, hoping the added endearment would drive him crazy. He didn't seem like a "honey," "sweetie," or "honey bunches" type of guy.

Turning to the attractive redhead, Julia added, "You'll have to forgive Rick. It's like this is the first time we've been alone for a long time." *Technically not a lie,* she thought.

Rick's chortle earned him an elbow in the ribs. The motion was playful enough to fit right into the act. Melissa frowned.

"So, you're the secret girlfriend." Melissa grilled Julia as they sat in the kitchen several minutes later. Monica had suggested Julia ask Melissa to help get the food ready. Thankfully, Monica was there, too, since Julia had no idea where anything was in the kitchen.

"Yes, I guess you could put it that way." Julia chose her words carefully.

"How did you guys meet?" Melissa asked, continuing the interrogation.

"A college friend of Rick's introduced us."

31

Trying to turn the conversation away from the perilous ground of the subterfuge, Julia decided to start her work on Melissa.

"So, Melissa, tell me about yourself," Julia said. "I'm anxious to get to know all of Rick's friends."

"Oh, I'm nothing special." Melissa's tone indicating she felt exactly the opposite. "I've done a little modeling here and there, but I'm hoping to find that Prince Charming to set me up in his castle."

"A castle would be nice, but a cozy home would be nice, too, I think. Some castles can be cold and overwhelming—from what I've heard," Julia said casually. Melissa's false smile was proof that Julia's comment had hit its mark. "I'd rather have a cozy cottage with someone who loved me. But that's just me."

"You don't want nice things? How quaint of you." Melissa's tone had moved from being arrogant to patronizing. "I'm sure that's easy enough to say when you're with Rick Adams."

She's not wrong, thought Julia. *I need to keep focused on the purpose of this covert operation, but this is going to be more difficult than I expected.*

Rick came in from turning on the grill in time to hear Julia's response.

"Nice things are nice," Julia admitted, "but I'd rather have someone who loved me for me. I'm sure most men want someone who loves them for who they are, not what they have, where they live, or what they drive."

I wonder if tonight is too soon to propose, thought Rick.

6
The Relationship Coach

The burgers were ready, and the ensuing dinner was entertaining. The easy camaraderie meant that much of the time Julia forgot she was supposed to be acting. Rick stuck close to her side, only leaving her when Monica was with her. Julia saw the likable, easy-going friend that Sloan had described. She felt safe enough here to continue teasing him as she did during the charades game. Hopefully her dry wit and quick comebacks didn't offend him. Not that it mattered in the long run.

Rick was thoroughly enjoying himself. Thankful that Sloan had warned him of her "wicked" humor, he was able to give back as good as she gave. They were enjoying themselves so much, they didn't see that their behavior was being promoted by the rest of the team, and their wives, of course.

"She's perfect," Evan's wife Corina said to Monica and Carolyn as they watched Rick and Julia. "We need to make sure she doesn't disappear after this whole pseudo relationship is over."

Melissa had been very patient, or at least as patient as she could be. Finally, she cornered Julia on the deck as she brought in the last of the utensils to be cleaned. The tall aspiring model blocked Julia's way.

"I think you're a fraud," she said.

"What do you mean?" Julia's confidence waned suddenly. She had been enjoying herself so much that she had lost sight of the goal of the evening. She had wanted to protect Rick, but her main goal had been to reach out to this miserable young woman. She realized she had failed.

Lord, please help me here. I'm sorry I ignored Melissa for the last hour. Please give me an opening to reach out to her, she prayed quickly.

"I've been listening carefully, and I don't think you and Rick are a couple at all." Melissa's defiantly folded arms matched her accusatory tone. "Did he pay you?"

"No, he didn't pay me." Julia battled her own anger, trying to feel sympathy for this unlikable woman. "But you're right, we're not dating."

"I knew it!" Melissa exclaimed.

"To be honest, your pursuit of him was unwanted and I offered to help," Julia's calm words were not soothing Melissa. "My plan was to convince you that pursuing a man for his money and position is not healthy. It will only buy you unhappiness."

"Oh, so you're Miss Relationship Expert now, are you?" Melissa's voice rose with every word. Both Rick and Stephen heard the confrontation. Rick was the first to reach them. He quickly put his arm around Julia's waist, partly in comfort, and partly to restrain her. The clenched teeth and tense petite form let him know that Melissa had made her mad.

"I'm sorry, Melissa, for lying to you," he said, trying to stop the onslaught. "But Julia's right. Men don't like to be pursued so deliberately. I thought I had dropped plenty of hints, but you seemed relentless."

"You're saying you'd prefer someone like this?" She pointed insultingly toward Julia. "A mousy little doormat that waits on you, hand and foot, satisfied with living on a song and a prayer?!"

"You'd better watch what you say." Rick's fury was barely under control. "I think it would be best if you leave. And in case you really want the truth, the answer is, yes, I'd much prefer someone like Julia. Any day."

"I've called a cab for you, Melissa." Stephen pulled his cousin through the kitchen, already holding her coat. "I'll wait outside with you until it gets here."

"Julia." Rick reached for her hand as she pulled away from him.

"I need some air. Alone, please." She moved out to the deck. It was cold and windy that night, but the breeze felt good on her flushed face.

Well, Lord, I blew that one. Please let my words and actions not harden Melissa's heart even more. I know you can take even my feeble attempts and make them fruitful.

As she stood overlooking the subtly lit landscape, her thoughts shifted to her own heart. *What was I thinking, pretending to be Rick Adams's girlfriend? How ludicrous is that? This will be something to tell my grandkids.*

The longer she stood, the more she realized how wrong this was. From her vantage point on the deck, she saw Rick join Stephen and Melissa as they waited for the taxi. It looked like Rick was trying to apologize but wasn't having much luck. As she heard the cab pull in, she walked back to the kitchen.

She saw Sloan's keys on the counter where Rick had tossed them, and she grabbed them and slipped them into her pocket. She circled around, avoiding Stephen and Rick as they rejoined the others in the living room. Moving as quickly as she could, she quietly took her coat from the closet and slipped out the front door. Halfway across the driveway, she heard the front door slam. Walking faster but knowing that she couldn't outrun him, she moved steadily toward Sloan's sports car.

"Where do you think you're going?" Rick called after her. "Did you honestly think you were going to escape that easily?"

She ignored him and fumbled the keys, trying to get Sloan's car unlocked. Shaking hands and tears of frustration made the task impossible. Rick reached around her and took the keys from her hands.

"I'll drive," he stated simply. "Give me a second to explain to the crew." He led her around the car and placed her in the passenger seat. He returned a few minutes later as the garage door opened and Stephen backed Rick's truck out.

"Stephen will follow us and bring me back home." Rick started the car. As they pulled out of the driveway, Rick reached for her hand. She shook her head.

"I'm sorry, Julia," Rick said. "I should have never let you take on that responsibility. I need to fight my own battles." He held out his palm in a silent plea. She quietly placed her hand in his.

"I'm sad I couldn't get through to her." Julia's sadness was evident in her voice.

"I know." Rick rubbed her palm gently. "You tried, though."

Julia pulled her hand away, folding her arms against the guilt she was feeling. She felt strangely worse without the contact, but she knew she needed to distance herself from Rick.

"So, are you going to give me your address, or are we going to wander around the city all night?" Rick asked. "Not that I mind using up Sloan's gas. Consider it payback for abandoning you at our little party tonight."

She couldn't help but laugh, although it was barely audible.

"It should be in Sloan's fancy car here." She reached over and pulled up her address on the in-dash system. Sloan hadn't wanted to get such a fancy car, but the hospital insisted he have a navigation system for emergencies. Despite being one of the youngest, he was among the best anesthesiologists in the region, specializing in trauma situations.

When the address came up on the computer, he saw that she lived about twenty minutes away. That was a lot of time to fill, especially with the obstinate passenger next to him.

"Rick," Julia said, breaking the silence, her voice barely above a whisper. "How much did Sloan tell you?"

Rick reached over and gently grasped her hand once more. He felt her resist slightly, but he didn't allow her to pull away this time.

"Pretty much everything, Julia," he said quietly, not trusting himself to look at her, even though they were stopped at a light. "I'm so sorry you had to go through such tragedy."

"Thank you," she responded, her voice still barely audible. She had draped his arm across her lap and his breath caught as she leaned against it. Her quiet sigh filled the silence.

Dear Father, Rick prayed, *if this whole evening is Your design to bring this lady into my life, please help me not mess it up! Even though I just met her, I am so drawn to Julia that I can no longer imagine her not being part of my life. Please make my path clear. I don't want to go where You are not with me.*

7

Team Security

Julia's townhouse was in a gated community. James had insisted on taking out a life insurance policy right after he was hired at the engineering firm. The money allowed Julia to purchase the home, and the interest gave her a small monthly check. With that, and her part-time teaching job, she and the kids were doing okay, although their budget was tight.

As they pulled up to the gate, Rick rolled his window down. Julia leaned over to greet her good friend, Malcolm. The older African American man considered himself Julia's substitute father-protector. He of course recognized the driver but ignored him to lean out of the gatehouse and greet the young lady he considered a spiritual daughter.

"Miss Julia," Malcolm said, "how was your evening?"

"Eventful." Julia replied, somehow comforted that Rick was being treated to Malcolm's scrutiny.

"Young man," Malcolm finally acknowledged Rick. "My name is Malcolm Humphries. I consider Julia part of my family. You will in no way treat her as anything less than a lady. Is that understood?"

"Yes, sir," Rick answered automatically.

Julia hid a grin in response to Rick's noticeable terror.

"Malcolm, there's a truck behind us with another young man," she said, explaining Stephen's presence so he wouldn't have to suffer through a similar interrogation. "He'll be taking Mr. Adams home. Dr. Sloan had to respond to an emergency but left his car for me. Mr. Adams wouldn't let me drive home alone."

"Very good." Malcolm pressed the button to raise the safety gate.

Rick hoped the "very good" was directed at him. Seeking this older man's approval quickly moved to the top of his list, right behind the approval of Julia's kids.

"Will the kids still be awake?" Rick asked. "I want to meet them."

"Oh, yes." she said. "It's Friday night. We have quite a routine, including an extra late bedtime."

"Wait a second," Rick said as they pulled into the parking space Julia indicated. He leaned across her and motioned to Stephen. The younger man obediently came to Julia's side of the car.

"Go on in and let Julia's friend Terry know that we will be there in a minute." Julia had called her friend when they left Rick's house, so Terry knew Stephen and Rick would be bringing her home.

"Will do, boss," Stephen responded automatically. He started to turn away but stopped. "Julia, I'm sorry about tonight. I've about given up on Melissa and her antics."

"It's okay, Stephen." She patted his arm reassuringly. "It will work out, I promise." She watched him walk up the sidewalk to her townhouse apartment.

"Terry's going to flip out." She suddenly thought of her friend's reaction to the disarmingly handsome placekicker.

"Really?" Rick leaned to where he could watch Stephen's progress.

"Oh yes," Julia said. "He's gorgeous. We may find her in a puddle at his feet when we get there."

Ignoring the jealousy that her evaluation of Stephen's handsome looks evoked, he pulled her around to face him.

"Julia." He brushed a stray curl back from her face. "I can't begin to explain how badly I feel about how tonight turned out. Will you ever be able to forgive me?"

"It wasn't your fault, Rick," Julia said quietly. "I volunteered and I'm the one that messed it up. Maybe God will give me an opportunity to reach out to Melissa again. I hope some of what we said to her tonight got through. She'll be a miserable lady if she continues to rely on her looks and doesn't adjust her priorities."

"You're amazing." He pulled her into a hug. "Here you are concerned about the well-being of someone who said some incredibly ugly things to you. How do you do it?"

She dismissed his question with a shrug as he released her. She started to open the door, but he stopped her once again.

"Stay put," he ordered. "You'll get me in trouble with Malcolm." He came around and opened her door.

"Very gallant, Sir Richard," she saw him make sure Malcolm was watching his chivalry. She even let him casually hold her hand as they walked to the door of her townhouse.

"Mommy, Mommy, Mommy!" The cries as her son marched around them were infectious. Rick grabbed her two-year-old angel, Bethany, in response to the outstretched arms. *She never goes to anyone but Terry or me!* Julia stared as her sleepy daughter settle into Rick's arms, gently patting his cheek as she snuggled into his neck.

I'm in big trouble, Rick thought. He realized he was now under the spell of two delightful ladies.

"C.J. and Bethany, this is Mr. Adams." Julia made the introductions. "He's a friend of Uncle Sloan's."

"You can call me Uncle Rick." Rick knelt down and shook C.J.'s hand formally.

"Unka Rick," Bethany murmured, "and Stephen!" She pointed sleepily toward the young man watching the interplay from Terry's side.

"Okay, kiddos. Time for bed." Julia reached for Bethany.

"But it's Friday, Mommy!" her son reminded her.

"I haven't forgotten." Julia leaned down and whispered to her son. "Let's wait until our guests leave, okay?"

"But Bethany is almost asleep," C.J. pointed out. "She'll miss it."

"Miss what, may I ask?" Rick shifted the angel in his arms.

Terry and Stephen watched the showdown between Rick and Julia. It was clear that Julia wanted them to leave, but Rick was holding his ground.

Julia's husband had started a Friday night tradition when C.J. was about one. They would end their special Friday evenings with a routine that included crazy dancing, jumping on the bed, and loud, but not too loud off-tune singing. They had found it helped release that final energy and assured a quickly sleeping toddler. After his accident, Julia continued the practice. They took turns picking the song, usually a rock classic, although C.J. had gone through a Christmas carol phase last March. Julia was glad when his choice the second week in April wasn't "Jingle Bells."

"It's a silly family thing." Julia hesitated to share this intimate side of her home life. It was one of the few things that kept her connected her to James. She pried Bethany from his arms and turned toward the stairs.

"Thank you both for the escort home." She offered a handshake to each man. "If you two would make sure Terry makes it home safely, I'd appreciate it. Good night."

Julia made her way upstairs without a backward glance. They had been dismissed.

"Yes, Your Highness." Rick raised an eyebrow.

"I'll walk Terry to her apartment," Stephen volunteered and earned a nod from Rick.

"There's fresh coffee in the pot, if you like," Terry said.

"Perfect. Thank you, Terry." Rick knew this young woman played a major role in Julia's life. He pulled Stephen aside while Terry gathered her coat and backpack. Julia had told him Terry was finishing her graduate degree. She had brought her books to study for her final exams.

"Half an hour, Stephen," Rick told him. "You will have me to answer to if you are anything less than a gentleman."

"You too, Rick," Stephen met his team captain's gaze squarely. "And you'll not only have to face me, but also the security guard I saw at the gate, Sloan, and probably the rest of the team if you mess this up!"

Hunting through the cabinets for mugs and spoons, Rick heard the distinct notes of a classic rock hit coming from the bedroom above. Unable to resist, he moved silently upstairs to peek at the trio.

C.J. was jumping on the bed as Julia twirled Bethany around. The little girl's voice was repeating the only words from the song that she knew, "I think I love you," but of course it sounded more like, "I sink I wuv you." Rick liked the new version as much as the old. As the notes of the song trailed off, Julia bounced onto the bed on her back, her daughter giggling in delight. Rick dashed back downstairs.

Julia smelled the coffee as she tucked both kids in for the night. She looked out the window and saw that Rick's truck was still outside. She made her way back downstairs.

"I thought you left." She accepted the cup of hot coffee Rick offered as she entered the kitchen. He took a seat at the dining room table.

"Nope." His one-word answer was accompanied by his pulling out the chair next to his. "Sit," he directed.

"Where are Stephen and Terry?" Julia inquired, her calm words concealing her rapidly drumming heart.

"He walked her home." Rick swirled the drink in his mug, watching Julia intently. Julia took a sip of coffee. She tried to fill the silence.

"Thank you for fixing my coffee."

"Terry told me how you like it." He continued to watch her expressions.

"Thank you for bringing me home, even though you know it wasn't necessary," she continued. *Why is he staring at me?*

"You know we disagree on that point." Rick put down his coffee and took her mug from her hand. He set it down next to his and pulled her chair toward him.

"I'm going to kiss you, Julia," Rick stated plainly. "If you don't want me to, you need to tell me now."

She responded with silence. The brief kiss held tenderness and hope. She sighed.

"Thank you for everything. Rick tilted her chin up and placed quick kisses on each cheek and at the end of her nose.

Rick scooted his chair back and stood up. "I'm going to leave now. I'll talk to you tomorrow."

"Good night, Rick."

"Good night, Julia." He turned as he opened the door, hesitating when he caught the enigmatic expression on Julia's face.

"What's so funny?"

"Just thinking," she said.

"About?"

"Nothing, Rick." Julia bit her lower lip to hide her laughter.

"Oh, no," he said. "That won't work on me. Spill it." He took a step toward her but stopped as she raised her hand.

"It's been more than three years since I've been kissed," she said, "and you've managed to kiss me—quite expertly, I might add—three times in one evening."

"Would you like another?" He took another step closer.

"No, Rick. Go home," she said, and then added with a smile, "but, thank you."

Her words hung in the air as she watched him leave.

Rick and Stephen stopped at the gatehouse as they left. Rick gave Malcolm a business card with his personal phone number.

"Will you call me if you think Julia ever needs anything, Mr. Humphries?" Rick asked the older man.

"What are your intentions in regard to Miss Julia, son?" Malcolm asked. Rick knew he had to convince this man that he had Julia's best interest at heart.

"She is a fascinating young lady, and I'm praying that she'll let me be a part of her life," Rick answered honestly. Malcolm's spiritual insight made him an excellent judge of character.

"I will pray the same," Malcolm promised.

8

The Play Call

"Rick Adams? *The* Rick Adams?" Mr. Pearson's voice conveyed his skepticism.

"Yes." Julia's mother held out the phone. "He wants to talk to you."

"Hello? This is Robert Pearson." Julia's dad covered the phone and turned to his wife. "Gotta be one of the guys from church." He and his friends were known for their playful humor.

"Mr. Pearson." Rick could not believe how nervous he was. "My name is Rick Adams. I'm a friend of Sloan Mackenzie." Sloan had reluctantly given the Pearson's phone number to Rick.

"How is Sloan?" Mr. Pearson played along. He turned to his wife again. "Whoever it is, they're good. He at least has the voice down. It sounds exactly like him!"

"He's fine." Rick could tell Julia's father thought this was some sort of prank. "But I'm actually calling about your daughter, Julia."

"Is everything okay?" Concern crept into the father's voice.

"Yes, she is fine," Rick continued. *More than fine, I'd say.* Rick thought. *Focus, Rick.* "What I'm calling about is that, uh," he hesitated as his nerves gave out again. "I'm hoping to pursue a relationship with Julia. I know she's a grown woman, and has been on her own for several years, but I won't go forward if you have any concerns."

"A relationship?" Robert's voice showed definite confusion now. Rick took a deep breath.

"Yes, sir," Rick said. "Sloan introduced us at a Sunday school party and I was..." Rick deliberated the wording that best suited his feelings, "...captivated."

"Captivated?" Julia's mom heard her husband's responses and saw his look of disbelief.

"I know this is sudden, but I think Sloan will vouch for me." Rick relied on the backing of his good friend. "I know Julia has had a rough couple of years, and frankly I have avoided dating, myself, because of my job. I honestly wasn't looking for a relationship, but, Mr. Pearson, I can't describe it any other way except that I..." Rick's words trailed off. He didn't know how to convince her dad that this was serious.

"You met her at church?" Mr. Pearson's voice relaxed as he decided to show some sympathy.

"Yes, sir." Rick slowly released the breath he had been holding. "I recently moved across town and started attending Sloan's church. Monday night's Sunday school party was the first chance I had to attend anything other than the Saturday evening service."

"How does Julia feel about this?" Mr. Pearson asked. The last time he spoke to his daughter, she was still firmly avoiding any discussion of a relationship.

"Honestly?" Rick asked. "I'm not sure she'd admit it, but I think she likes me, at least a little. I know my friends would tell you that she has a wit to match mine. Although it was at my expense, I must say it was quite comical."

"I can imagine." Mr. Pearson laughed. "These friends, are they solid people? What do they think about this?" The wisdom of age meant Robert knew the importance of a friend's objectivity. He had seen enough people get into relationships against their best friend's advice, and then suffer later for their foolishness.

"They love her." Rick said. "I know they've been concerned about me. I've avoided relationships for so long that they're thrilled to see a godly young lady tolerate my presence without throwing herself at me, wanting my money, or looking to take advantage of my position."

"Have you met Malcolm?" Mr. Pearson knew the gatekeeper well, having vetted the apartment complex and its security before Julia moved in. He and Malcolm spoke regularly, sharing a passion for fishing and Old Testament stories.

"Yes. Mr. Humphries was the first, besides Sloan, of course, to ask what my intentions were." Rick remembered the respect, mixed with a little fear, he felt for the older man. "Julia is fascinating, and I'd like the opportunity to get to know her better. I told him, as I'll tell you, I don't want to take this any further if God is not clearly involved."

"Good answer," Mr. Pearson said.

"I'd like to work my way slowly into her routine," Rick explained, "but my time is limited for the foreseeable future. A teammate plans to ask her to tutor his son a couple times a week and he suggested that I join them for dinner on those evenings. Would that be acceptable?"

"That sounds fairly safe." Mr. Pearson said. "I appreciate your caution, but I reserve the right to interfere if I get the sense from Julia that she's uncomfortable with your attentions."

"I would want nothing less," Rick assured him.

"Honestly, we're thrilled that she is considering getting out again," Julia's father confessed.

"I'd appreciate your prayers, too," Rick added.

"Of course," Mr. Pearson promised. "Thank you for calling, son. Give my grandkids a kiss for me."

"I will," Rick said. "Thank you."

Robert stared at the phone before placing it on the counter.

"Well?" she asked.

"Rick Adams asked for permission to court Julia. Eerily similar conversation to one I had with James. several years ago."

"Oh my," Joyce Pearson said.

9
A Most Eligible Player

On Sunday morning, Julia and Terry were running late for the early morning worship service. They slipped into the back pew, and Julia settled her son next to Sloan. Terry was holding Bethany so the little girl could see over the crowd as the opening hymn was ending.

As the pastor finished welcoming the congregation, he introduced the short time of greeting. Julia turned toward the couple sitting on the other side of Sloan. They were new to the area, and their son Trenton was C.J.'s age.

"I'll show you where their children's church classroom is when they dismiss the kids," Julia offered.

As she turned back, Julia saw Terry handing an eager Bethany into the arms of Rick Adams. He winked at the little girl's stunned mom.

"What are you doing here?" she whispered. Rick and the other team members that were part of the church normally came to the Saturday evening service. They had no game today, which meant he was free to attend this morning.

"Thank you for your warm welcome to worship," he teased her. She felt the warmth creep across her cheeks.

"Are you stalking me?" One slender eyebrow rose.

"And if I was?" Rick gulped. *She's adorable.* Rick forced his attention back to the front of the sanctuary as the worship leader began the next song. *Focus, Rick,* he told himself.

As they shared a hymnal, he bounced Bethany to the beat of the modern praise piece. Their church combined traditional and more modern worship styles in the early service. Saturday evening was a contemporary worship service, and the later service that morning would be more traditional.

Julia reached for her daughter as the announcement came for children's church. Rick shook his head and moved out of the pew, indicating he would follow her. Julia waited for the new little boy and his mother. C.J. had already pointed out the direction, and the two boys were hurrying ahead.

"Thank you, Julia. It looks like he will be fine." The young mom returned to the sanctuary as Rick followed Julia to the two-year-old class.

The church had quite a few famous members, and the leadership made a point of creating a safe atmosphere at the church. The pastor and elders strove to make it a place where these fellow members of the Father's family felt safe and free of harassment.

Still, the sight of the very eligible pro-football player delivering Julia Fitzgerald's daughter raised a few eyebrows. The older nursery worker gave a strong warning look to the young worker whose eyes had widened at the sight of Rick with Julia.

As they walked back to the sanctuary, he placed a hand lightly on the small of her back, more as a protective gesture than anything else. She jumped. Rick laughed.

"If you're going to jump every time I touch you, this is going to be an interesting courtship," he said as they moved into the pew. She scooted as far from him as possible. He responded with a raised eyebrow and crooked grin.

Sloan caught Rick's eye when Julia bent to retrieve her Bible from her large handbag. He gave Rick a thumbs-up sign. They had talked for over an hour yesterday morning. Rick wanted to get Sloan's take on all that had happened after he left the party.

"You should write a screenplay," Sloan had told him after hearing the story of the Melissa fiasco. "Sorry I missed it!" Julia hadn't been in when Rick called on Saturday as promised. "Either that, or she screened my call," he had lamented to Sloan who had refused to give Rick the number to Julia's cell phone. What Rick would later learn was that she and the kids had been on a long walk when he called. With her phone left at home, it was an excuse to avoid Rick's call.

As the sermon started, Rick turned his full attention to the message. Julia stared. The change from his earlier playfulness was surreal.

After the service, Rick waited as Julia gathered the kids. He didn't want to push his luck in offering to get them on his own. He saw her heading to the parking lot, avoiding him completely, and trotted after her.

"Running away?" he asked as he easily caught up.

"No." She didn't slow her pace toward her car, but her son dropped her hand and ran to hug Rick's leg.

"Don't believe you." He swung C.J. onto his back. The five-year-old was thrilled with his new, and very high, vantage point.

"Be careful," she cautioned, not really frightened since James had routinely done the same thing. Watching him with her son brought a painful longing.

"I need to get home," she stated curtly, turning her attention to getting the kids into the car. Two children and all their paraphernalia made even the simplest of trips an adventure.

"No chance you'd go to lunch with me?" Rick asked, knowing what the answer would be. She was obviously anxious to get away from him.

"No, Rick." She confirmed his fear. "It was nice seeing you. Good luck at practice this week. We'll be rooting for you next weekend."

He was being dismissed again. *She obviously does not know how stubborn I can be.* Rick leaned down and whispered in her ear.

"This isn't over, missy." He placed a quick kiss on top of her head, away from prying eyes.

10

Assistant Coaches

On Monday morning Rick called after practice, knowing her class she'd be home already. Julia taught math at a charter high school that employed both certified and non-certified teachers for many subjects. Like her, some teachers only taught one or two classes. This year Julia was teaching algebra and geometry. The situation was ideal since her kids were able to attend a preschool next door.

"Hey," he said as she answered on the second ring.

"Hey," she answered without thinking. "How was practice?"

"Brutal. I'm too old for this."

"Yes, you're ancient."

"How was your class?" He struggled to find a topic to keep her on the phone. There were hours and hours' worth of conversations he wanted to have with her, but right now, his mind was blank.

"Brutal." She mimicked his words. "I'm too young for this."

"Too young?" he asked. "What do you mean?"

"My methods are not what the older teachers at the school expect," she explained. "I get lots of weird looks when teachers walk by and my algebra students are all laughing."

"You're probably their favorite teacher," Rick said.

"Whatever." She brushed off his compliment. "Did you need something?"

"Just wanted to hear your voice," Rick started to say but caught himself in time. Instead, he chose the less honest, "Just checking in."

"Okay." She tried not to laugh at him. "I'm fine, you're fine, and the kids are fine. Is that good?"

"Yup. Can I call you tomorrow?"

"Will the conversation be as scintillating?"

"Promise."

"Looking forward to it," she said. "I think."

She groaned as she hung up the phone. *What is it about this man that brings out the silliness in me?* Julia thought. "What is he doing to me?" she asked aloud.

"Who, Mommy?" C.J. asked.

"Uncle Rick," she responded automatically.

"I like Unka Rick!" Bethany bounced around the room. "Unka Rick! Unka Rick!" she sang.

Julia's brow furrowed. *I am fighting an uphill battle*, she thought.

Tuesday had been uneventful despite the inner battle she had been fighting all day. Rick hadn't called today, and she was disappointed. That disappointment led to frustration. Julia was not willing to admit why not hearing from him annoyed her. The ringing phone interrupted another session of contemplation.

"Julia? This is Monica." The friendly voice came through the phone. Julia's

"Hey, Monica." Julia's day brightened. "What's up?"

"Garrett heard through the grapevine that you were a math teacher," the lineman's wife explained. "Is that true?"

"Yes," Julia said. "Not a popular career choice, I know, but I enjoy it."

"Do you do private tutoring?" Monica asked, explaining why she asked. "Our twelve-year-old, Gary, is struggling with the latest concepts and we're at a loss. Would you be interested in meeting with him a couple times a week?"

"Sure," Julia offered without thinking. "When would you like me to start?"

"Tonight, if possible," the preteen's mom said hesitantly. "He has a test tomorrow and I got a call from his teacher today. She is concerned because he didn't do well on the practice test this morning."

"No problem. Do you want to bring him here, or would he be more comfortable at home?"

"Would it be possible for you to come here? I have to take his sister to dance class, but he usually stays home and watches his younger brother. Would four o'clock be okay? I know it's short notice, but you could bring the kids and stay for dinner."

"Sounds fun." Julia said honestly. She had enjoyed her time with the couples. Spending time with Monica and Garrett, away from Rick, would be nice.

At three thirty, Julia and the kids were on the road. She had asked Monica to send her an e-mail with the specific topics the test would cover, so she could bring some extra practice worksheets.

The kids were excited. Julia realized that her children didn't get to see other kids outside of church and preschool.

Monica and Garrett's house was smaller than Rick's, but it was still located in an exclusive neighborhood. Her observant son noticed.

"Wow, that house looks like a castle," C.J. remarked as they passed a Tudor-style mansion. "Maybe they have a dragon in the basement!"

"Dwagon!" Bethany parroted her brother.

"You guys are silly." Julia laughed.

Monica and her youngest son, Lucas, greeted them at the door. The eight-year-old seemed quite excited to have company, even if it included a two-year-old girl. Monica was on her way out the door to drop off Crystal, her budding ballerina. Before they left, their hostess introduced the boys to C.J. and Bethany and settled them into the toy-filled playroom. She had put up all the toys that had small parts, not knowing if Bethany would try to put things in her mouth. Julia had thanked her for her foresight.

"Why didn't my teacher say it like that?" Young Gary Stahl asked after Julia explained a tricky concept. "That makes so much sense."

Gary was a bright young man, but his new teacher was experimenting with some techniques picked up at a summer seminar. The methods were confusing some of the students. Normally at the top of his class, the thought of not getting an "A" on every test concerned the preteen.

"Don't forget that teachers are people, too," his new tutor gently reminded him. "She has a lot of students, and each one of you may understand a concept in a different way. At least she cares enough about you to make sure you got help before the test."

"Yeah," the young man reluctantly admitted. "I guess you're right."

"So, are we good here?" Julia stacked her papers up and slipped them into her bag.

"Thanks, Miss Julia." The polite young man carried her bag to the front door. "Can I go play with the kids now?"

"Sure," Julia said, releasing her newest pupil. "If it's all right with your mom." Monica had returned from dropping his sister at dance class.

"One of the other dance moms will bring Crystal home," Monica explained as Julia helped get dinner ready. "I hope spaghetti is fine. Garrett is ravenous after practice, and it's one of his favorites. They should be here soon."

Julia assumed that 'they' meant Garrett and his daughter. As the door to the garage opened minutes later, she realized her mistake. Rick had come home with Garrett. Julia missed the wink between Monica and her husband.

"Hello, Mrs. Fitzgerald." Rick pretended to be surprised she was here. Acting wasn't his field of expertise.

"Hello, Mr. Adams," she responded in kind, trying to hide the effect he had on her. "Are you here for math tutoring?"

"No, for the food," Rick said, settling at the counter next to her, reaching for celery and a knife to help her with the salad. "Are the kids here?"

"No, I left them at home," she replied. "I hope they'll be okay. I think C.J. has about figured out how to use the microwave, but not sure about the can opener."

"Very funny." Rick waved a stalk of celery under her nose. "Are they in the playroom?"

"Yes." She waved a carrot under his chin. "I'm sure Bethany will let you play with the dolls she brought if you ask nicely."

"Can't wait!" Rick finished the celery, dumped it into the salad bowl, and headed for the playroom.

Monica and Garrett stared at the young woman.

"What?" she asked, catching their gaping expressions.

"No one," Garrett explained, shaking his head in amazement, "and I mean no one, gets away with talking to Richard Adams like that. How do you do it?"

Julia's puzzled look made the couple laugh.

"You two are so cute," Garrett muttered as he went to greet his kids.

"What on earth does he mean?" Julia asked.

"It's fun seeing someone able to give Rick a run for his money," Monica told her. "Rick looks like a different man than he did even two weeks ago. The only thing that has changed is you."

"Me?"

"Yes, you."

"But—" Julia started to protest.

Monica sat in the chair Rick had vacated. "Listen, Julia, I know you don't know us well, but the group at the party is a close-knit one. We care deeply about each other. We have all been concerned about Rick, not only about Melissa, but since his last birthday, he's been consciously trying to reprioritize his life."

"I know there have been reports that next year will be his last season." Julia repeated the rumors that had circulated widely. "Is that true?"

"We'll see," Monica said. "He's not actively looking for a relationship, though. That's what makes this all so exciting." Monica hugged Julia impulsively.

"'Relationship'?" Julia stared at her new friend, brows furrowed. "As in me and Rick?"

"Yes." Monica returned to the spaghetti sauce, which was now bubbling on the stove.

"But we're not in a relationship!" Julia busied herself with finishing the salad. Monica stirred the sauce and glanced at Julia, who paused with the salad tongs poised over the large bowl.

"Julia, at least promise me you won't slam the door without even considering the possibility."

"No, no, no," Julia shook her head and stabbed the salad vigorously. "I'm not ready for a relationship."

"But you're not saying, 'absolutely not,' right?" Monica asked. The guys chose that moment to return to the kitchen, so Monica's question went unanswered. Julia was glad for the interruption.

Dinner was a lively affair, with Rick getting to see the joys and sorrows of feeding a finicky five-year-old and a messy two-year-old. Bethany managed to get spaghetti sauce on every exposed inch of her face.

While Rick helped load the kids into Julia's car after dinner, Garrett was pretending to help his wife clean the kitchen. They were discussing the budding romance between Julia and Rick.

"I'll be so disappointed if this doesn't work." Monica reached around him to load the dishwasher.

"You'd better not push too much," Garrett warned. "I think she's pretty wary of the whole idea. You can't always expect a happily-ever-after."

"I know," Monica admitted. "She's perfect for him, though."

"I agree." Her husband pulled her into a romantic embrace. "I think he knows it, too. It's Ms. Julia that we'll need to convince."

"Get a room, you two," Rick said from the door. Monica threw a dishtowel at him.

11

Quite a Catch

"No." Julia was adamant. "I do not charge for tutoring my friends' children. It's a ministry."

"Julia, sweetheart," Monica tried her sweetest Southern charm. "You have to let us do something. Gary is finally excited about school again. Your help over the last two weeks has worked miracles."

"How much do I owe you for our dinners?" Julia asked sweetly.

"Point taken," Monica conceded. "Not that I'm happy about it. You may have to face Garrett, too. He wasn't too happy when I told him you wouldn't take the check last week."

"He'll get over it." Julia shrugged. "Maybe I'll make him an apple pie for tomorrow."

"Sounds good." Monica switched to player's wife mode. "Now to the real reason I called. We'd like you to go with us to the game this Saturday."

With three games left in the season and Christmas coming, this would be the last game many of the wives attended. It was the team's only Saturday night game, and while technically it was an away game, it was close enough to make the trip reasonable.

"Go to the game?" Julia's mind started racing. She would love to see Rick play in person, but her wary nature started listing all the reasons it wouldn't be a good idea. Despite seeing him at dinner after her tutoring sessions, and phone calls on the other days, Julia was still not sure about the idea of a relationship with Rick Adams.

"Yes. The wives and…" Monica hesitated, "…invited guests usually sit together, and the game is only a couple hours away."

Julia heard the hesitation and figured Monica almost said, "wives and girlfriends." The idea of being labeled Rick's girlfriend added to her desire to rationalize her way out of going. Monica seemed to read her mind.

"Is there someone besides Terry that could watch the kids?" Monica asked. "We were thinking she could come with you. I'd like to meet her, since Stephen talks about her all the time."

Julia knew Terry would be embarrassed and thrilled at the same time. She and Stephen had decided over the last couple of weeks that they should stick to friendship, since Terry would be moving after graduation, and neither of them was ready for a serious relationship. Still, Terry would love to go to a professional football game. It would be a welcome reprieve from the pressures of her graduate class work.

"Well," Julia heard herself say, "my parents live a few minutes from the stadium and they had asked to see the kids one weekend before Christmas."

"You really aren't sure about this, are you?" Monica asked.

"You must have mind-reading powers, lady," Julia told her.

"You've got to give him a chance."

"I know," Julia's voice was barely audible, "but it's scary."

"Not if it's meant to be."

"Like that ever happens in real life." Julia said with a sigh. "Especially to someone like me."

"You mean a godly, faithful young woman who loves God, loves her kids, and has a tremendous capacity to love a husband, as she has already shown?"

"Okay." Tears gathered in Julia's eyes.

"Okay, you'll go?"

"Yes," Julia said.

"I'm so glad, my friend," Monica said. "I know this is a big deal and I know you won't regret it."

"We'll see."

Julia called her parents to give them the news of the unexpected visit. They were understandably excited. Julia was not quite as happy when her dad delivered his news.

"He called you?" Julia was annoyed that her parents hadn't told her of Rick's call.

"Yes," her father answered his semi-hysterical daughter. "He wanted to ask my permission before he spent any more time with you."

"Oh." Julia quieted quickly. "That's nice—I think."

"You think?" Her dad teased her. "I hear he's quite a catch, my dear."

"Really, Dad?" Julia's voice rose. "Quite a catch?"

"So, you're not after his money, or fame, or big house?" Robert knew his daughter was not the type to date a celebrity of any sort, but continued to tease his daughter. Their relationship had always been strong, the obvious love expressed often in teasing and silly inside jokes.

"No," she told him, 'I'm not sure I even like the man. He's infuriating." *And handsome, kind, and funny*, she added in her mind.

"Honey," her mom's voice interrupted their humorous interchange. "What's your concern? Rick sounds like he's trying to do this right. I know you don't like the idea of living in the spotlight, but from what I can tell, many of these celebrities, and athletes in particular, can lead normal lives if they choose. It's the ones that make bad life decisions that end up in the headlines."

"I know," Julia conceded, "but the thought of seeing my name or worse, the kids' names, in print or on the news, terrifies me."

"I'm pretty sure Rick wouldn't let that happen," her dad said. "Not if he could help it."

"I know," Julia repeated. "I think you may be getting a little ahead of yourselves, too. I've seen the guy all of six times, all in very casual, open settings," she said. Well, she thought, except for the few minutes in the library, in Sloan's car, and in her kitchen. She chose not to tell her parents about those.

"So, you'll be bringing the kiddos by Saturday morning before heading to the game?" her dad asked. "We can hardly wait. We'll bring them back to you on Monday. Spoiled rotten, of course."

"Aw, thanks, Dad." Julia laughed.

12
A Monster Hit

The game was in one of the few remaining outdoor stadiums, which meant that weather often played a factor. Not today, though. Forecasts were for sunny skies and a light breeze.

After dropping the kids at their grandparents' house, Monica navigated through the line of cars at the stadium. The players had reserved seats for their family and friends about halfway up behind the visitors' bench. Julia spotted Rick right away. Monica had told her that the players rarely acknowledged their families before or during the games, mainly because they were so focused on the competition. What she didn't tell her was that the men were aware of exactly where they were in the stands, which was evident if any one of them got hurt in the game. Within minutes an usher usually showed up to deliver a message to the ladies. Monica decided Julia didn't need to know this, since it would merely serve to remind her of the violence most of the wives tried to forget.

The team was expected to win this game handily, since the opposing team had two star players out with injuries. True to the predictions, they were ahead by a comfortable margin heading into the fourth quarter.

Julia was hoping the coach would take Rick out for the last few plays, already sensing the inherent danger in the game. Almost as she was evaluating why she suddenly felt such concern for his well-being, the unthinkable happened.

"Quarterback Rick Adams just took a monster hit!" The announcer told the fans what they already knew. Rick was surrounded by a group of concerned teammates. Julia paled.

"He's going to be fine." Monica patted Julia's hand. "Don't panic. Look, he's talking and moving his feet and hands. They'll probably put him on a stretcher, though, so don't be alarmed."

"Why would they do that unless he's really hurt?" Julia took a deep breath and stretched to see over the fans in front of her.

"Partly because it's a league rule, and partly to lure the opponents into a sense of security. If next week's team thinks Rick is not at full strength, they will think they've got it made. It gives us a psychological advantage."

Monica's explanation hadn't prevented Julia from watching what was happening down on the field. The trainers had indeed put Rick on a stretcher, but he was sitting up, smiling, and waving to the fans as they wheeled him off.

"I hope the usher gets here soon," Monica said to Terry, who was sitting on her other side. The young lady's questioning look went unanswered as—almost on cue—an usher appeared next to their row.

"Ms. Fitzgerald?" he spoke quietly to Julia. "Would you come with me please?"

"Go," Monica said. "They'll take you to talk to Rick."

Julia's face was a picture in disbelief.

"Yes." Monica said. "Go!"

The usher led Julia to a private suite and pointed her to a house phone.

"When you pick up the phone, the trainer will get Mr. Adams on the line for you," he said.

"Hey, sweetheart," Rick greeted her. "Did I scare you?"

"Yes," Julia answered honestly. Picturing him in the training room blurred her vision.

"You need to be back on the field in two minutes, Rick," she heard someone say.

"Back on the field?" Julia asked. "They're joking, right?"

"He means on the sidelines," Rick assured her. "To show the fans I'm okay. It will be quite spectacular. Lots of cheers and confetti and such."

"Stop!" Julia's begged. "This is not funny." She didn't care that he knew how frightened she had been.

"I'm fine," he said. "I will never lie to you, Julia." His calm words didn't help. She stared blindly at the wall, blinking away tears.

"Let's go, Rick," the trainer called.

"I'll talk to you right after the game, okay?" Rick said quietly. "I'm not hurt, I promise, Julia."

She sat quietly before letting the usher take her back to her seat. She didn't want Monica to see how upset she was. Picturing Rick in the training room, surrounded by medical personnel, brought back oppressive memories. She took a deep breath and rejoined the group in the grandstands.

Pulling out of the parking lot after the game, Monica merged into the line of cars trailing the team bus. The players were required to ride back with the team.

"I'm sure you wouldn't want to know what goes on in that bus tonight." The veteran team wife's running commentary was a not-so-subtle attempt to take Julia's mind off Rick's injury. Terry and Monica had both noticed Julia's quietness since returning from speaking to Rick. They knew Rick was fine and wondered about the change in Julia's mood.

"Monica?" Julia asked quietly from the passenger's seat. "Would it be too inconvenient for you to take me to my parents' house?

"Oh, Julia," Monica begged, "please don't let what happened today scare you off."

"It's not only today." Julia said. "I'm not ready for this. Please. If you want, you can drop me at the edge of the parking lot and my dad will come get me."

"No," Monica said. She sighed and reluctantly gave in. "Rick's not going to be happy, but he'd be furious if I just dropped you off somewhere."

Monica walked Julia to the door when they arrived at her parents' house. Mrs. Pearson met them on the porch. She had been watching for the car since Julia had called to tell of her change in plans.

"Thank you so much." Julia hugged Monica. "I'm sorry I've delayed your trip home."

"That's okay, but please promise me you'll at least talk to him. He's going to be frantic." Monica was already dreading the phone call she'd have to make when she got in the car. She had told Terry not to say anything to Stephen yet.

"Thank you for bringing her by." Mrs. Pearson walked Monica to the car after making sure Julia got inside.

"What can I do?" Monica asked. "I feel so helpless."

"I think she's simply scared," Julia's mother explained. "That's the best answer her dad and I have come up with. Rick will need to give her some time, and some space. I hope he understands."

"I think he's so convinced that she's 'the one,' and he would do almost anything to win her." Monica said wryly.

"Well, hopefully he won't have to do anything too drastic," Joyce said. "I'm sure Julia would appreciate your prayers. I know we would."

"She's been on our family prayer list since Sloan brought her to the party several weeks ago. It was evident then that Rick was smitten." As she walked back to the car, Monica dialed her husband's number.

"Wife!" Garrett's boisterous voice boomed through the phone. "You'll have to talk louder. The party is noisy tonight!"

"I just dropped Julia off at her parents." Monica figured straightforward was the best answer, especially given the noise restrictions.

"What?!" Garrett yelled into the phone.

"Ow! That was loud!" Monica replied, holding the phone away from her ear. "Did you hear me?" She could tell from the sounds in the background that Garrett was trying to find a quieter part of the bus.

"Are you saying Julia is not coming home tonight?" Garrett wanted to make sure he got the message right. "Are the kids okay?"

"Yes." Monica didn't know how much more she should tell him.

"What on earth am I supposed to tell you-know-who?" Garrett asked desperately.

"I don't know!" Monica's frustration was evident. "I think she is scared, and today's incident didn't help any, by the way."

"Well, I don't think he purposely got hurt, if that's what you mean."

"What are you going to do?" She ignored Garrett's condescending tone, knowing it was purely from frustration.

"I vote you call and tell him." Her big, masculine, not-so-brave husband offered his solution.

"Nice try, but no."

"Guess I better get it over with," he said. "I'll call you when we pull in to find out how far out you are. I love you."

"Love you, too." Monica hung up and backed the car out of the driveway. Terry had moved up to the passenger's seat and was taking in the whole situation.

"Well, what are we going to do about Ms. Julia Fitzgerald?" Monica asked her.

"Love potion or kidnapping seems to be viable options at this point," Terry offered.

Monica could picture Rick Adams going for either one, or both. "Better not suggest either to Rick, or we might be charged as accessories!"

13
The Referee

When Julia made her way upstairs, her children were already asleep, thankfully. They had special beds in the extra bedroom, and Julia got to sleep in the room she occupied all through high school. Her mom found her curled up, softly crying.

"Oh, honey." She gathered her daughter in her arms. "What is wrong? Can you tell me what you're feeling?"

"I miss my husband." The sobs grew stronger. Her mom rocked her gently until the tears slowed and eventually stopped.

"It's okay to miss James," Joyce told her daughter. "But you need to figure out why the sadness all of a sudden."

Julia pushed away from her mom and pulled the covers up over her head.

"Get some rest and we'll tackle this in the morning," Joyce said.

"He'll probably call." Julia mumbled from under the covers. She couldn't even bring herself to mention his name.

"We'll tell him you're asleep," her mom promised. "I won't have to stretch the truth, since from what I can tell, you already are."

Julia smiled as she snuggled under the familiar covers. Her mom was the most honest person she knew.

As she fell asleep, she thought she heard her phone ring downstairs, the football-themed ringtone she had designated for Rick's number slipping into her dreams. Joyce grabbed the phone and waved her husband into the room.

"May I speak to Julia?"

"Rick, this is Joyce. Julia was almost asleep when I left her a few minutes ago. I think she needs her rest tonight."

There was silence on the other end.

"Rick?" Joyce thought she heard a deep sigh.

"Will you tell her I called?"

"I will," she promised him. "And Rick?"

"Yes, ma'am?" Rick responded, his voice sounding tired.

"Don't give up on her, okay?" Joyce said.

"What did I do wrong?" Rick asked. "She was fine when I talked to her from the locker room, or at least I thought she was."

"She needs some time and some space, but don't give up," Joyce repeated her advice.

"I'll be honest, Mrs. Pearson," Rick admitted. "I'm struggling here. A lot. My feelings for Julia are as strong as they are unexpected. I've never felt like this before. I know that sounds like a bunch of romantic mumbo jumbo, but I don't know how else to put it."

Joyce smiled. Her husband, realizing it was Rick, motioned for the phone.

"Rick, this is Robert," he said. "How are you, son?"

"Not well at all, Mr. Pearson," Rick said. "I don't know what I did to frighten Julia."

"Your injury wasn't serious, was it?" Julia's parents had watched the game, so they were aware that he had returned to the sideline fairly quickly.

"No," Rick said. "We even talked on one of the house phones. I thought she knew I was okay. I wish she could've been in the locker room. Maybe then she'd believe that I wasn't hurt."

"Oh, no, no," Mr. Pearson quickly interjected. "That would've been worse!" Julia feared hospitals and had completely avoided them since James died.

"I don't understand," Rick said. Her dad remained silent for a moment. The pieces of the puzzle were falling into place. Rick deserved to know the obstacles he was up against, but Robert knew he had to let Julia and Rick handle it, no matter how he wanted to step in. He decided he could drop a couple hints so that when all the details came out, Rick would already be prepared to a point.

"I think there are a couple of issues at play here, Rick," Julia's dad said. "Some parts of my daughter's story she's going to have to share herself." Robert decided to reveal a little of what he suspected was one of the many issues bothering his daughter. "She is still skittish about your status and wealth, based on her experience with her in-laws. Has Sloan explained that situation to you?"

"Yes, he told me, but I thought Julia had started to see me differently." Rick's tone conveyed his rising concern. "She still teases me about being rich and famous, but I thought she had begun to forgive me for it."

"Well, Julia will need to tell you it all herself, but I can tell you that the relationship with her in-laws was more than unpleasant," Mr. Pearson said.

"You said there were a couple of issues." Rick wanted as much information as her parents were willing to give.

"Yes," Robert said. "I don't want to betray her confidence. All I can say is that this may take some time. Hopefully she will open up to you soon."

"So, you don't have a magic solution for me?" Rick asked, trying to sound more light-hearted than he was.

"Just be patient with her," Mr. Pearson repeated his wife's advice. "I know you've been praying about it, and at this point that's the best advice we can give you."

As the conversation ended, Rick asked Julia's dad to tell her he had called.

Before he hung up, Mrs. Pearson last statement gave him hope. "We'll plan on seeing you next week. We're spending Christmas with Julia and the kids."

"Thank you, Mr. Pearson."

The next morning, Julia's dad handed her a cup of hot coffee and reached for a warm cinnamon roll. "I think I know what's going on here." He waved a half-eaten pastry at her.

"That makes one of us," Julia grumbled. Her dreams had been filled with bizarre football clowns and ambulance rides. Strangely, the handsome paramedic bore a strong resemblance to Mr. Richard Adams. She was sure some dream specialist would have a great time analyzing her latest subconscious adventures.

"I think your reaction to Rick's injury means that you're more attached to him than you want to admit." The armchair psychologist sitting across the breakfast table continued. "You have feelings for Mr. Adams."

"'Feelings'?" Julia childishly rolled her eyes. *I need to break that habit. C.J. does it all the time, and I'm sure Bethany will pick it up if I do it every time Rick is mentioned.*

"If by 'feelings' you mean confusion, annoyance, and distrust," Julia listed, "then, yes. I do have feelings for him."

"I think you need to add attraction"—her dad raised one eyebrow—"and fear."

"'Fear'? I'm not afraid of Rick," she insisted. "What on earth would I be afraid of?"

Turning the tables suddenly, her dad went to the core issue.

"Do you feel like you're being unfaithful to James?" Tears flowed as Julia simply nodded.

"Why do you think the game yesterday was so difficult for you?" Her father pressed even deeper. He and his wife had discussed their daughter late into the night. They suspected the true reason behind Julia's reaction, but they knew she needed to come to the realization on her own. They were hopeful that three years of resistance were finally coming to an end.

"Daddy, I don't want to talk about it."

"I know," he said, sympathetically, "but you know that you need to. It's unfair to Rick to leave him out on a limb like this."

"He's a big boy." Her pouting response told her father more than she probably intended. "I'm sure there are plenty of other women for him to choose from."

Her dad called her on her attitude "Julia Lynn. That is beneath you." He stood and cleared his place.

"Sorry."

"Sounds like you're a little jealous, if you ask me." Her father left her to her thoughts.

The next morning, Julia was still struggling. Attending the church where she grew up was more difficult than it had ever been. After taking the kids to their class, she rejoined her parents. Struggling to concentrate on the pastor's words, she silently prayed for understanding.

Lord, I don't know what to do. I find myself apparently in the middle of a relationship that I did not remember asking for. Rick is so different from James, yet I am strangely drawn to him. But I know I am not ready for any type of commitment. It doesn't seem fair to him to string him along while I am so unsure. Daddy was right. I feel like I'm being unfaithful to James and his memory. The fear I felt when they wheeled Rick off the field yesterday brought back painful memories of the phone call I received on that awful day three and a half years ago. Please, Father, help me.

The starting notes of the closing hymn were a welcome sound. She was desperate to escape. Unfortunately, it had been several months since she had visited, so she was inundated with friends and well-wishers. The worst were the ones who still offered sympathy, still amazed that she had survived this long after such a tragedy. She wanted to yell, "That's not the kind of support I needed today, people!"

While her dad took the kids upstairs to change clothes, Julia and her mom set out the lunchmeat and sandwich fixings.

"You know he called last night, right?" Her mom broached the subject she was avoiding. "You need to let him know you're okay."

"Who?" Julia almost asked but knew her mom wouldn't find it funny. "I know." Julia was hoping to catch Rick away from his phone so she could get away with leaving a message. "I'll go call him right now," she said, thinking that church back home wouldn't be out yet. Maybe his phone would still be on silent and she could avoid talking directly to him. She wasn't so fortunate and nearly dropped her phone when he answered.

Rick had been up half the night. Sloan let him vent for an hour, but Rick had a sense that Sloan was holding back some vital information. His friend's doubts about his pursuit of Julia were unsettling. Needing encouragement, Rick had called his parents. They were in London visiting his sister and brother-in-law at the army base where he was currently stationed. Given the time difference, Rick waited until almost two in the morning to call. His parents knew of his interest in Julia and had already cautioned him to go slowly. Last night they let him vent and then gave wise, if somewhat stinging, counsel.

"Give her some space, son," his father had warned. "You can't possibly expect Julia to be ready for the kind of culture she's being thrust into. If you care for her, as we think you do," he said, "be patient."

Patience. Great, he thought. Not willing to face his church family that morning, Rick had decided to listen to the live stream. Julia's call shook him out of his slide into despair.

"Julia." Rick took a deep breath. Patience, Rick, patience. "Are you okay?"

"Yes. I'm sorry about yesterday. I should have called you when I decided to stay here." She somehow managed to keep her voice stoic. Not trusting herself to explain any further, she left it at that.

"That's it? 'I'm sorry, I should have called'?" His fatigue turned to frustration. The grand plan to show patience and kindness if she called was forgotten as the morning wore on. It was now mid-afternoon.

"Rick, I can't do this right now." She was struggling to keep the tears back. She didn't want him to know how much this was affecting her. It'd be better for him to think she was merely another cold and cruel woman. There was no response, and she thought he had hung up.

"Rick?" she asked quietly.

"I'm still here."

"I don't know what you want me to say." Julia now knew it was a mistake to have called without a better plan of explanation.

Gathering his courage, Rick laid out the speech he'd prepared last night. "I know you don't feel the way I do about this relationship. And it is a relationship, whether you believe it or not. I'm not going to go away easily, but I'll give you the time and space that you need, within reason." His forthright tone was so different from the way that James would've handled this that she wanted to stand and salute.

"Sir, yes, sir!" She couldn't hide the humor in her voice. He thought she was mocking him.

"Fine. We'll leave it at that for now, then. I'll talk to you later."

"He hung up on me!" She stared at the phone in her hand. Her mom had joined her in the den.

"What did you say to make him mad?" Joyce asked her daughter.

"Thanks, Mom, for taking his side!" Julia stomped out of the room. Even as she did, she knew both she and Rick were acting like children.

Perfect! We are certainly bringing out the best in each other!

14

Not Playing Fair

A week before Christmas, Julia and the kids returned home. When Rick had called again during the week, Julia had been out shopping with her mom. She desperately wanted to know what Rick and her dad had talked about but refused to admit her curiosity.

Her tiny living room had been decorated since before Thanksgiving, and it made her think of the sparsely decorated mansion of Mr. Richard Adams. She thought how fun it would be to decorate such a large space, but she brushed aside those thoughts almost as quickly as they surfaced. Christmas was her favorite holiday, and she seemed every year to find one or two, or three or four, more decorations that were perfect for her home.

Julia knew that the team would have an unusual practice schedule leading up to their next to last game, which would be a couple days after Christmas. Barring something tragic, it looked like the two-year-old expansion team would make the playoffs. This was such an unusual occurrence that the local stations, and many of the national outlets as well, were all focused on the team as they prepared. She couldn't turn on the TV without some reference to the Wolves. She had resorted to listening to Christmas music.

After pressure from her parents, Sloan, and even Terry, she agreed to see Rick the evening before Christmas Eve.

"You've got to give the guy a chance," Sloan said. "For my sanity, please!" Rick's daily phone calls made it clear that Julia's hiding out at her parents' house had been frustrating.

"The last time we talked, he wasn't very happy with me." Julia was still ashamed of her childish behavior during their last conversation.

"Yeah, I heard about that." Sloan said. "He feels bad about hanging up on you, but he was afraid he was going to lose it if he stayed on the phone. But, Julia, you need to stop hiding. He's a good guy, and I know he cares about you. Admit it. You like him, at least a little bit, right?"

"I'm not admitting anything, but I will see him," she said. "The kids miss him."

Sloan recognized her not-very-subtle ruse, and he passed on the message. The next day, plans were set. They were going on a real date to a fancy restaurant on the outskirts of town.

Rick picked her up early so he could meet her parents and get some time in with C.J. and Bethany. It felt like it had been months, not merely a few days, since he had seen them.

Julia's parents could hardly wait to meet Rick but hid their enthusiasm from their daughter. Rick had called and talked to her dad more than the once during the week, a point her father kept from her. With each conversation, Robert Pearson felt more and more confident about this man. Now, if only Julia would give Rick a chance.

As Julia came downstairs, she saw Rick reading a book to her children. Bethany was perched in his lap while C.J. was draped along the back of the couch, his little arms around the quarterback's neck and his chin on Rick's shoulder.

A wave of longing swept over her. It was such a domestic scene that she fought to get her clear-headed objectivity back. *He's perfect,* she thought. *Just not for me and not right now.*

"Julia." Rick set Bethany on the couch as he stood, nearly knocking C.J. off the couch. Thankfully, the boy thought it was great fun.

The dark blue chiffon dress made Julia's skin glow. The long, flowing sleeves gave her an angelic look, and the pleated bodice accentuated her petite form. She looked lovely and somehow vulnerable. Her wrap was a lined silk scarf decorated in a green, blue, and purple paisley print. Rick had to remind himself to breathe. Her tentative smile further upset his equilibrium.

Mr. and Mrs. Pearson watched the smitten athlete's expression.

"Now you two kids, don't stay out too late, you hear?" Robert's teasing tone helped wake Rick out of the trance he had fallen into since she came down the stairs.

"Are you ready?" he asked when he moved to her side and slipped the wrap around her shoulders.

"Yes." Julia hoped her voice didn't sound as breathless as she felt. The distraction of Rick in his dark gray, well-tailored suit would make dinner tonight quite eventful.

Rick recovered enough to kiss the kids good night and shake Robert's hand.

"Have fun, you two," Julia's mom called as they left the apartment.

"You are beautiful." Rick pulled her around to face him before he opened the car door.

"Thank you." Julia dropped a quick curtsy, adding playfully, "So are you."

Before she could object, he dropped a quick kiss on her cheek. She slid into the passenger seat after he opened the door. As he moved around to the driver's side, he saw her gently touch her cheek. He hid his grin as he slipped behind the steering wheel.

The restaurant was several miles outside the city. Rick knew there was less chance of people bothering them the farther out they went. Still, he had called ahead to ask the staff to make sure they had privacy. The maître d' led them to the back corner, away from the main seating area. Rick sat facing the dining room so he could be aware if anyone recognized him and attempted to interrupt their meal.

"Are you hungry?" he asked as they opened their menus.

"Famished." Hopefully, he wouldn't mind having a date that didn't insist on eating tiny portions. Waiting for her prime rib and his lobster, they shared an appetizer sample plate. Despite the fanciness of the restaurant, it was known for hands-on food, and they thoroughly enjoyed the somewhat messy eggrolls and gooey cheese dip.

Without thinking, Julia leaned over and fed the last half of her eggroll to Rick. As her fingers touched his lips, she realized her mistake. Too late to pull back, he had taken hold of her hand. After he munched the enticing bite and dramatically licked his lips, he kissed the palm of her hand.

Julia was glad that the low lights of the restaurant would keep him from seeing that she wasn't immune to him. Rick raised an eyebrow and Julia realized that it wasn't as dark in the room as she had hoped. She pulled her hand away.

"You're not playing fair," she said.

"Never said I would." He recaptured her hand.

Their meal turned into a two-hour feast. Thankfully, there was enough time between courses for recovery.

"I wish I could cook like this," she said wistfully. "Not that C.J. or Bethany would eat any of it. I guess I'll have to be satisfied with hotdogs and mac-and-cheese for a few more years."

She hated to admit it, but she was genuinely enjoying the evening. As if they knew this was a pivotal point, the conversation had been filled with a depth that didn't normally happen on a first date. They talked about everything from childhood memories to child-rearing philosophies. The one subject they didn't address was her reaction at the game.

As she took the last bite of cheesecake off the fork, he waved in front of her, she leaned back contentedly.

"That was delicious." She sighed. "Thank you. I'm forever spoiled for sure."

"Glad to be of service," Rick said as he paid the tab. Waiting for the receipt, he gently took her hand.

"Julia," he said softly, "there's one thing we haven't talked about, you know."

"Hmm?" she asked distractedly, mesmerized as his thumb made circles on her palm.

"We need to talk about why you were so upset after the game last week," he reminded her.

Crashing back to reality, she tried to pull her hand away.

"Not so fast." He held on. The waiter brought back his card and their receipt. As they stood, Rick released her hand long enough to help her out of the booth. They picked up her wrap from the coat check and Rick settled his arm on her waist as they walked to his car. She was glad he had driven the sports car and not the truck. Trying to look dainty and ladylike would be difficult while trying to climb in and out of that monstrosity.

Rick turned to her before starting the car, reaching once again for her hand. She was helpless at this point to resist him. "Do you want to talk now or when we get home?" he asked. "Pick one."

"Start driving and I'll talk on the way." In her mind she knew if he were driving, at least he wouldn't be able to stare at her while she talked. Unfortunately for her, he correctly interpreted the attempt to maintain control of the situation.

"Nice try. Here or home?"

They were parked at the edge of the large, tree-lined parking lot, so the spot was quite private.

"Here," she conceded. Steeling herself for the difficult discussion, she took a deep breath.

"Julia," Rick said as he tugged her hand so she would face him. "Something is scaring you. What happened after we talked at the game?"

"Ever since James's accident, I hate hospitals," she blurted, deciding honesty was the easiest course. "Seeing you wheeled off the field brought back all those memories."

His look of dismay would have been comical under different circumstances. Since she had dealt with this fear over the past few years, Julia was actually better equipped than Rick at this point.

"It's okay, Rick." She reached over and touched his cheek. His next action confused her. He abruptly got out of the car and came around to the passenger's side.

"C'mon." He pulled her out of the fancy sports car. "We do need to talk."

The restaurant was located along a picturesque river surrounded by a series of beautifully landscaped walkways and the evening was unseasonably mild. Rick's sudden change of attitude was disarming.

"Are you up for a walk?" he asked. "Or is it too chilly? I'll keep you warm if you like." His blatant attempt at flirtation earned him a giggle from Julia.

"That'd be nice." He led her down the stone walkway that snaked along the riverfront.

"The walk or the offer to keep you warm?" Rick pulled her closer as a slight breeze came off the water.

Both, she thought. The warmth of his arm around her waist was comforting. They stopped along a secluded bridge. Julia leaned over the wide stone wall, watching the gently flowing river that was softly lit by a series of hidden path lights.

"It's so beautiful."

"Yes, you are." Rick opened his blazer and wrapped her in its warmth. Both arms around her now, he rested his chin atop her head.

"You must have had too much wine," she said, effectively contradicting her protest as she leaned back into his warmth.

"I had one small glass, as you very well know." His voice was muffled, as he placed a chaste kiss on the top of her silky hair.

She felt so perfect in his arms, and he knew he was treading on dangerous ground. He decided conversation would help move his thoughts into safer avenues.

"Tell me about James."

15

Scouting the Competition

His request hung in the air.

"What do you mean?" she asked. Their evening had been almost magical up to this point, and she started to struggle slightly in his embrace.

"Be still." Her squirming let him know that he had finally pushed her stoic control off-balance. Maybe now he would be able to get to the real woman behind her calm façade.

"What on earth could you possibly want to know about James?" Her voice held a slight sense of panic.

"Julia." His voice was soft but insistent. "James was an important part of your life. I want you to be able to talk about anything, including James and your life together, without fearing it' will upset me. He fathered your children, and they already have enchanted me, so I need to know who he was."

"You're bizarre," she said.

"True." Rick agreed. He leaned over and kissed her gently below her ear. Her breath caught as he whispered, "I'm waiting."

"What exactly do you want to know?"

"For starters, how did you meet, and what was he like? Funny? Serious? Stubborn? Kind?"

"Sloan introduced us, but you knew that," she said. "We met at a church picnic during the spring of my sophomore year. He was in the graduate school engineering department. He and Sloan were on an intramural soccer team."

"Soccer," Rick shuddered.

"Don't be a football snob, Rick. Soccer is more popular, you know."

"Yes, if you count the populations of all seven continents," he said, "and all the planets."

He heard her giggle once again, and he realized that it was rapidly becoming one of his favorite sounds. He vowed to arrange to hear it as much as possible, even if it meant sacrificing any dignity he possessed.

"So, he was a computer whiz but athletic, too?" Rick asked. "That's an unusual combination."

"Not as unusual as you might think," she said. "You did know that Sloan was on the chess team in high school?"

"You're joking!" Rick tried to picture his handsome, arrogant, and athletic friend bowed over a chessboard. "That's priceless information!"

"You can't tell him I told you!" She tried to turn to face him, but he shook his head.

"Stay put, I told you."

They stood silently for a few moments.

"Continue, please," Rick said. "James was obviously smart and had fabulous taste in women." He paused, hoping for another chuckle. None came.

"He was quiet, but solid. There were times when I wanted my way and would stomp childishly around the house, and he'd simply let me rant. Then, we would end up doing what he had said in the beginning. Looking back on it, I was quite silly at times. I don't know how he stood it."

"Although I'm not an expert on you, yet," he paused, "I think you're being hard on yourself."

"Well, he did appreciate my humor, which was so different from his. But he was much quieter and kinder." Rick could hear a hint of regret in her voice.

"Go on."

"My sarcasm may be endearing to some, but I know I used it as a weapon at times. James tended to have more self-control than I did, so he rarely used sarcasm, and never at anyone else's expense."

Another breeze blew across the bridge. Rick wrapped his jacket tighter around Julia in response to her slight shiver. Knowing he may not ever get her to open up like she seemed willing to do tonight, Rick posed a loaded question.

"What do you miss most?" He held his breath. He saw her blink away tears.

"There are too many things to list," she said quietly at last. "I wouldn't know where to start."

"Try." Rick turned her gently in his arms so he could see her face. She instead buried her head on his chest, her arms still folded against the cold. He rested his head against the top of hers, now snuggled against him.

"He was kind, calm, and gentle. But sometimes I feel bad because I miss silly things, too."

"Like?" Rick asked, bracing himself for what she would say.

"Kisses, foot rubs, sitting on the couch watching a movie." Her muffled words evoked pictures of the woman in his arms being embraced by a man Rick had only seen in photographs. Rick held his breath.

"And, yes," she answered his unspoken question, "I miss sleeping with my husband."

"Completely understandable." Rick's forced response was a superb acting job, but he couldn't hide his sigh of frustration.

"I don't think you understand completely." Julia leaned her head back to meet Rick's troubled look. "I don't mean what you think I mean, at least not entirely." She hid her head again. "I mean literally sleeping with my husband—snuggling next to him, waking up next to him, kicking him gently in the middle of the night when he was snoring. All of it."

Rick tucked a curl behind her ear. When she looked up again, he kissed her gently.

Suddenly her arms were wrapped around his neck, her fingers in his hair. She clung to him as he deepened their kiss. Moments later, he set her slightly away, his hands still gripping her slim waist. Her eyes, blurry with passion, showed confusion as his face came into focus.

"I'm sorry, Julia." He set her away from him quickly. "It was wrong of me to take advantage of you. It won't happen again. I'll take you home."

Julia winced at his clipped words and followed him silently to the car.

Right before they reached her complex, he broke the silence that lasted their entire return trip.

"Julia," he said quietly but clearly, "thank you for opening up about James. I want you to know that you can always talk to me about him. He played a major role in your life, and that's important to me. He loved you, he loved his children, and that means we have more in common than you may realize."

Julia merely continued to stare out the window at the passing scenery. Thinking her lack of response meant she didn't understand what he was trying to say, or she was rejecting him outright, he turned on the radio. The noise drowned out the last few minutes of their silent ride.

His anguish turned to prayer. *Father, please guide me. I know the kiss we just shared was a mistake, but You know my feelings for this young lady. Please repair any damage I've done to the relationship I hope to have with her. Guide my words and actions as I try to let her know how much I want to be part of her life.*

Rick silently walked her to the door. The kids were already in bed, and he resisted the urge to ask for permission to check on them. He said his good-byes to Julia's parents before they left Rick and Julia alone.

"This conversation is not over," he told her as he kissed her hand. At the door he turned and left her with one last request. "My parents and sister will be here on Sunday. They'll probably arrive while I'm still at the game. I want you and the kids to come over to meet them." He shut the door without awaiting her answer.

16
Throwing the Penalty Flag

Julia slipped out of her fancy dress and hung it in the laundry room. She was using the room as her makeshift dressing room while her parents were visiting. She put on one of James's old sweatshirts and a pair of sweatpants, her typical nightwear.

As she flipped on the television and flipped through the sports channels Rick had insisted on adding to their cable subscription. "So you can watch me in all my glory," he had said. Unable to relax, she thought back to the evening. Even though she was alone, she blushed at the thought of how passionately she had kissed Rick. *I need to apologize,* she thought. *Otherwise, he will think I'm 'that' kind of woman.*

Knowing she wouldn't be able to do it face-to-face, and not wanting to risk even talking to him, she sent him a quick email message. She had no idea if he would read it tonight or not, but she knew she had to do it while she still had the courage. Of course, she could have sent a text message instead, but opted for email, subconsciously hoping he wouldn't get it tonight.

She turned her laptop computer on and typed quickly.

Rick, I'm sorry about my wanton display tonight. I hope it didn't completely ruin the evening. I don't know what I was thinking, throwing myself at you like that.

I hope you can forgive me. I had a nice time tonight. Thank you for the special evening. ~Julia

She read and reread the message, considering changing "wanton" to "excessive" or "passionate," but she decided the old-fashioned word fit her actions best. She knew her apology was halfhearted, but she didn't want him to know how much she had thoroughly enjoyed their kiss.

"Do you want to talk about it?" her mom asked the next morning over an early morning breakfast. Although it was barely daylight, they were up ready to head out for some last-minute shopping.

"No," Julia said. She had tossed and turned all night. Normally she loved sleeping on the foldout couch, its comfortable mattress unusual for a sleeper sofa. Last night she hadn't even bothered to open it up.

"Rick seems nice, Julia," her mom said. "You need to give the guy a chance, you know."

"He is, and I know," Julia answered, "but I don't want to." She knew her folded arms and protruding lip would remind her mom of Bethany defiantly refusing to pick up her toys. As expected, her mom laughed as she caught sight of her stubborn daughter.

"What happened last night?" Joyce asked.

"Nothing. It was a magical evening," Julia waved a piece of toast airily. "The restaurant was marvelous, and we walked through a moonlit park after dinner. It was all quite romantic." *Until I threw myself at him after spilling my guts about James,* she added in her mind.

"I don't believe you," her mom said. "I think you're ready to move on, and you know it, so I'm not sure what you're afraid of anymore. It's time. James wouldn't have wanted you to give up your life, too. That would be a double tragedy."

"I kissed him." Julia took her empty cup to the sink and began washing up the few dishes that were there. Her blunt confession didn't surprise her mother.

"Understandable," Mrs. Pearson said. "He's a nice-looking young man."

"No, Mother." Julia turned and tossed the dishtowel on the counter. "I mean I really, really kissed him. Like practically attacked him, right after he had made me tell him everything that I missed about James. It shocked him so much, he couldn't wait to get away."

"You two talked about James?" Her mom's quiet question merely served to frustrate Julia.

"Yes." Julia retrieved the towel and turned back to the sink. "I told him I missed sleeping with my husband." She looked over her shoulder, thinking she would finally shock her very proper parent. Instead, Joyce simply sipped her coffee. So Julia added, "And then I kissed him. Thoroughly."

Her mom continued her stoic silence. Julia wanted to shout, *"How can you be so calm about this? I kissed a man who was not my husband, and I thoroughly enjoyed it."* She waited for her mom to respond.

"I'm going to ask you a pointed question, Julia. Your honest answer is extremely important." Her mom's serious tone won Julia's full attention. "Were you thinking about James when you kissed Rick?"

"No." Julia's quiet confession hung in the air. "I was thinking about Rick."

"I see," Joyce said quietly.

"Does that make me a terrible person?" Julia moved back to the table and sank her head onto her crossed arms.

She peeked up at her mom. "I had just spent half an hour listing the wonderful things about James and had described how much I missed his kisses and snuggling with him in bed and then, boom! I was clinging to Rick Adams, kissing him without a single thought of my husband."

"Your late husband." Her mom's calm reminder was pointed, but necessary.

"I'm a terrible person."

"No, you're not. You're a lovely young woman who has a great capacity for loving. You love your children and your family, but you have plenty of love and affection to go around. Do not discount the idea that God may have brought Rick Adams into your life." Joyce stood and left Julia alone with her thoughts. She and her thoughts were not alone for long.

When the phone rang, just a few minutes later, Julia moved outside to the patio for privacy, not knowing when her mother would come back downstairs.

"Rick," she said. The air was cool on her flushed cheeks.

"Hello, Julia." He chose his words carefully. "I got your message. It confused me a little bit, though."

"I'm sorry. I thought it was pretty straightforward." She was glad he couldn't see her blush. "I needed to apologize for ruining the evening."

"Is that what it said? I must be using the wrong secret decoder ring, then," Rick laughed. "What makes you think you ruined the evening?" Julia laughed and Rick relaxed his tight grip on the phone. "I thought our conversation was deeply revealing. I'm glad you felt free enough to talk about James so honestly. I know that you miss him."

"Yes, I do," she said, "but that's part of the problem." Rick's grip tightened once more.

"Why is that a problem? I know I could never take his place." Rick's words tumbled out. "That's not what I want. But I do want to be part of your life."

"I know that." She paused.

"Talk to me, Julia," he said. "Tell me what you're thinking, please. I can't read your mind and it's driving me crazy!"

"I don't want to shock you."

"Shock me?" he asked. "Now I'm totally confused. What on earth could you possibly say that would shock me?"

"You were so kind to let me ramble on about James. Yes, I do miss him. But, Rick, when I kissed you, I felt guilty."

"Guilty?" *Here it comes,* he thought.

"I had just talked about how much he meant to me, and then seconds later I was passionately kissing you."

"You regret kissing me after talking about James?"

"No," she said, her voice almost inaudible. "That's why I feel guilty."

"Julia," Rick's voice was pleading now. "Explain exactly what you mean, please. When you kissed me, were you thinking about James? Or me?" The question had plagued him since last night.

"You, Rick."

"Julia." Rick paused and finally exhaled the breath he had been holding. "You have probably just saved my sanity. You weren't disappointed when you realized it was me and not him?"

"Oh, no," she said, "far from it." There was relief, and a hint of humor, in her voice.

"Are you flirting with me, woman?"

"Maybe a little."

"You should be thankful that I'm twenty minutes away and that I have an early morning practice to go to."

"Why?" she asked playfully.

"Stop," he said. "You're not playing fair."

"Sorry." She changed the subject. "Are you still planning to come to the Christmas Eve service?"

"Yes," Rick said, "and we don't have to be on the bus for the airport until mid-afternoon on Christmas."

The next-to-last game of the season was against a weaker team that had been riddled with late-season injuries. Of course, the coach's interviews typically insisted that the team didn't plan to take anything for granted. The only evidence of the coach's confidence was the concession of shortened practices on Christmas Eve and Christmas.

Rick was confident that the team would practice harder and more efficiently than they would if they had to suffer through longer practices. This confidence meant he didn't feel guilty inviting himself to join her for Christmas.

"Subtle, Mr. Adams," Julia responded.

"Don't forget that I need to get the kids' Santa gifts to you, too." A bright pink tricycle for Bethany and a big-boy bike with training wheels for C.J. were sitting in his garage. He insisted that they be from Santa so that he could give them another present from "Uncle Rick."

"I'm still not thrilled about that, you know." Julia renewed her objections to his generous gifts for her kids. "But, since you're so stubborn, I guess I'll have to give in."

"So?" Rick asked.

"Would you like to bring them over on Christmas morning?" Julia asked, trying not to laugh at his impatience. She figured he was ready to invite himself if she didn't give in.

"Well," Rick sighed dramatically, "if you insist."

"The kids will be up early, you know," she said.

"Yes, and you know I don't care how early it is. I want to spend Christmas morning with you," he said, then he added after a slight pause, "and the kids. I'll see you guys tonight at church and we'll discuss the details then. Save me a seat."

"Okay." Julia didn't trust herself to say more.

"Julia," Rick said. She could hear the smile in his voice. "Thank you for last night—all of it."

"Go to practice, Rick," she said, but added, "please be careful, though."

"For you," he said, "always."

17
Home Field Advantage

The atmosphere at church that night was festive. Casual attire was the norm at their community-friendly church. Except for Christmas Eve. Elders and deacons that regularly came to church in jeans or khakis sported three-piece suits, complete with bright Christmas-colored ties. The ladies wore fancy dresses, and even the children were decked out in their finest. Julia loved the formality, and although her deep emerald dress was one of her bargain-hunting successes, she felt elegant. The knee-length dress had billowy sleeves and an empire waist. She paired it with her grandmother's pearl necklace and earrings. Her long hair was carefully twisted into a stylish bun.

"Mommy, you look like a princess!" C.J. said as she walked carefully down the stairs. The high heels were not her usual footwear.

"Why, thank you, son," she said. "You look like an especially important young man. I will be honored to be escorted by such a handsome knight this evening."

"Look at me, Mommy!" Bethany twirled through the kitchen and into the living room, amazingly keeping her balance.

"What a lovely princess you are!" Julia bent to adjust the tiara atop her daughter's blonde curls. "I think we are all dressed perfectly for celebrating the Savior's birthday, don't you?

"Hey, what about us?" Julia's dad called from the couch. "Don't we look nice, too?"

"Yes, you do, Daddy," she said, "but not as good as Mother." Her mom wore a tea-length dark blue dress that lent her a regal air.

Being dressed up seemed to help the kids' normal wiggly antics as they settled into their usual pew at the back of the sanctuary. Julia had chosen this spot when she first started coming to the church, afraid of disturbing the other worshippers if she had to leave with one of her children.

Rick was already there. *He is gorgeous,* Julia thought. His dark suit and light green shirt were obviously not bargain-basement deals.

He moved out into the aisle, allowing her parents to move down next to Terry and Stephen. Julia had planned to place C.J. strategically between her dad and mom, but the young boy made it clear he wanted to sit next to Rick. Realizing there was no logical reason to deny his request, Julia let Rick scoot in after her son, Bethany already in his arms.

As the first hymn began, she was once again holding the hymnal for the two of them. C.J. was standing on the pew so he could see over the congregation, Rick's arm securely holding him. Julia caught Terry's amused glance at the familiarity.

With Bethany between them, Julia moved closer so that Rick could see the hymnal. He tried not to gloat. As they settled into their places for the message, C.J. had transferred his attention and was now sitting between his grandparents. Rick shifted Bethany to his other side and slipped the now-free arm along the pew behind Julia. He saw her slight frown and winked. She looked away quickly. He wasn't physically touching her, but the gesture spoke volumes to her, her parents, and anyone else that saw it.

After the message, the service ended with candle lighting. Thankfully, the extra hands made the prospect of open flame combined with two youngsters less treacherous. Robert was awarded the privilege of holding Bethany who was mesmerized by the flicking flame. As the light from the candles made its way back from the front of the sanctuary, Julia was struck with the majesty of it. The simple exercise so poignantly represented the spread of God's love to the world at His Son's birth that it had always been one of her favorite Christmas traditions.

Rick's arm was now around her waist, and he bent quickly and placed a chaste kiss on top of her head. Instead of resisting, she moved slightly closer. He loved her childlike excitement. Honest with himself, he knew he loved everything about this woman.

"You look enchanting tonight," Rick said after the service, as they trailed behind the others in the parking lot.

"So do you," she replied as he stopped and pulled her around to face him. She pretended to straighten his already perfectly arranged tie.

"What time do you want me there in the morning?" he asked her, capturing her hands beneath his so he could think clearly. "Is seven too early? Or too late?"

"Seven will be good," she answered. "I think I have a couple years before C.J. figures out the super early Christmas morning routine."

"I have the gifts in the truck already, and I'll put them right outside the door when I get there, okay?"

"Sounds good," Julia said. "I'll watch for you, and if they happen to already be awake, I'll distract them."

"I'll see you in the morning," Rick said, kissing her again as they reached her car.

In the morning, Rick was able to bypass the check-in process since Julia had given him the pass code the second time he brought her home. She'd been watching for his truck, so the front porch light came on as he backed into the parking space. After getting the kids' gifts unloaded, he returned to the truck and retrieved a large bag. He knew Julia would be mad that he had purchased additional gifts for the kids, her, and her parents. There was nothing elaborate, since he knew she would object even more if he went overboard.

For the kids, he had team pajamas, including furry wolf slippers for Bethany. For Mr. and Mrs. Pearson, he had purchased tickets to their local symphony orchestra's winter concert, based on a brief reference to classical music during one of their conversations.

A copy of his favorite author's latest novel was the only thing he had wrapped for Julia. Their banter in the library the night of the party made it clear that he would have to convince her of the author's overwhelming talent.

An additional gift would be waiting for her and the kids when they came to his house later that week to meet his parents. He had cleared the special purchase with Joyce and Robert, and he had gotten input from Terry as well. He was sure the kids would love it, but he was nervous about Julia's reaction. *Oh well, I'm going to live dangerously. All in, as they say.*

As he stepped into the kitchen, the enticing aroma of cinnamon rolls greeted him as Julia opened the oven, revealing the golden delights. Rick hid the bag of gifts in the corner and grabbed a potholder from the counter.

"Smells heavenly!" He took the pan from her hands.

"It's a family tradition," she said. "We always have cinnamon rolls and a breakfast casserole on Christmas morning. It fills us up, so we can eat a late Christmas dinner."

Rick helped her ice the pastries and swiped some of the sticky goodness across her cheek.

"Here, let me get that for you." Her eyes widened as he wiped icing across her lips. He lifted her to the counter in front of him.

"Merry Christmas." He leaned in and kissed her. Her arms wrapped around his neck as he kissed her jaw line, below her ear, and then her forehead, before abruptly putting her back on the floor. She protested with a pout.

"Enough," he said, tweaking her nose. "I hear movement upstairs."

"Uncle Rick!" C.J. came bounding around the corner of the stairs. "Did Santa come?!" Julia's mom was close on her grandson's heels, with a still-sleepy Bethany in her arms.

"Good morning, Rick," Joyce said, automatically handing the little girl to Rick.

"Thank you for letting me invade your family time," he said around Bethany's hand that was patting his face. He settled Bethany on the couch as she started squirming, finally fully awake.

"Coffee ready?" Robert's voice came down the stairs. "Something smells marvelous!"

"Santa came, Grandpa!" his grandson announced.

"Did he bring me anything?" The look of confusion on C.J.'s face was evidence that the thought of Santa bringing something to any so old was a new idea. Mr. Pearson shook Rick's hand and accepted the cup of coffee his wife had prepared for him.

"Glad you could make it this morning," he said. "What time does your flight leave?"

"Not until later this afternoon," Rick said. "Most of the guys have young kids, so this works out best. Coach doesn't mind most of us missing out on a large, heavy holiday meal the day before a big game, either."

After breakfast and the gift giving, Julia and her mom were getting the kids' helmets strapped on for their inaugural bike and tricycle rides, while Mr. Pearson got all the details for the post-Christmas surprise.

"You have everything all set?" he asked Rick.

"Yes," Rick said, watching to make sure Julia couldn't overhear them. "You're still sure she's not going to be mad?"

"I don't think she will be," Julia's dad assured him. "She mentioned it again last night, wishing she had followed through and gotten one herself."

"Good." Rick was relieved, until her dad continued.

"Of course," Mr. Pearson said, "she'll probably be upset with you at first. She doesn't like surprises, but be patient. You can always blame it on us, or Sloan, or Terry. We were all in on it, so take your pick."

"Thanks," Rick said, appreciating the help, "but I'll take the full brunt of her displeasure. I don't think she'll be able to stay mad for long, given that she is going to fall in love with it anyway."

"That's true. It was a good call, for sure." Robert and Joyce had discussed the surprise last night. Julia's dad was struck with how quickly Rick had figured out what would mean the most to Julia and the kids.

"I've got pictures, if you and Mrs. Pearson want to see before I leave." Rick pulled his phone out of his jacket pocket and slipped it to the older man. "I'll distract Julia."

"How perfect!" Julia's mom said, trying to keep her voice down. Rick and Julia were escorting the kids around the complex. "I wish we could be there. She's going to be so excited."

"She's not going to be so happy when she finds out we were all in on it, you know."

"True," Joyce conceded, "but there's no way Rick would've dared do this without making sure it would be okay." Mrs. Pearson was delighted to see Julia finally enjoying life again. She had watched her daughter bear the burden of raising her children and supporting herself without complaint, but she knew Julia was lonely. Seeing her daughter light up when Rick walked into the room was an answer to her prayers.

The older couple watched as Rick, Julia, and the two children appeared from around the corner of the building.

"They make a lovely couple." Mrs. Pearson said.

"Yes, they do," agreed her husband as he pulled her closer to his side.

18
The Mascot

Julia's parents stayed a couple more days, and they enjoyed watching the game with their daughter. Even more fun was watching *her* watch Rick, while pretending *not* to watch Rick. They returned home right after the game.

The Wolves had won, as expected, and Coach had rested Rick during the last quarter. It was evident from the quarterback's body language that he disagreed with the decision.

"He's pouting," Julia observed, from her vantage point in the kitchen where she was refilling the chips and dip. "But that's good. It means he's not injured."

Her mom elbowed her dad.

"Ow!" he said.

"What's that, Dad?" Julia asked.

"Nothing," he said, winking at his wife.

Rick called later that evening, making sure Julia hadn't changed her mind about meeting his parents. His mom, dad, sister, and new niece had arrived while he was at the game. They had brought his surprise gift with them.

"What time do you want me to come get you in the morning?" he asked Julia after assuring her that he was indeed not injured.

"You don't need to drive all the way over here to get us," she said. "I'm a big girl, and I can get to your house all by myself. I promise." *Plus, that means I can leave when I want, too*, she thought.

"No, I'll come get you guys," Rick said, then unwittingly verbalized her thoughts. "That way you can't skip out before I'm ready for you to leave."

"I know we said no more gifts," Julia said, "but we do have a couple for you, and I have one for your parents and sister." On Christmas Day, they had given Rick a coffee mug that read, "Eat, Sleep, Football." Julia had added a bag of his favorite candy.

An antique, but pristine, copy of her favorite novel, Jane Austen's *Persuasion,* was her Christmas Day gift to Rick. The night of the party, she had been appalled to learn that an English Communications major hadn't read the classic. Of course, she groaned when she opened her gift, but promised to read the spy novel, agreeing that she too needed to expand her literary horizons.

Rick's favorite gift from the kids was the family portrait that C.J. had drawn. Julia had matted and framed it and it was now prominently displayed on his mantle.

She had the sense that he had more gifts for the kids, and she wasn't thrilled with the idea, but she also hadn't told him that she had also saved out a gift for him to bring with her. The kids had insisted on getting him a castle for the fish tank she had described after the party. They wanted to wait until they were at his house to give it to him so they could help put it in the large freshwater tank.

The gift Julia was bringing from herself would contradict her insistence that they were just friends. Rick had seen a T-shirt quilt that she had made for James. He mentioned it to Sloan, who also had one she had put together for his college graduation. Knowing he had a stack of old high-school, college, and random other T-shirts sitting in the back of his closet made Rick consider asking her to make one for him. He decided it was too much to ask, because of both the amount of time involved and the level of commitment to their relationship that it would imply.

What he didn't know was that Garrett had retrieved the bags and put them in her car during one of Gary's tutoring sessions. The quilts weren't difficult to make, although she had worked steadily on it for the last three weeks. She tried to deny her own thoughts that the gift would convey more than it should.

"My parents and sister are eager to meet you." Rick's voice stopped her musings.

"No pressure though, right?" Julia asked. He knew how nervous she was to meet Mr. and Mrs. Adams. Now she had the added pressure of meeting his older sister, who had returned with them for an extended visit while her husband was deployed.

"They'll love you." Rick let his words hang in the air.

"Fine," she said. "Pick us up at nine thirty?"

"Nine it is," Rick said. He planned to show up at eight thirty, but she didn't need to know that yet.

"Get some rest, okay?" Julia knew he was always sore after a game, and would be tonight, too, despite having not played the whole game. "Did you hit the hot tub after you guys got back?"

"For a little while, but probably not long enough," Rick admitted. "I was anxious to get home. I'll probably regret it in the morning. Maybe I'll get the kiddos to pound out the kinks for me tomorrow." One evening at Garrett's he had let Bethany bounce on his back and had declared it, "One of the best massages ever!"

"I'm sure they'll be happy to oblige," Julia said. "I'll see you in the morning."

"Julia, I know it's a big deal for you to do this, and I don't want you to feel pressured," Rick said, his voice quiet again. "It means a lot to me that you're willing to give this a chance."

"I know, Rick," she said. "Please be patient with me, okay?"

"For as long as it takes," he said. "Good night, Mrs. Fitzgerald."

"Good night, Mr. Adams."

As Rick hung up the phone, the sleeping puppy in his lap decided it was now time to play, clawing his way up Rick's shirt to his face.

"Stop it, silly!" Rick cradled the tiny dog in his large hand and rejoined his family in the living room.

"When's the last time Mighty Mouse went outside?" he asked his sister.

"Right before you got home," his older sister Miriam answered. "It would probably be a good idea to take him out again. He's close to being house-trained, but being in a new environment may set him back some."

The three-month-old Yorkshire terrier mix was undeniably cute. Knowing C.J. battled seasonal allergies and might be allergic to some animals, Rick had researched breeds when he decided to get them a puppy.

"Oh, and you'd better stop calling him Mighty Mouse," Miriam said. "I'm sure the kids will want to name him themselves."

"I know, I know," Rick said. The puppy was now on one shoulder, enjoying the bird's eye view of his new surroundings. Once outside, he did his business right away and then wanted to play, alternately attacking Rick's feet and exploring the bushes. Rick's mom watched from the window.

"I hope Julia doesn't get too mad," Elaine Adams said to her daughter. "I know both Rick and Sloan insist that she had considered getting one for the kids herself, but I still think she may not be thrilled."

"She may be mad at first, but, Mom," Miriam said, "look at him! How could anyone resist that face?"

"Do you mean Rick, or the puppy?" her mom asked. Miriam laughed.

"You have a shadow, son," Mrs. Adams said as the tiny dog adoringly followed his hero. The incongruous sight made the two women laugh even harder.

Glen Adams joined his family in the living room. "So, tell me more about this young lady we are to meet tomorrow." Rick sat on the floor, continuing to play with the puppy.

"I know this has all happened quickly," he said and noted his parents' nod. "But it feels right. Julia seemed to appear unexpectedly, right at the time God was convicting me about my loneliness and grumpiness. Turning thirty-three last spring was quite a shock, too."

"You had forgotten how old you were?" his sister teased. She had slipped out to retrieve her newborn daughter who had awakened from her nap. Miriam placed Olivia in her Uncle Rick's outstretched arms. She kept to herself her surprise at how comfortable he looked.

"Yes, sis," he said. "Too many hits to the head." He saw the look of concern between his parents.

"Relax, Mom," he said, quickly confirming his clean bill of health, "I have gotten bumped around some over the last couple of years, but no concussions—mostly sore arms and twisted ankles."

"So why the sudden change in your future plans?" his father asked.

"It wasn't like I woke up the day after my birthday and thought, 'I need a wife.' It was more like I realized my decision to not pursue a relationship was made without considering if that was what God wanted. So, I put the car in neutral and let Him steer it wherever he wanted."

"And He steered you to Julia?"

"Not right away. We didn't meet until a month ago. Wow." He paused. "It's hard to believe it's only been a month."

"Tell us, tell us!" His sister, the born romantic, was eager to hear the love story. "We want details."

"Well, late last spring when Stephen Schmidt was signed and he and I became good friends, his cousin Melissa showed up." Rick's family knew about the pretend girlfriend that had been invented, but they did not realize there was a real situation that had made the subterfuge necessary. Rick spent the next few minutes describing Melissa's pursuit, his avoidance, and Julia's intervention.

"I had about sworn off women, tired of the games and uncertainty, when Julia showed up."

"So, she pretended to be your girlfriend, but then told Melissa the truth later that evening?" His mom was intrigued. "Interesting."

"Even more interesting, she didn't avoid me after that," Rick said. "Well, at least not completely. It took some convincing, but I think she's finally beginning to let me into her life."

"She likes you?" Miriam couldn't help teasing her little brother. "Are you sure she's not delusional?" She took Olivia back from Rick, as the baby girl was fully awake now and ready to be changed. Miriam wasn't sure Uncle Rick's fascination with his new niece extended to willingness to change a diaper.

"Funny," Rick said. "Don't you have a diaper to change?"

"Save the juicy parts of the story until I get back," Miriam said as she headed to her bedroom.

"So, you've met her parents and have their approval?" Rick's dad asked. He had always emphasized the importance of family support in any relationship. "You marry the whole family, not just the girl," he had told Rick on numerous occasions.

"Yes, I called them soon after the party and talked a long time with her dad. He helped me understand what she'd been through the last couple of years. It helps, too, having Sloan here. They grew up together and their families are still close. He introduced her to James," Rick said, "and me, which is ironic. He has quietly encouraged her to give me a chance, I think."

"I'm sure you've covered this in prayer, too, son," Glen Adams said. "Correct?"

"Yes," Rick said. "Garrett and Monica, Sloan, her cousin Jocelyn, her good friend Terry who babysits her kids, Stephen, her parents, and a lot of people are praying for us."

"You still seem to be concerned about something, baby brother," Miriam said when she and Olivia returned.

"Money," Rick said simply.

"Money?" all three asked at once.

"Like you don't make enough?" His sister's incredulous look was priceless.

"No. I make too much." Knowing he needed to explain, he chose his words carefully. "Julia's family is not wealthy," he said. "They're not poor, but have worked hard for what they have. I know it bothers her to hear the salary amounts being bandied about during contract negotiations and to see the cars some of the guys drive. This house didn't help change her attitude about rich, spoiled professional athletes, for sure."

"But you're not like that!" Miriam exclaimed.

"Not in attitude, maybe, but c'mon, Miriam, look around. I have a huge house. I drive a brand-new, fully equipped truck, and I have a nearly new fancy sports car in the garage. I eat at fancy restaurants, wear expensive clothes, and buy expensive gifts."

"You also give a lot of money away, support several missionaries, do a lot of community service, much of which never makes the news, and you're …you're…normal!" His now-distraught sister insisted.

"Thanks for the vote of confidence, sis." Rick laughed. "Glad to know you think I'm normal!"

"You know what I mean."

"Yes, I do," Rick said, "but there's more. Her in-laws were extremely wealthy. They didn't give their blessing to the marriage, and blamed Julia for their son's death. They've treated her very badly."

"Wow." Miriam digested this new information. "How could they do that?"

"I don't know. I try not to think about it because when I do, I get really angry," Rick admitted.

"Still," his mom injected, "is she starting to see that you aren't like that?"

"I think so," Rick said. "Spending time with Garrett and Monica has helped, plus Sloan had already taken her to a couple of fancy parties over the last few months. I think she dreads them, because I know she doesn't like the wasteful spending she sees at the events, and she isn't always comfortable around 'high society' people.

"Since she and Sloan are more like siblings than childhood friends, she's his cover date. It protects him from the unwanted advances of money-hungry women on the prowl for a doctor husband. He's actually engaged to her cousin Jocelyn."

"You like this young lady, don't you, son?" Mr. Adams asked.

"Yes, Dad, I do," Rick said. "It's deeper than that, though. I only hope that I can convince her to give this a chance."

19
Facing the Fans

The next morning, at eight thirty sharp, a knock sounded on Julia's townhouse door.

"Come in, Rick," she called from the kitchen. "I see you still can't tell time."

"You knew that I'd be here early, so don't pretend you're surprised," Rick said. She helped prove his point as she handed him a cup of coffee, already prepared to his liking.

"I'm psychic."

"Sure," he said, "we'll go with that for now. Is everybody ready?"

"Yes, the kids are brushing their teeth," she said. "I need to go check upstairs and then I'll be ready."

He heard the kids at the top of the stairs.

"Butts down!" Julia called. She had taught Bethany to sit and work her way down one stair at a time. The apartment was a split-level, so the kids traversed several stairs and then scooted around to the lower flight. It was quite efficient but comical to watch, especially on a day like today when they were both so excited.

"Unka Rick! Unka Rick!" The two-year-old girl cried as she bounced on each stair. "We're going to your house!"

"Yes, yes, you are!" He swung her up as she reached the bottom step. "You get to meet my mom and dad and my sister and her new baby."

"We got you another present, too!" C.J. chimed in.

"Quiet!" Julia called from upstairs, having heard the whole interchange. "It's a secret surprise. No telling!"

"It's not really for you, though," C.J. said. "Mommy won't let me even tell Bethany what it is 'cause she'll blab it."

"Well, you need to obey your mom, then, and don't tell me," Rick said. "I don't want her mad at me, too! Is this the box that's going?" He pointed to a box sitting next to the door.

"Yes," Julia answered as she made her way downstairs. Rick thought she looked like a teenager in the light pink sweater and dark blue jeans she was wearing. The outfit matched the youthful spirit that hid beneath Julia's carefully controlled exterior. He knew not to verbalize his thoughts though, afraid she might turn around and go change into something she considered more age appropriate since she was meeting his family.

Minutes from the house, Rick decided to prepare Julia for the surprise. He was still afraid she was going to reject his gift outright, even if it meant disappointing her children. With each passing mile, he thought perhaps he should have asked her first. *Oh well, too late now.*

"Julia." Rick hesitated. "I've done something perhaps a little foolish, and I want you to know I did it with the best intentions. I'm not going to tell you what it is, but I want you to try to be open-minded, okay?"

"You have me a little concerned, Mr. Adams," Julia said. "What on earth did you do?"

"It's not bad, I promise. But I probably should have asked you first."

"Well, as long as it's not a surprise birthday party or something else that would totally embarrass me, I can't imagine that it's too terrible."

"Well, we'll see if you feel the same way in a few minutes," he said. "Besides, your birthday is not until late summer, so I haven't even started planning that one yet."

"I do hope you're joking," Julia said, shuddering. "A surprise birthday party would be the worst thing anyone could ever do to me. I went to a friend's surprise party when I was a teenager and remember thinking that I would pass out from humiliation on the spot if someone did this to me."

Rick filed the information away. *Guess that eliminates a public proposal,* he thought, smiling to himself. *Good to know in advance.*

Julia was nervous as they reached his house. Now she had the added fear of his surprise on top of meeting his family. Thankfully, the two events didn't coincide. His parents and sister greeted them at the door.

Elaine Adams was several inches taller than Julia, but her husband was obviously the one responsible for Rick's height and frame. They were an adorable pair. Rick's sister Miriam was taller than her mom and her light brown hair was several shades lighter than Rick's.

Introductions were made and included letting the kids peer into the bassinette to see the sleeping newborn. Miriam's daughter Olivia was six weeks old, and the look of awe and wonder on her children's faces was adorable.

"I need to get this over with soon," Rick said to his mom. "I told her I did something slightly foolish, and I think she may be scared to death of what I've done."

"Wait a few minutes and let her get settled. Let's have some coffee, and I'll bring the kids some hot chocolate and donuts."

As they walked into the kitchen, they found that Miriam was already cooling down mugs of hot cocoa for Bethany and C.J. and had a tray of donuts ready. Julia was pouring herself a cup of coffee, and she smiled at him as he came to her side.

"They seem quite nice," she said quietly to Rick.

"Were you afraid they'd all have two heads, sharp teeth, and scales?"

"You know what they say about genetics," she said.

"Very funny," he said, kissing her gently on the cheek.

Rick's mom's laugh from the kitchen doorway made Julia looked around for a means of escape, so she volunteered to deliver the tray of pre-meal snacks to Rick's dad and the kids. Bethany and C.J. were snuggled next to the older man. Miriam settled Olivia in her playpen and came to take the tray from Julia.

"Aren't they cute?" Miriam asked. "Daddy says he can't wait for Olivia to be old enough to do more than eat and sleep." Julia stopped and listened to the conversation between her son and Glen Adams.

"Yes, I'm Uncle Rick's Daddy," Mr. Adams said. "Miriam is Rick's sister, just like you're Bethany's brother."

"Oh," the little boy said as he climbed onto his lap. "My Daddy's in heaven."

Julia shut her eyes and forced herself to breathe normally. When she ventured a glance, she saw that Miriam was wiping tears away. Julia turned quietly and headed back to the kitchen. Out of the corner of her eye, she saw Rick in the kitchen doorway. He had overheard C.J.'s comment and appeared torn—not sure if he should intervene. Deciding she needed more privacy, Julia scooted past him.

Rick reached for her as she spied the dining room doorway. She slipped out of his grasp and was through the door before he could stop her. Rick knew immediately when she spotted the puppy's crate.

Mighty Mouse had chosen that moment to wake up and reveal his unhappiness at being left alone again. His yipping wasn't loud enough for the children to hear from the living room, but Julia heard him right away.

"What have you done?" She turned on Rick, and then fled through the dining room and into the hallway, seeking the one place of retreat she knew in this monstrosity that he called a home.

Rick detoured back through the kitchen and told his mom to keep the surprise quiet.

"I don't think I'm going to be able to give it to them today. I blew it, big time." He found Julia where expected, in the library, curled up in the corner of a loveseat. Instead of a forlorn woman, he was shocked at the immediate verbal attack.

"Get out."

"It's my house."

"Fair enough. I'll leave instead." Despite her words, Julia didn't move.

"You're being unreasonable." He flipped on the lamp next to the loveseat and knelt beside her.

"Go away," she said.

"Are you upset about the puppy or about what C.J. said to my dad?"

"You had no right to get my children a dog."

Okay, we'll deal with that first, Rick thought as he settled next to her. "Let me explain, please, Julia. You have to give me a chance."

"Why? What good will it do at this point?" She stood. Arms folded, she faced him as she continued on the offensive. "Are you going to take it back? What happens if they find out? What happens if they ask where their surprise is?" She knew she was being unreasonable, but she couldn't stop the tumble of words.

Rick let her vent, giving her a chance to calm down. He watched as she moved across the room and stopped in front of the family pictures that had caused such a stir only weeks ago.

"I'm going to explain whether you like it or not," he said finally. "I know you had thought about a puppy for the kids this year."

"So what if I did?" She glanced back over her shoulder. *Now we're getting somewhere*, he thought.

"I know that allergies are a concern, since C.J. has had a couple bouts with hay fever, so I did some research. The puppy is a Yorkshire mix, a breed that is good for allergy-sensitive homes."

"Nice job on picking a good breed for *your* new puppy." She was still not happy with him.

"C'mon, Julia, you're killing me here. Honestly, I didn't do this to make you mad. I talked to Sloan, Terry, and your parents. Even Garrett and Monica know how much your kids love their dogs. I would never have done this if I didn't know it was already something you were considering."

"Why did you do it?" Her quiet words let him know she was relenting.

"Look at me." Joining her, Rick turned her gently. He brushed the hair back and lifted her chin up with one finger. She pushed his hand away and moved back to the loveseat.

"Let me do this for you." Leaning against the bookshelf behind him, he crossed his arms, mirroring her defiance. "Whether you're willing to admit it or not, I am part of your life now. How quickly and how much I get involved is up to you, although we both know my preferences. For now, accept this as a grand gesture from a friend."

Her arms were wrapped around her knees, and she had pushed herself as far into the corner of the loveseat as she could get.

"Just a 'grand gesture from a friend'?" She lifted her head slightly.

"Yes," Rick rejoined her, sitting closer this time. "At least for now."

"Okay," she said quietly. Rick gently pried her arms off her knees and pulled her toward him. Despite her previous anger, she came willingly.

"Can we talk about the other thing?" Rick knew his dad and sister would be concerned about her reaction to Bethany's simple confession. Rick felt her tense.

"No, Rick. I don't want or need anyone's pity. If I were to get upset every time James was mentioned that would traumatize my children more than necessary."

Wisely deferring the discussion, Rick kissed the top of her head softly. "I'm sorry I didn't ask you about the puppy first." Placing her arms around his neck, he held her close against his chest. "Shall we go meet the latest addition to the family?" Knowing his parents were probably wondering where they were, he wouldn't put it past his father to come looking for them.

"I'm embarrassed that I acted like a child," she said, "and I'm sure I look terrible."

His response was a deep and passionate kiss that left them both a little breathless.

"I'll send C.J. with your purse if it will make you feel better," he said. "Personally, I think you look beautiful, vulnerable..." then added as he left, "...and sexy."

A few minutes later, she and C.J. rejoined the others. While she had retouched the little bit of makeup she usually wore, her son spent the time spinning in one of the stools at the game table.

"Can we give Uncle Rick the castle now?"

"Yes, in a few minutes, I think we can." She knew that once the puppy made an appearance, all thoughts of other gifts would disappear.

Still feeling ashamed for her display, she hesitantly stepped back into the living room. Rick's mom gave her a quick hug. Rick had warned them not to mention C.J.'s innocent comment.

"At least I get to say, 'I told you so' to my very stubborn son," Elaine said. "I knew it wasn't a good idea to try to surprise you."

Julia managed a slight smile in response to his mom's kindness. Rick pulled her down next to him on the couch, the spot familiar to her from the charades episode at the Thanksgiving party. He leaned over and asked when they should reveal the surprise.

"The kids want you to open their gift," she said. "I know they'll forget afterward, so can we do that first?"

Rick was dutifully, and genuinely, thrilled with the new castle for his tank. The whole group had gathered around the tank for an official installation ceremony. Rick stole a quick kiss before suggesting they head back toward the dining room.

"If Little Bit's whining gets any louder, they're going to hear him, anyway."

"Okay, but I want pictures, so let me get my phone first." His mom offered to take play photographer so she could enjoy the surprise with the kids.

Rick positioned the kids in front of the swinging kitchen door that led to the dining room and created an elaborate story about Santa delivering their gift to him because he knew Uncle Rick would take good care of it until Christmas. They had to both promise to be good and gentle and help Mommy with the present. The five-year-old could hardly stand still from the excitement, Rick's story having worked him into a frenzy. His sister didn't completely understand what Uncle Rick was saying, but knew whatever was happening was wonderful, if her brother's reaction was anything to judge by.

"Stop torturing the children, Rick," his sister said from behind him. "Are you ready, Julia?"

Elaine had the camera poised, so Rick pushed open the door.

"You'll have to listen carefully to find it," he said. The two children fell completely silent, just long enough to hear the yips coming from the crate under the table. C.J.'s eyes were round with surprise as he turned to his mom.

"It's a puppy!"

"Puppy!" Bethany echoed.

Rick bent and pulled the crate toward them, opened it, and lifted the squirmy bundle and placed it in C.J.'s outstretched arms. The Yorkie wiggled in delight, covering his newfound friend's face with puppy kisses.

"Sit down, son, and let your sister see the puppy, too."

Rick settled the pair on the dining room floor with the puppy between them. Julia joined her children on the floor. The puppy's instinct led the tiny ball of wagging dog to settle into her lap, knowing a safe refuge immediately.

"Smart dog," Rick leaned over and whispered in Julia's ear, loving that he could make her blush so easily.

"Let's take him outside, okay?" Julia carried the puppy out, already instructing the children in the potty training that would be crucial over the next few weeks. He immediately took care of business and then bounded on short legs back to the kids.

Rick's parents watched from the window as their son grinned ear to ear over the antics of the puppy and children. Julia reached out to hold Rick's hand. The gesture did not go unnoticed.

"I think she's forgiven him," Mrs. Adams said.

"Looks that way," her husband agreed. "Do you think he knows yet?"

"That he's head over heels in love with her?" Elaine asked. "Yes, I'm pretty sure he does. I don't think he's told her yet, which is good. Her reaction to what Bethany said shows she may still be leery of the whole idea."

"Yes, she may be, but that's understandable." His father watched the young mom as Rick pulled her closer.

"Her children are precious. It's so tragic that they lost their dad. Sometimes I struggle with trusting that our Heavenly Father knows best, because it seems so unfair."

As C.J. turned toward them, playing a game of chase with the puppy, Rick's mom was struck anew with how much he looked like Rick as a child.

"I'm so glad Rick warned us about C.J.," she said. "It's sort of eerie, isn't it?"

"I know that it troubles Rick to think that if they end up together, people will assume the kids are his biological children and how unfair that would be to James," Mr. Adams said. "But I think James was the type of man that would be thrilled to know there was another godly man that loves his children. It's obvious that Julia does a good job of talking about James to the kids. Rick said she keeps his pictures around and even has video for when they get older. I trust our son to handle the situation."

Not used to her quiet husband making such a long speech, Mrs. Adams merely stared up at him.

"I don't think we need to get ahead of ourselves just yet, dear." Mr. Adams playfully teased his wife. "It's a puppy and not an engagement ring, you know." She wrinkled her nose at him, and he rewarded her with a kiss.

The rest of the day was filled with puppy frolics, opening the few presents they had brought for Rick and his family, and a tasty but nontraditional Christmas meal. The homemade lasagna and New York-style cheesecake made a delightful end to the day.

Rick drove them back home later that afternoon, with the puppy, crate, and supplies tucked carefully in the back seat between the kids' car seats.

Julia carried the still-unnamed puppy through the townhouse to the backyard area to help get him acclimated to his new surroundings. She praised his contributions to the environment and led him back into the house.

"We've decided on a name," Rick announced. He had shared his ideas of Mighty Mouse and Little Bit, but the kids had decided on one based more on their observations.

"And?" Julia asked.

"Bouncer!" the kids yelled in unison.

"Perfect, right?" Rick asked, lifting the newly named pup onto Bethany's lap as she sat on the couch.

"Yes, it is," Julia said, surprising Rick with a quick kiss. "Thank you, Rick."

"My pleasure," he said, knowing she understood the double meaning behind his words.

20
The Bonus

Julia, the kids, Sloan, Jocelyn, Terry, and Rick's family were all gathered at Monica's for the last game of the season. The outcome would determine if the two-year-old expansion team would make the playoffs, an unusual feat in professional football.

The team had flown out on New Year's Eve, a couple of days before the game. Since it was an early game, and a short flight, they might be back home by early evening. Rick made Terry promise that she would make Julia and the kids ride with her, so Rick and Stephen would have an excuse to take them all home. They had seen little of Rick over the last week since Coach had ramped up practices now that there was a possibility the young expansion team would make the playoffs.

Bouncer was intrigued with the larger, older dogs, who in turn were alternately avoiding and shepherding the newcomer in and around the kids. Julia rescued the little one for a nap in the crate, reminding her children that they promised Rick they would take good care of the puppy.

"He needs to take a nap, just like you do sometimes," she told them. "We'll let him sleep for a little bit and then he can come back out and play."

"So, you weren't mad at Rick for the puppy?" Monica asked when they were alone in the kitchen.

"Well," Julia said, her hesitation telling the story for her, "I wasn't thrilled, but I got over it."

"If they make the playoffs, they'll be gone most of the week, right?" Julia was still getting used to the routine, which Monica seemed to take in stride.

"Yes, since the game will be away, Coach wants them to get there as soon as they can so they can get rested and have as much time as possible on the actual field."

"And after the playoff game?"

"Well," Monica said, "don't ever say this to the guys, but it's unlikely that they'll win more than one playoff game, but we're hoping for at least a good showing. Anything besides a blowout loss will seem like a victory. It's so unusual for a young team to get to the playoffs. Still, the male ego being what it is, they'll all be miserable for several days after a playoff loss, so be prepared."

"Then what do they do?" Julia hadn't thought of pro athletes and their off-season time before.

"I wouldn't be surprised if Rick gets a call from one of the networks to do some commentary during the playoffs. His degree in communications is a big bonus, and he has experience because he anchored the sports segment on the college television station during the spring sports seasons."

"So, he'll be gone covering the games every weekend?"

"Most likely," Monica said. "Has he talked about what he plans after he retires?"

"With me?" Julia asked, surprised at the question.

"Yes, with you, silly. Who else would he discuss it with?" Monica asked as she took a tray of sandwiches to the den where the crowd was watching the halftime show.

Two hours later, Monica, Julia, and Terry all received calls within minutes of each other. The plane had landed, and Coach had released the guys to head home. They would all come home with Garrett and celebrate making the playoffs.

Rick greeted C.J., Bethany, and the puppy first, before lifting Julia into a bear hug followed by a long, dramatic kiss.

"We made the playoffs," he said quietly, against her neck.

"I know, I heard," she whispered. "Congratulations."

"Why thank you, Mrs. Fitzgerald." He slid her back to the stool he had lifted her from and kissed her again. "Your support is most appreciated."

"When do you have to fly out?" she asked. Rick moved around the counter and filled a plate with food, rejoining her with a well-stocked array.

"We leave Tuesday afternoon, but the good news is we won't practice on Monday." He glanced over her shoulder and winked at her. "So, my whole day is free." His hint was so lacking in subtlety that it was funny.

"Is it unusual for Coach to give you that much time off?" Julia smiled sweetly at him, her chin resting innocently on her hands.

"A little, but I think he knows the adrenaline is running pretty high and he wants to give some of these youngsters a couple days to settle down, otherwise they might get hurt before the game." He finally looked up from his feast long enough to catch her amused look.

"Am I boring you, ma'am?" he asked.

"On the contrary," she answered. "You are quite fascinating, sir." She enjoyed watching him talk about the game he loved so much. She had always been a fan, but now she had a new perspective and deeper appreciation.

"I aim to please, madam," he said and fed her a grape followed by a kiss to reward her patience with his rambling.

"Scrumptious," she said, meeting his gaze squarely, daring him to continue their flirtation.

"I agree completely," he said. "Scrumptious, indeed. I might even say addicting." He leaned in for another kiss, but she playfully pushed him away as she heard Sloan and Garrett coming down the hall.

"I need to go check on the puppy," she said, making her escape.

"Coward," he called after her. She turned at the doorway and blew him a kiss. The illustrious Dr. Mackenzie saw this last gesture, which meant Rick had to endure several minutes of merciless teasing from his friend.

An hour later, Rick drove Julia home while Stephen and Terry followed in Julia's car, puppy and kids in tow. The younger pair had volunteered for the challenge. Even though they were not romantically involved, Stephen and Terry had become good friends. They had a friendly, if unspoken, competition for the affection of Julia's kids.

The mood in Rick's truck was relaxed and comfortable. Julia even thought to herself that she never would have dreamed a month ago that she'd be alone in a vehicle with the famous professional athlete, their hands touching gently on the seat between them while they talked about the upcoming game. Unfortunately, the idyllic atmosphere was shattered quite unexpectedly.

Rick's phone rang, and he asked Julia to answer via the speakerphone on his dashboard.

"Rick, my man!" Morris Longworth, Rick's agent, was on the phone. "We made the playoffs!"

Rick rolled his eyes, and Julia laughed. He had told her how annoying his agent could be. Rick mouthed the word, "We?" He had mentioned how Morris loved to take credit for any successes, however remotely he may be tied to them.

"Yes, *we* did," Rick said. Julia hoped Morris couldn't hear the sarcasm. "What can I do for you this evening, Morris? I'm pretty beat and was hoping to relax a little before the craziness of the week begins."

"Hey, buddy," Morris said, again with the overly familiar attitude of a born salesman. "It's not what you can do for me, but I'm all about what I can do for you." This earned another eye roll from Rick. "So, you remember how hard I worked for you during the contract negotiations a couple years ago, right?" Morris asked. In the back of his mind, Rick remembered some big coup that Morris had gone on and on about when he arranged for the trade to the new expansion team. He racked his brain as Morris droned on about how hard he had worked to get the right deal.

A feeling of dread filled Rick as he remembered the juicy caveat in his new contract. He had forgotten all about the obscure agreement because when he signed the contract, it was so unlikely to ever come into play. It was too late to hit the mute button. Rick could feel the mood change in the cab as Julia heard his agent's news.

"You, my friend, just made a sizable chunk of change!" The enthusiastic agent could hardly contain his excitement. "I know you didn't believe in yourself like I did, but aren't you glad now that I slipped the line in about making the playoffs by your second year?"

"Thrilled," Rick said, his tone making it clear he was anything but thrilled. He was pulling into Julia's complex, and he tried to wrap up the conversation before any more damage could be done.

"I need to go now, Morris," Rick insisted, desperate now as he saw Julia staring out the passenger window, wishing to be anywhere but with him.

"Will do, bud," Morris said. "I'll call you tomorrow."

"Julia," Rick said, reaching across her to prevent her from jumping out of the car, "let me explain."

"Exactly how much is a 'sizable chunk of change'?"

"The amount doesn't matter," Rick said. "I had forgotten all about the stupid rider Morris had slipped in to the contract."

"It may not matter to you, but it does to me," she said. "How much?"

"Two million."

"Two million dollars?!"

"Yes," Rick said, now staring out his own window. He had long ago dealt with guilt over the outrageous salaries that professional ballplayers made in this country, but he wanted Julia to understand.

"How can you sit there like it's okay for you to make more in thirty seconds than most people will make in four or five lifetimes?!" He heard disgust and panic in her voice.

"Let me explain." Rick turned and pulled her around to face him. He saw Stephen and Terry unload the kids and Bouncer quickly and head into the apartment.

"I can't handle this right now." Julia pulled away and opened her door. "I'll send Stephen out to you. I think it's best if you go home now." Rick watched in despair as she walked to the door and disappeared inside.

"Bad?" Stephen asked when he got into the truck a couple minutes later. "She seemed pretty upset."

"Yes, bad," Rick said. "Really bad. Morris called to remind me that making the playoffs meant a two-million-dollar bonus."

"Ouch," Stephen said.

Rick was still in shock. Stephen sat quietly as Rick leaned his head back, contemplating his next move. He needed help and needed it quickly. Rick sat forward suddenly and grabbed his phone from the dashboard connection.

"Sloan."

21

Questioning the Call

"Hey, Rick. What's up?" Sloan's voice came through the speaker. Rick didn't care that Stephen could hear his conversation. "Did Julia leave something here? Jocelyn and I haven't left yet." Jocelyn was staying with Julia while she was in town working on wedding details.

"Sloan," Rick said. "Help!"

"Is Julia okay? The kids?" Sloan's response to Rick's anguished voice was immediate.

"Yes," Rick said. "Sort of, I guess you could say."

"Explain yourself, brother," Sloan said. "What did you do?"

"Thanks for the vote of confidence," Rick said, glaring at Stephen. The young kicker seemed to appreciate Sloan's presumption of blame.

"Apparently the whole idea of dating a millionaire has suddenly become repugnant to Mrs. Fitzgerald."

"Suddenly?" Sloan asked. "I don't think she's ever been thrilled with the idea. Based on her previous experience with the rich and famous, and compared to her own upbringing, I'm sure she's had a hard time accepting it."

"I thought we were beyond that point," Rick explained. "At least it's not a topic of conversation anymore."

"Was it ever a topic?" Sloan asked. "I mean, have you two discussed it? Really, truly discussed it?"

"Apparently not."

"What exactly happened to set her off?" Sloan asked. "She was fine twenty minutes ago."

"Morris called. Two-million-dollar bonus for making the playoffs. I had forgotten."

"Ouch."

"Exactly what Stephen here said."

"Hi, Stephen," Sloan said, realizing that the young man was listening in. "Did you see her reaction? What do you think Teddy here should do?"

"She's pretty upset. Went straight up to her room. Asked Terry to get the kids ready for bed."

"Wow," Sloan said.

"Let me know if you want me to stay out of it," Stephen said calmly to Rick, "but I think you need to go handle it right now."

"I'm sure she won't talk to me," Rick said.

"I think you can make her listen," Stephen offered. "Even if she stays locked in her room, you can talk to her through the door."

"Wise advice, my young apprentice," Sloan said in his best movie-mentor accent. "I think the kid has the right idea, Rick. Go talk to her."

"Exactly what am I supposed to say to her?" Rick asked, his tone signaling his lack of confidence in his friends' advice. "I'm not especially happy with her right now either. She jumped to judgment and bolted. That seems to be her go-to reaction when she doesn't like what's happening."

"I know you worked through these issues when you came into the league," Sloan said. "But remember the perspective she's coming from. I know you care about her, and the good news is I think she's beginning to like you a little, too."

"I'll say." Sloan's last comment elicited a loud chuckle from Stephen. Rick gave him a warning look, and the young placekicker wisely shut up.

"I know she's upset and I'm not happy that she didn't let me explain, so this may not be very productive," Rick said. He thanked Sloan and then asked Stephen if he'd help Terry with the kids and then make sure she got home safely.

"Gladly," Stephen said, always willing to spend more time with the kids.

"Well, here goes nothing." Rick's anger hadn't ebbed much as he reached the doorway. It was still unlocked, and he pushed in without knocking.

Terry had gotten the kids into their pajamas. She was at the top of the stairs as Rick bounded up.

"Is she still in there?" he asked, pointing to Julia's bedroom. Terry nodded, eyes wide. She looked relieved to see Stephen come up the stairs behind Rick.

"Uncle Rick looks mad," C.J. said, peeking around Terry's legs.

"I think he just wants to talk to Mommy." Terry tried to downplay the level of drama, not wanting to concern the kids. "Let's get you two into bed, okay? Maybe Uncle Stephen will read you a book." Stephen grabbed Bouncer who was intent of helping Rick charge into battle.

The young couple scooted the children back into their room, trying to distract them from the sight of Rick's arms on the frame of Julia's closed bedroom door.

"Julia, stop pouting."

"Go away."

"We need to talk."

"Well, I don't want to talk to you right now."

This conversation is not going well, Rick thought.

"Terry and Stephen are putting the kids to bed. You need to come out so we can talk, or I'm coming in after you."

"You wouldn't dare."

"Yes, I would." Rick opened the door. Julia stood next to her bed, hands on hips and tapping the foot of one flannel covered leg. She had already changed into an oversized sweatshirt and cartoon character pajama pants.

"You have one minute," she said.

"We are going to talk—but not in your bedroom." Rick moved so fast that Julia was on her way downstairs before she knew what had happened.

"Put me down!" Rick had grabbed her by the waist and hoisted her over his shoulder in one lightning-fast movement. He plopped her down on the couch and sat on the coffee table in front of her.

"Fine." Julia sat with legs crossed and arms folded.

"All I'm asking is for you to listen. I don't know if what I say will change your mind, but you owe me at least the courtesy of letting me explain."

She met his steady gaze.

"You, my dear, are a poverty snob." Rick saw the color drain from her face, but his anger was still simmering, so he continued. "I'd say you are so proud of being able to survive and do so successfully on a limited income that it's drawing you to be judgmental. I think your pride has grown to the point that you're prejudiced against anyone who doesn't have your financial skills, abilities, and thriftiness."

"Prideful and prejudiced? Well, *Mr. Darcy,* pray tell how living as a single mother on an income that flirts with the poverty level, raising two young kids equates to pride?" Julia moved to stand up, but Rick pushed her gently back on to the sofa.

"You seem to think that being poor means that you're somehow a better person than those of us that have wealth, *Miss Bennett,*" Rick said, continuing the allegory from her favorite author's classic novel. She opened her mouth, but he stopped her response with a quickly raised finger.

"Let me finish, please."

"By all means," she waved a hand inviting him to continue.

"When I came into the league and the magnitude of the change in my status finally hit me, I struggled with what I perceived as the injustice of the situation. I felt guilty and confused. I was ready to quit the whole scene because I couldn't wrap my head around how this all could possibly be part of God's will."

Her refusal to meet his gaze let him know his words were getting through. His anger was subsiding as he realized how important this conversation was to their future. He loved this woman and had to make her understand. He took her hand as she finally lifted her head.

"I went to my pastor, and he was quite patient with my immature and selfish tantrums."

"'Selfish'?" she asked, confused as to why giving up millions of dollars would be considered selfish.

"A lot of people, even in the church, think that because I have money, and lots of it, I don't worry about anything. They think I don't need God since I don't have to worry about my next meal, a roof over my head, or any other basic needs." Rick took a deep breath.

"The pastor told me what I needed to hear. There is no sin in being wealthy. I had to accept that this life, my talents, and this job, however long it may last, are all gifts of my Heavenly Father. It is my duty to use those gifts in the way He wants me to."

Julia was watching him intently now. He was not apologizing for his money as she expected him to do. Instead, he was accusing her of being the snob. It was unsettling.

"Yes, God has blessed me with more money than I could ever need, but that does not mean I don't need Him. On the contrary, it's all His money, anyway. I feel like I have a serious responsibility to be a steward of His money. Have I always used it wisely? Probably not, but I am trying. Just like you, Julia."

"You really think I'm a snob?"

"That was a little harsh, I know," he said, smiling in apology. "Forgive me?"

"What did you mean?"

"You're an amazing woman. What you're able to do on such little money is incredible." He paused, hesitating, then carefully chose his words. "You've become so good at managing that I think you may be forgetting to depend on God as much as you should."

Her look was part disbelief, part confusion. He watched patiently as she processed his gentle rebuke.

"I don't want to be rich." Her simple words stated her fears more eloquently than she realized.

"I know," he said, brushing a strand of hair back from her face. "I agree that riches do make dependence on God harder, but I think you have such a fine-tuned control over your life that you're in danger of falling into the same trap."

Rick scooted her over and joined her on the couch, resting his arm along the back. He cradled her face in his hand, obliging her to look at him.

"Do you think that maybe, just possibly, being in a relationship with someone like me might require a step of faith on your part?" Rick asked. "Do you think you might consider the possibility, however remote, that God might be leading you into this? Is it so unreasonable to think that He could use us, the money, our situation, my job, for His glory?"

"I don't know." Her emotional exhaustion was evident as let him gather her in his arms. A few minutes later, they heard Stephen and Terry coming down the stairs. Stephen indicated that he was walking Terry home and pointed questioningly to his watch.

"Ten minutes," Rick said quietly.

As the door closed, Julia lifted her head and moved out of Rick's embrace.

"Well?" Rick asked.

"I can't think straight when you're here," Julia said. It was not what Rick expected her to say.

"You want me to leave?" he asked, somewhat confused.

"Yes," she said simply. "I need to think about this, and I can't do it when I can reach out and touch you."

"Okay." He stood up quickly and moved across the room to sit on the edge of the recliner. "Far enough?"

"Nice try," she laughed. "But no."

"Tell me what you need me to do," Rick said. "Short of giving up on us, I'll do whatever will help you get used to the idea."

"I just need some time right now," Julia said.

"How much time do you need?" Rick asked, looking at his watch.

"Funny," Julia said. "I will let you know." She moved to the kitchen and started a pot of coffee, knowing she wouldn't be able to sleep anytime soon. "Besides, Sloan and Jocelyn will be here soon. Good night, Rick."

"Julia." His voice was gentle but commanding enough that she put down the mugs she was holding and turned toward him. "We leave Tuesday afternoon for the game. I'll call you before we get on the plane."

She watched out the window until his truck left the complex.

22
A True Fan

His patience stretched thin, Rick waited until an hour before the plane's schedule departure before he called Julia. Forcing himself to show restraint, he called Sloan first.

Sloan was shocked that he had held out that long.

"Good job, Teddy," Rick's friend said, teasing him. The dreaded nickname was appropriate, Sloan felt, based on the emotional mess that would've described the professional quarterback over the last two days.

"You'll keep an eye on her this week, right?" Rick asked for Sloan's assurance. "I don't want her to make any rash decisions while I'm out of town."

"I think if she was going to run away, she would've done it by now."

"Hopefully, you're right," Rick said. He ended the call with his close friend and dialed Julia's number.

"Rick." She answered on the first ring.

"Hey," Rick said. "Waiting anxiously by the phone for my call?"

"Hey, yourself," Julia said, "and no, I just happened to be walking by when it rang."

"Sure you were," he said.

"Are you ready?" Julia ignored his comment. "How are the youngsters? Are they beyond excited? Do you think they'll be able to settle down enough to play well?"

Nice try, avoiding what we actually need to talk about, Rick thought, but he decided to humor her.

"Yes, they're wound pretty tight. I think Coach was wise to get us over there as soon as possible. Maybe some of the excitement will wear off." He moved out of earshot of the rest of the team.

"You know we're not likely to win, right?" he asked her, confessing what he wouldn't share with anyone else. "I just hope we don't embarrass ourselves."

"I know that's what the experts are saying, but you weren't supposed to make it this far, remember?"

"True," he said. "Thanks for the encouragement. Just promise to turn off the TV if it's a blowout, okay?"

"No way! I'm a true fan, in it until the end, better or worse." Julia regretted immediately her choice of words.

"Better or worse, huh?" Rick asked.

"You know what I mean," Julia said, desperately trying to think of a way to change the topic.

"Julia," Rick's voice was low as he tried to find the right words to make things right between them. "Tell me we're going to be okay. The last two days have been torture."

"You know, I think you need to thank Ms. Austen for her intervention," Julia said. Her biggest spiritual weakness was her pride, and she had struggled with it all her life. That she was so willing to admit it to this unlikely man convinced Julia that this relationship was different.

"How so, Miss Bennett?" Rick knew exactly what she was implying.

"I'm so sorry. I was wrong, you were right," Julia was surprised at how her confession lightened the heaviness that had settled on her with the agent's fateful news. "You were right about it all."

"Julia," Rick said. Repeating her name was all he could manage.

"Rick," she said, a teasing tone creeping in. It was obvious that she had shocked him.

"Are you saying that you're willing to give this a chance?" He held his breath.

"Yes," she said. "You were right about my pride, my prejudice, and my lack of faith. I realized I had stuffed God into a box, limiting what His will is to what I thought it should be."

"I wonder if Coach would mind if I took a later flight."

"You're being silly now," Julia said. "Go get on the plane. Don't keep the Baby Wolves waiting."

"You know that Sloan's nickname for the team could get me in a lot of trouble, right?"

"Yes." Julia laughed. "But you have to admit it's perfect."

"They've called us to board," Rick said. "I'm not sure what our schedule is going to look like, so I may not be able to call again before the game," Rick said. "Kiss those kids for me, okay?"

"I will," Julia said. "And Rick?"

"Yes, ma'am?" Rick asked, responding to her motherly tone.

"Have a good time," she said. "I know you know that this is a special event, but make sure you enjoy it. Don't beat yourself up if things don't go perfectly."

He hesitated, wanting badly to tell her the words he knew she wasn't ready to hear. He resolved to be patient. Not happily patient, but patient.

"You're making it difficult to get on the plane. I'll call when I can," Rick said, finally ending the call. He boarded the plane with a much lighter mood.

The game was surprisingly close, which made the loss even tougher. Still, as a team leader Rick had to face the press with an upbeat attitude.

"Yes, it was a tough loss, but I'm proud of the team. No one expected us to make it this far in our second year, so we're pleased with how quickly we came together as a team," Rick answered one of the reporters bombarding him with questions at the after-game press conference.

To the casual observer, he didn't look devastated by the four-point loss to the team that most experts predicted would be the eventual champions. He was upbeat and smiling, and he made sure the reporters and fans knew he was proud of how well the young team had done, despite the loss.

As he left the conference room, he saw that he had a message on his phone. It was from Julia.

"That's a bunch of hooey and you know it."

"Excuse me? Hooey?" Rick typed a response and sent it back to her.

"You may have the press and the fans fooled, and maybe even the team fooled, but I know you are VERY disappointed."

"How do you know that?"

"I saw right through you."

Garrett stopped Rick as he got on the bus and pushed him into the vacant seat across the aisle.

"What's so funny?" Stephen asked. The kicker was sitting with Garrett and had seen Rick's grin.

"Julia saw right through my spiel," Rick said, holding up his phone. "Remind me to never play poker with her. She knows me too well."

"That's because she's in love with him." Garrett said under his breath to Stephen, who failed to contain his chuckle in time.

"Why is that funny?" Rick looked pointedly at the young man.

"No reason," Stephen's response was accompanied by a raised eyebrow.

"You said what the fans and press wanted to hear," Garrett interjected. "That's exactly what the youngsters needed going into a long off-season. Besides, it's true. We did rather well and much better than expected."

"I still can't help being disappointed that the season is over," Rick said, almost to himself. "I know I'm heading into the long, dark abyss of winter and springtime. This time tomorrow I'll be throwing a royal self-pity party, like every other year." He knew this year's post-season melancholy had the potential to be deeper, given next season was probably his last. The rumor had been circulating, but Rick hadn't confirmed it with anyone. For some reason, he wanted to talk to Julia about it first.

The thought of Julia lightened his mood. He stretched his legs out into the aisle, and the linebacker in front of Garrett untied his shoe. Rick kicked him. Normally playful pandemonium would ensue, but they were all too tired.

"Maybe it won't be so bad, though," Rick said, as he settled back in his seat. "How late do you think it will be when we get home?"

"Do you mean will it still be early enough to go to her house?" Garrett asked. The flight was another short one, so it was a possibility. "You're whipped." Rick punched him and got a pillow in his face.

23

A New Team Trainer

Three hours later, Rick was knocking on Julia's door. The emotion of the game and the end of the season had caught up to him. She pulled him into the apartment, sat him down on the couch, and deposited Bouncer in his lap.

"Puppy therapy," she said. "Lots cheaper than regular therapy."

The children were waiting patiently, sitting together in the recliner across the room. Julia had instructed them to stay put until she gave them permission to move.

"Uncle Rick is going to be sad when he gets here," their mom had explained. "We're going to let Bouncer cheer him up first, okay?"

Rick was amazed at the restraint from the normally squirmy boy and restless toddler princess. Their looks of concern were his undoing.

"Come here, you two," he said. "Save me before this beast licks me to death!"

"We made you pictures!" C.J. proudly presented his masterpiece to Rick.

"Me, too!" Bethany climbed into Rick's lap, waving her picture under his nose.

Their sweet offerings were Rick's undoing. Julia quietly wrapped her arms around his neck from behind as she saw tears in his eyes. She kissed him on the cheek and then moved back into the kitchen.

C.J.'s picture was a brilliant work featuring some sort of battle. Apparently, the young boy's view of football was that it would be better if it included multiple grenades. As Rick studied the picture more closely, he realized the grenades were, in fact, footballs.

"Fantastic, C.J.!" Rick said. He agreed with the boy's concept. The games would be quite a bit more interesting if each team could have several balls in play at the same time.

Bethany's picture was just as elaborate, if far more abstract. It featured a lovely array of pink and purple swirls. Julia had let her use the finger paint.

"This is lovely, Bethany!" Rick said, looking desperately at Julia for assistance. She quickly made a heart with her hands, saving him. "It's the prettiest heart I have ever seen," he said. The two-year-old princess beamed.

Julia returned with a plate of cookies. She rescued Bouncer from the pile and moved her daughter to the floor between Rick's feet. As Rick reached over the toddler to get a cookie, Julia noticed his wince.

"No time to visit the trainer after the game, huh?" she asked.

"Curse of the visiting team," Rick said. "Some of the guys got right off the bus and walked straight to the locker room when we got home." He paused. "I had other priorities."

Knowing she may regret the offer on so many levels, Julia still couldn't stop herself as the words left her lips.

"I've been known to give a mean massage," she said. "At least that's what James always said."

Rick forgot how to breathe.

"I could even get the kids to help," she offered. "You won't be able to move tomorrow if you don't work those kinks out tonight." He groaned, and she realized her choice of words were not the best.

Trying to reassure him, she stood and tossed a pillow in front of the TV. She pulled out the video game system that was loaded with C.J.'s favorite racing game. She attached the extra controller and turned to her young son.

"I think Uncle Rick should come down here and race you," she said.

"Yippee!" C.J. immediately settled in, ready to play.

"This is not a good idea, Julia," Rick said. *She has no idea what she's doing,* he thought. Still, he stood and stretched out, pillow under his chest and controller in hand.

Julia had gone to the kitchen and returned with two wooden spoons. Rick looked at her in alarm.

"Relax," she said. "These are for Bethany. She's going to help."

Julia gave the weapons to her daughter and showed her how to beat on Uncle Rick's thighs and lower back, areas that Julia knew were best for her to avoid.

Trying to stay as objective with the process, she still had to admit that it was a pleasant experience to have the gorgeous man under her complete control. That her touch on his ankles and shins was having an effect on him was evident in how poorly he was performing against C.J. in the video race.

"You're killing me," Rick said. Of course, C.J. thought the statement was directed at him, so he sought to encourage his hero.

"You'll get better, Uncle Rick," he said. "You just need to practice more." Julia tried unsuccessfully to stifle her giggle.

Julia moved Bethany to Rick's back and demonstrated a karate chop. The little girl's blows were barely perceptible, almost to the point of tickling. Julia did not know yet how ticklish he was, and he hoped now was not the time she discovered his weakness. He was already completely at her mercy.

Julia moved to work his shoulders. He was now truly engrossed in the race, and she was glad the game was distracting him. Unfortunately, she didn't have anything to distract her from his muscular arms and realized she needed to stop, for her own sake.

"Well, we've done all we dare. You need a more professional massage," she said, trying to sound as stoic as possible as she lifted Bethany off Rick's back. As she did, the closely fought race ended with C.J. the ultimate winner.

"Can we race again?" C.J. asked his mom.

"No, it's way past your bedtime. I only let you stay up to see Uncle Rick," Julia said.

"Aww," her son said. His sentiments were echoed by his sister, and humorously by Rick, too.

"Let me at least get them tucked in." His offer was completely selfish, and she knew it but accepted anyway.

"Okay." She had started a pot of coffee but was reconsidering the gesture. While he was upstairs, she gathered his jacket and keys and placed them on the top of the container she had filled with the remaining cookies.

As he came back downstairs, she was putting away the dishes she had washed. He noticed the pile of his belongings on the counter.

"Am I being dismissed?" Rick asked. He had figured out this was a defensive ploy she used to avoid confrontation.

"I figured you were tired and wanted to get home." She kept her back to him as she slowly placed the silverware in the drawer.

"I still think there are things that we need to talk about," he said. He had wisely put the full distance of the kitchen between them as he settled into a chair at the dining room table.

Another shrug from Julia meant he was going to have to work at getting her to open up again. It was a task he was willing to tackle. He was in love with this woman and knew it was time to tell her.

"Are you okay with the money thing?" he asked.

"I'm not thrilled with it, but I understand your perspective now."

"Well, that's a start, I guess." Rick decided to raise another issue, not sure if she even remembered admitting it.

"You said something else that has me curious," he said. "You said that you couldn't think straight when you were around me." She shrugged and turned to add more cream to her coffee.

"I don't know," she said. "You're intimidating." She was lying, and he knew it.

"Really? I got the sense that you meant something else completely."

"You're not going to let this go, are you?" She turned to face him, arms folded.

"Nope." He smiled.

"I am no different than every other woman in the country. You're quite attractive, and when I'm in your exalted presence, I find that quite distracting."

"Every other woman in the country?" he asked, standing now. "Surely you exaggerate."

"Okay, ninety percent of them," she said.

"What's wrong with the other ten percent?" he asked as he took a step closer. "Insane? Blind? Soccer fans?"

His false indignation made her smile. Despite her doubts, she loved this part of their relationship. She missed having someone she could tease that would tease back.

"You are not exactly like every other woman in the country, though," Rick said, his tone more serious now.

"How so?" Julia took a deep breath.

"I think you know the answer to that question," Rick said, closer now. "What frightens you most about this?"

Julia met his gaze, trying not to squirm under his intense stare.

"That my feelings for you, and yours for me, are based purely on physical attraction." Her admission surprised him. He quietly took a step back.

"The women that are attracted to me for my looks and my money are not what I'm looking for and not what I need."

"I know."

"I need and want someone who loves me for who I am, not for how I look or what I have. I don't believe you're attracted to me because you think I'm good-looking—which I don't understand to begin with—and definitely not because of my money."

"More like in spite of it," she said reluctantly.

"Are you saying what I think you're saying?" Rick knew he was teetering on the edge of a cliff, wondering if she was going to throw him a lifeline or not.

She steadily met his gaze as he took a step back towards her.

"Is that a yes?"

"Yes," she said.

"I love you, Julia," he said.

"I know."

"Don't push me, woman!" He growled lightly.

"I love you, too, Rick."

"Now I have the difficult choice of whether to kiss you senseless or show you that my love for you is not purely physical."

"I am not going to make that choice for you," she said, moving back to lean on the kitchen counter. "I've already explained my lack of clear thinking in your presence."

"For such a level-headed woman, your response to me is a surprise," Rick said. "On the other hand, I've noticed that my thinking seems to become clearer when you're around. I've never been as focused and sure of what I want in my entire life."

"Although that's nice to know, however suspicious I am of its truth, it still does not solve your immediate quandary."

Rick stood silently.

"I'm going to compromise," Rick said finally. "I am going to kiss you tonight, but for the next couple of weeks I'm going to prove to you I can control myself. I want you to be one-hundred percent sure that this is the real deal."

As he explained his decision, he gently lifted her onto the counter, as he had on Christmas Day. Her hands moved up to his shoulders and around his neck. Rick kept his hands firmly on the counter.

For such a brief kiss, it left them both breathless.

"I'm going to leave now," he said after he kissed her again.

"Okay," she said, taking the opportunity to place gentle kisses along his jaw line.

"I've got to get out of here," he said, removing her hands after she ventured a soft touch inside his collar. She shook herself out of the stupor his kisses had caused as he placed her back on firm ground. At the door, he paused. "Good night, Julia."

"Good night, Rick."

24
The Off Season

The early morning message on her phone let Julia know Rick wouldn't be at church. Coach had asked the team to clean out their lockers by noon. She was both disappointed and slightly relieved. She was unsure how to act around him now that she had admitted her feelings, both to herself and to him. Doubts still nagged at the back of her mind.

The activity of getting the kids buckled into their seats gave her a chance to reflect on the insightful sermon. The pastor spoke about living on faith and being willing to move out of the carefully constructed comfort zones that everyone had.

Ouch! Julia had thought in response.

She turned her phone back on before heading out of the parking lot. There was a message from Rick asking her to meet him and the team for brunch. Garrett's family and most of the other spouses and kids would be there, he told her.

"We just got to the restaurant. The coach had already reserved it but hadn't told us yet. He didn't know if this would be an end-of-the-season party or a celebration."

"I don't know anyone, Rick," she said. Honestly, she was more concerned that everyone would see the change in their relationship. She forgot that he appeared to be able to read her mind.

"Please, Julia. I promise to behave," Rick needed her to take this step.

"Monica will be there? And the kids?" she asked.

"Yes," Rick said. "And Stephen told me that Terry is heading your way to ask for a ride."

On cue, her friend tapped on the passenger door.

"Okay, we're on our way." *Nothing like having to apply a sermon's truth immediately,* she thought.

Rick greeted Julia with a kiss despite her unspoken objection but rescued her by glaring at the teammates who dared make catcalls over the display. Garrett and Stephen shared a high-five behind Rick's back.

The team was in a surprisingly good mood, mainly due to Coach's encouragement and the leadership of Rick and Garrett and the other the veteran players. Despite her reluctance, Julia had a good time. Bethany and C.J. were simply happy to be with Uncle Rick, Uncle Stephen, and the Stahl kids.

Rick's phone rang as they headed to the parking lot. He was carrying a sleepy Bethany to the car. The large meal and her approaching naptime meant she was ready for bed.

"Intriguing," Rick said to Julia as he deposited the little girl gently in her seat. He proceeded to strap her in as if he had been doing this for years.

"That was the network," he said, referring to the sport's newest television association. "They want me to consider joining the studio team through the Super Bowl."

"Wow!" Julia said. "That's fantastic!" His background in communications made him a perfect choice. As she watched him process the news, she wondered why he didn't seem as excited.

After she finished strapping C.J. in, she tugged on his jacket, regaining his full attention.

"What's wrong?" she asked.

"It means flying to New York tomorrow," he said.

"And?" she asked. "What's the problem?"

"You wouldn't consider going with me, would you?" He asked her as he pulled her closer. He kissed the palm of first one hand, then the other. She tried to pull them away, but he refused to let them go.

"Are you that afraid?" she asked, smiling up at him. "What would your adoring fans say?"

He didn't answer immediately, instead leaned down for another kiss. Bethany interrupted their "discussion."

"Mommy, Mommy, Mommy!" The little girl sang. "Unka Rick kissed you!"

"Yes, I did," Rick leaned in the open car window and made a face at the two kids. Their giggles continued as he turned back to their mother. "So, you won't go with me?" He moved his hands up to cup her face.

"No," she said. "I will not go to New York with you, but you knew that. What's really going on in that thick head of yours?"

"If I leave, you may change your mind," he said, pulling her into a hug. He tilted her chin up and kissed her again, and then hoped Julia didn't notice the cheers that came from several team members.

"What happened to the whole 'I'm not going to touch you for a couple of weeks'?" Her question incongruent with the fact that her arms were wrapped around his waist, preventing him from moving away.

"Sorry," he said and gently moved out of her hold. "You promise not to dump me while I'm gone?"

"I promise," she said. "I'll at least wait until you get back." The horrified look on his face was priceless.

"Kidding." She pulled him down for a kiss of reassurance before she got into the car, putting some much-needed distance between them. He was much too tempting for her well-being.

"You are a cruel, cruel woman," he said, then leaned through the window to say good-bye to C.J. and blow kisses to Bethany, who was starting to nod off. His proximity offered Julia an opportunity for one last touch, but she kept her hands firmly on the steering.

"Go call them back and pack your bags. This is a perfect chance for you, and you know you'll enjoy it."

He leaned in the window. "I love you," he said, his breath brushing her cheek.

"I love you, too."

***

The next three weeks were a whirlwind. Rick was in town two nights a week, flying back to New York for the weekend games. He spent his days studying team and individual player statistics and biographies. He was having a blast. Julia could hear it in his voice when he called each night.

"I knew you were perfect for this," she told him the week before the conference championship games.

"You think I'm practically perfect at everything," Rick said. She had no idea how these nightly conversations were the reason he was doing as well as he was. It was strange to him to think that a woman he had met less than two months ago was now vital to his emotional and physical welfare. He almost panicked at the thought of living without her.

Sloan had promised to keep an eye on her and the kids while he was gone. This wasn't a big deal, since before Rick got involved, Sloan regularly spent a couple evenings a week at her house. The doctor had been busy over the last few weeks with wedding plans, since his engagement to Jocelyn was now official.

Sloan was the first to know about Rick's plans to propose within a few weeks.

"You sure you're not moving a little fast there, big guy?" Sloan had cautioned.

"No, I've prayed about this, and I've even talked to her dad," Rick revealed. "I know she still has some doubts, but I think this time apart has helped. The conversations we have each night are important. She knows how I feel, and I've made it clear where this is leading."

"Yes, I can see that, now that you mention it," Sloan said. "She is definitely more content and secure than I've seen her since James died. Just don't push too fast. Her reaction would probably be to run as far and as fast as she could the other way."

"Well, I wouldn't be against you getting a take on how you think she'd react," Rick said. "I'm not talking about asking her the day after the Super Bowl, and I'm not going to ask her to elope."

"Okay, I'll see what I can do," Sloan said. He added some sobering thoughts, though, before ending the call. "I do agree that the time you've been gone has been good in that it's helped solidify your emotional and spiritual attraction," Sloan was aware of the pact Rick and Julia had made to help her believe the relationship was not purely physical. "But I do think it has also insulated her from what life with you would really be like. I still have a hard time picturing her being completely comfortable with the money and status. It's something I know you're probably going to have to deal with off and on for a long time."

"I will deal with it," Rick insisted. "I'm not giving her up without a fight." It was a fight that was soon to become more difficult.

The Super Bowl was over, and Rick was on his way when Morris had called to remind him of an upcoming charity event. He had forgotten about the Bachelor Auction that raised money for the homeless shelters in the area. Julia wasn't going to be happy. On the flight home, Rick called Monica for advice.

"We'll take her with us," she said. "We'll secretly pool our money and bid on you ourselves." Many of the married team members came out to the gala, one of the city's largest annual events. Garrett enjoyed teasing the bachelors over the whole ridiculousness of being sold to the highest bidder. Last year he and a coach had bid on one of the young players and won. They made the young rookie mow the practice field for his 'date.'

"I still don't think she'll agree to go," Rick said. "She'll complain about not having anything good enough to wear, she'll say she has no one to watch the kids, and who knows what other excuse she'll come up with."

"Let me handle Julia," Monica said. He could hear the excitement in her voice and decided he could trust her. "I'll even break the news to her so you don't have to."

"You're a gem," Rick said. "I owe you big-time."

"Just make sure I'm invited to the wedding," Monica said, laughing as she hung up.

It took some steady work to convince Julia to consider the charity event. Monica appreciated her perspective, since it was one she hadn't thought of herself. The fact the civic club sponsoring the auction would spend tens of thousands of dollars to put on an event that would raise barely a hundred thousand seemed ludicrous to Julia.

"Why don't they have it in a high-school gym?" Julia asked. "They could then use the money for the homeless instead on fancy decorations and expensive hors d'oeuvres."

"Good point," Monica said, "but we won't change any minds by not showing up. I know some of the people on the committee and I'll try to drop some hints about scaling back the grandeur. There are a lot of choices made in the decorating and promotion that could be done less expensively. We need someone like you to hold them accountable."

"I still don't want to go," Julia said. The thought of watching Rick being sold to the highest bidder made her uncomfortable. And jealous. And furious.

"Well," Monica said, "you'll leave me with an angry team captain, and he may take it out on Garrett. You wouldn't want that, now would you?"

"He wouldn't do that, and you know it." Julia succumbed to her friend's tactics. "Okay, I'll go, but under protest."

"Yippee!" Monica said. "I'll pick you up tomorrow morning to go get a dress."

"Oh," Julia said, her voice sinking. "I didn't even think about a dress."

"My treat," Monica said. "I won't take no for an answer. If you add up the hours you've spent tutoring Gary, I owe you much more than what a simple evening gown will cost. Plus, we get to go shopping, without the kids!"

Rick, Garrett, and the kids had volunteered to watch C.J. and Bethany while the ladies went shopping. Rick hadn't seen them since getting back from the last broadcast, so he arrived at the Stahl's house early.

Monica and Garrett wisely left the two alone for a few minutes. Rick had committed to not pushing for physical contact, but the culmination of so much time away from her was challenging his self-control. He let Gary take Bethany inside, followed by an eager C.J., and then pulled Julia onto the front porch swing before she could follow her children inside.

He resisted pulling her into his arms and instead sat quietly, holding both her hands in his. The circles he made on her palms with his thumbs made it hard for her to breathe.

He has to know exactly what he's doing to me, she thought. She was certain the whole neighborhood could hear her heartbeat.

Content to simply stare at her, Rick battled the desire to propose on the spot and ask her to elope. Tonight. He shook his head at the thought of Sloan's reaction.

"What's so funny?" Julia asked.

"Just thinking," he said mysteriously.

"About what?"

"Sloan," he answered. At her look of surprise and confusion, Rick tugged her closer and kissed her lightly on the nose.

25
The Handoff

Two weeks later, Julia was rebelliously glaring at her reflection.

"I can't believe I agreed to this!" She stared at the stranger in the mirror.

"You are stunning!" Terry assured her. "Monica has superb taste. I can't believe she found this off the rack, and it fits you like it was custom-made."

"Except for the hemming," Julia reminded her. The dress had to be shortened, even with the three-inch heels the two ladies had convinced her she needed.

She turned again to look at the elegant woman in the mirror. The dark-violet, strapless bodice faded into lighter shades of lavender with each layer of chiffon. Terry's aunt, a whiz at fancy hairdos, had arranged Julia's long hair up into a simple style, with one smooth curl falling over her shoulder.

Julia decided to wear her grandmother's antique amethyst necklace, one of her few expensive pieces of jewelry. It had a tricky, old-fashioned clasp, and she had to have assistance to get it hooked. Terry was going to have to help her get the dress unhooked later tonight, too. The bodice was tight but not uncomfortably so, despite requiring both Terry and Mrs. Hampton to zip it up.

Terry's aunt had volunteered to help Terry with the kids, since Mr. Hampton was working the graveyard shift. Plus, she wanted to get the scoop on the evening when Julia got home.

"Mommy! You're pretty!" C.J.'s exclaimed.

"Why thank you, kind sir." She swept him an elaborate curtsy.

She lifted the hem of her gown to show Bethany the purple beaded anklet that she wore. Crystal Stahl had helped the little girl make it to match the dress when Julia and Monica had returned from shopping.

"It matches my dress perfectly, sweetie." Julia gave her daughter a quick hug. She wondered if Rick was wearing the matching bracelet that Crystal and Bethany had made for him. Julia knew that Monica's ten-year-old daughter was promoting the relationship as much as her mother was. Crystal was concerned that Rick would forget who his girlfriend was in the excitement of the auction. She had even contributed a whole three dollars to the pool of money her mother and father had collected to bid Rick for Julia.

When Julia found out about the money being collected to assure she won the date, she threatened to not attend the event.

"I thought you understood how much I would freak out to be the center of attention like that," she had told Rick. "I'm not going."

After a quick conference, the crew had decided on a compromise. Taking a cue from Garrett's former antics, Sloan would bid on Rick. If questioned, he would say Rick owed him and he was going to make the quarterback paint his garage.

Monica and Garrett were picking her up in a limo. Julia had protested that this was too much like a prom date and objected to the ridiculousness of it all.

"Humor me," Garrett said. Knowing the huge linebacker was more afraid of Monica, and Rick, for that matter, that he ever would be of her tiny self, she gave in.

"They're here!" C.J. was on lookout duty. "Wow, look at that car!"

Garrett came to the door and escorted Julia to the limo.

"Too bad my mom's not here to take pictures," Julia mumbled. "I feel like I'm in high school."

"Relax, you're going to have a blast," Garrett assured her. "You are going to knock his socks off, too!"

The man in danger of losing his socks was anxiously awaiting the arrival of the limo. He had promised not to jog to the curb to get her out of the car, since Julia had insisted that they pretend they were not a couple.

Now as they pulled up to the venue, Julia's courage was failing.

"I can't do this," she said. "Please tell the driver to take me back home."

"No way," said Garrett, "Rick would kill me!" He shuddered.

She laughed at his antics. "Okay, I'll go in, but only to save your skin."

"It will be fine, I promise." Monica leaned over and gave her a quick hug. "You look so lovely. All the bachelors are going to be begging you to bid on them. Rick will be green with envy."

Rick and Sloan were standing at one of the large bay windows. As they watched the limousines pull in, Rick waited patiently as each door opened, expecting to see Garrett at any time. Finally, he saw the linebacker make a not quite graceful exit from their car, then turn to assist his wife.

Rick's breath caught as he spotted Julia. As the driver handed her out of the limousine, the velvet wrap she had borrowed from Monica, slipped from around Julia's shoulders.

Sloan squeezed Rick's shoulder. "Steady, Teddy!" Rick was too stunned to verbalize anything. Sloan, on the other hand, seemed unable to shut up.

"My, oh my, oh my," he said. "What a looker we have here, Rick, my boy!" Realizing his friend was still bordering on catatonic, Sloan shook him firmly.

"Wake up, Rick. She's almost to the ballroom. You'd better intercept her now or you'll miss your chance to talk to her at all this evening. As soon as the barracudas get one look at her, you won't be able to get within ten feet."

"Let's go." Rick sprang into full-out attack mode.

Garrett and Monica had planned ahead, knowing Julia would cause a stir. They slowed their entrance to give Rick time to find them.

Julia's eye lit up.

"She's spotted him," Monica told her husband. "See if you can see where he is."

"There he is," Garrett said, pointing to their left. "By the window."

Rick had positioned himself directly in their path, knowing Julia would see him. He tried to look and sound casual as they approached.

Pretending they were meeting for the first time, the Garrett made the introductions. The purple bracelet peaked out from under Rick's tuxedo sleeve. Julia smiled as they were introduced.

"You look lovely this evening, Mrs. Fitzgerald." Rick stopped a waiter and asked for two glasses of sparkling water. When he had ordered a glass of wine on their fancy date, he hadn't known that Julia didn't drink.

"Having a husband killed by a drunk driver tends to affect you that way," Sloan told him later, apologizing for not warning Rick. The sparkling water was fine tonight, anyway. He handed her a glass as they moved away from Monica and Garrett.

"Would you like to look around the ballroom at some of the pieces that will be auctioned off?"

"Excuse me?" She nearly choked "You want me to shop around?" She looked at him in shock. He was grinning at her.

"It's not just bachelors being auctioned tonight, is it?" she asked, her cheeks reddened as she realized her mistake.

"No." He kissed her hand. "You are adorable."

They had moved through the crowd to a more secluded alcove, and he took the opportunity to let her know how stunning she looked—at least that's how she interpreted his perusal as he twirled her slowly in front of him. He confirmed her suspicions.

"I'm struggling to find the right words to tell you how beautiful you look." Rick accompanied his humble words with a quick kiss on her cheek. The intrigue and secrecy of the game they were playing was intoxicating. Choosing a more innocent subject seemed prudent.

"Nice bracelet, Mr. Adams." She turned to admire the elegantly decorated tree that hid them from the view of the ballroom. "I have one almost exactly like it." Julia turned back to him and glanced around to make sure no one was watching. She lifted the hem of her dress slightly so he could see the bright purple beads.

"I hear they are much sought-after pieces of jewelry by an up-and-coming designer," Rick said and smoothed her dress back into place.

Julia lightly ran her fingers through his hair before putting more distance between them.

Rick knew he couldn't monopolize her for much longer, so he led her back through the crow to look for Sloan. They found him at the appetizer table.

"Couldn't wait for dinner?" Rick asked.

"These are marvelous," Sloan said inelegantly around a mouthful of a delicate crab and lobster puff.

"I'm passing the lovely lady back into your safe hands," Rick said. "Figuratively speaking, of course." His warning gaze was pointed.

"I'm a happily engaged man!" Sloan reminded him. "But, seriously, I will take care of her. I think you've already pushed your limit, anyway. From what I could tell, you two were starting to draw attention."

"I don't really care," Rick said, kissing Julia's hand once more before moving off.

"He's in a bit of a huff tonight, isn't he?" Sloan asked Julia as he handed her a plate of tempting appetizers.

"It's completely understandable, Sloan," she said. "He's being offered up to the highest bidder. With his Melissa experience, you can understand his reservations."

"Julia! Sloan!" An excited voice reached them. As if speaking her name had conjured her up, Melissa Schmidt was making her way toward them. She had a slender gentleman in tow. He reminded Julia of her English professor at college. The incongruity between the image he presented and the type of man Julia expected to see with Melissa was remarkable.

The gorgeous brunette hugged Julia as if they were long-lost friends.

"It's so good to see you!" Melissa's enthusiasm was confusing. Sloan's mouth was hanging open.

"You, too, Sloan." Melissa turned to her companion. "This is Julia that I told you about, and this is Dr. Sloan Mackenzie. He's a friend of Rick's." Sloan and Julia stared at the couple as Melissa continued her excited chatter.

"This is Dr. Levi Harris," Melissa said. "He's a professor at State. We met at church. Isn't he adorable?" She gazed adoringly at her date. Then she abruptly surprised Julia beyond imagining.

"I have you to thank for this, Julia." She wagged her finely manicured finger at Julia. "Your words that night at Rick's party hurt me deeply."

"I'm so sorry, Melissa," Julia said. "I tried to contact you for days afterward, but I understand why you were upset with me."

"No, no! Let me finish." Melissa patted Julia's hand as if they were old friends. "They hurt at first, but Stephen continued to lecture me about it for a long time. He even called my parents."

"I don't understand." Confusion was evident in Julia's voice.

"You were right!" Melissa hugged her again. "Thank you so much for setting me on the right track. Lee and I met, and I fell head over heels immediately. But I had learned my lesson, so I kept it to myself. You can imagine my shock when he called several days later to ask me out!"

The reserved, seemingly shy, professor was obviously smitten.

"I just wanted to thank you. If there's anything I can ever do to help you and Rick, you let me know," Melissa said, hugging Julia one last time. "Are you bidding on him tonight?"

"No, I am," Sloan said.

The look on Melissa's face caused both men to laugh.

"Yes." Sloan explained. "Julia refused to be part of the crew's plans, so we've pooled our money. I'm going to bid on him, supposedly so he can paint my garage, but it's actually for Julia. We want to keep their relationship quiet."

"Great idea," Melissa said. "Good luck. We'll see you guys later."

"Wow," Julia shook her head as they watched Melissa and her new beau walk away.

"Yes, wow," Sloan said. "That about sums it up." He was looking forward to sharing the news with Rick.

The large circular table held Rick's entire group. Garrett sat on Julia's right and Sloan on her left. Rick knew he wouldn't be able to hide their relationship unless he was several seats away from her, so he placed himself next to Monica.

Dinner was delicious. It was a formal affair, but thanks to a gourmet cooking and etiquette class her college roommate tricked her into taking, Julia was not completely at a loss over which utensil to use and when. Still, the fancy table settings weren't helping her doubts. She felt like an outsider. She nervously fiddled with her napkin.

Several times she noticed that her presence was garnering comments from people at neighboring tables. She quietly asked Sloan why that was, covering her concern with a falsely calm sip of her iced tea.

Sloan explained that the high society crowd tended to roam in a big pack, going from one glitzy event to another. Rick's group was unusual because they didn't do the charity events just to be seen. So, when they show up to an event, they tended to get more attention.

"Plus, they've never seen you before," he explained.

"Oh." Julia's fears were not alleviated much by his explanation. "All these people know Rick well?"

"Somewhat," Sloan said. "Because he's rich and eligible and not bad to look at, he gets more attention than some of us." Julia forced a chuckle at his false humility.

"Relax, though, Julia," he said, seeing that she wasn't completely at ease with the attention. "They're just jealous. Especially since he's not doing a very good job of hiding his interest."

Julia's blush let Sloan know she was aware that Rick was watching her intensely.

"I wish he wouldn't do that," she said.

"I'm sure he can't help it. You look ravishingly beautiful tonight," Sloan said, placing a quick kiss on her cheek. Rick dropped his fork. "See what I mean?"

26

The Fumble

They were finishing their dessert when the emcee came to the podium. Julia sipped her coffee, hoping to appear uninterested in the upcoming proceedings.

"Will all the bachelors up for auction tonight please make their way backstage?" The dignified city councilman was obviously proud of the power he had behind the microphone. Julia turned her attention to Sloan as Rick slipped out of his seat but watched him out of the corner of her eye. His body language was that of a grouchy two-year-old being sent to clean up his room. Her chuckle must have been louder than she thought.

"What's so funny?" Garrett asked. He had been watching her watch Rick.

"He's pouting," she said.

"You're right!" Garrett's laugh caused Rick to stop and turn, leveling a warning look.

"That's hilarious," Garrett said, after Rick had gone behind the curtain.

Monica leaned over and spoke across the table to Sloan. "We have a thousand dollars."

"What? That's ridiculous!" Julia was shocked. Heads turned at the two neighboring tables. Retrieving her conveniently dropped napkin allowed her overheated cheeks to cool down.

"It'll be fine." Sloan slipped his arm around her shoulders. "I've never seen anyone go for more than six hundred, and that was some big-name country music star that was here a couple years ago. Rick will be a bargain. I may even throw in some more of my own money. I desperately need my garage painted." He had made sure his last words were loud enough for the tables of noisy onlookers to hear.

Rick was the fourth man up for auction. It was painful to watch him pretend to be excited to be there. His acting ability had improved since his attempts during the Thanksgiving charades game. He looked almost enthusiastic. Almost.

The bidding started at two hundred dollars.

"He owes me! I'm going to make him paint my garage! Three hundred dollars!" Sloan called out, working his angle loudly.

Rick's crew made a show of emptying their wallets and tossing money toward Sloan. It was quite comical.

"Five hundred!" A female voice came from the back of the room. Julia paled. So did Rick. Then, miraculously his charming smile widened.

How does he manage to do that? Julia thought. A frown crossed her brow. *Maybe he's enjoying this.*

"No way, miss," Sloan called playfully. "You should see my garage. It's a mess!" The doctor's antics were a big hit, with laughter erupting with each punch line. "Six hundred!"

"Seven hundred." The voice from the back sounded again.

"Eight hundred." Sloan was starting to get a little annoyed at this point. He stood and turned to see who was bidding against him. A tall, auburn-haired woman waved sweetly at him. A frequent subject in the society pages, she was a well-known, but former, television actress, rumored to be on the lookout for another rich husband.

Garrett refilled Julia's coffee cup as she clenched her hands in her lap. She thanked him quietly and then pretended to enjoy watching Sloan's battle. Hopefully some observers would assume she was Sloan's date.

"Nine hundred," the actress said. Her smiling invitation now turned full force on Rick. Julia had turned slightly in her chair so she could see the stunning woman. She felt sick.

"One thousand," Sloan said. Finally, the woman fell silent and lifted her hands in surrender, giving Sloan reason to relax.

"Going once, going twice," the emcee said.

"Fifteen-hundred dollars," the beauty called out.

The emcee turned to Sloan, who hung his head in defeat, not bothering to hide his disappointment.

"Sold to the lovely Lady Tiffany."

Julia tried to hide her anguish, with Garrett and Monica providing excellent cover as they teased Sloan loudly enough to hide their own distress.

"Sorry, Sloan," Evan added from Sloan's other side, seeing the looks of desperation from Monica. "Looks like you'll have to do a little hard work all by yourself this time. No more mooching off our good nature!" The crew's strained laughter was convincing enough, and the onlookers lost interest as the next bachelor made his way up on stage.

Julia waited several minutes before excusing herself. During that time, she had to endure the spectacle of Rick's auction winner hanging all over him as the press documented her win.

"Julia," Monica spoke around Garrett, "look at me."

"I'm fine," Julia said through clenched teeth.

"Keep smiling," Garrett said. "The busybodies at the next table will lose interest soon enough. It wouldn't hurt, either, if you laid a big one on Sloan. To comfort him for his loss, of course." Sloan donned the perfect face of disappointment.

Julia laughed, a little louder than necessary, but took his advice, kissing Sloan soundly on the cheek. She took a couple deep breaths, aware of the looks she was still getting.

Rescue came from an unlikely source. Melissa appeared at their table.

"Wasn't that exciting? Sorry you didn't win, Dr. Mackenzie. I guess you'll have to suffer with an ugly garage for a little while longer," she said. "Julia, darling, Sloan will be fine. Come with me while I powder my nose."

"I can't believe that woman!" Melissa's whispered outrage would have been amusing had Julia not known of the young woman's change of heart. "*Lady* Tiffany Ray is anything but a lady!"

Monica started to stand to join Melissa and Julia. "It's okay, Monica." Julia stopped her. "I'll explain later." She gathered her purse and let Melissa lead her from the ballroom.

"Thank you, Melissa," Julia said as they left the noisy gathering behind.

"You stay out here as long as you need to recover." Melissa gave Julia a quick hug. "I must say, you all did a marvelous job. I don't think anyone suspected what was really going on. You were very brave to even let Rick participate tonight. I don't think I could've done it."

Inside the elegant ladies' room, two young women exchanged looks of disbelief as they overheard Julia and Melissa's conversation. Covert sneers broadened as they caught sight of Melissa's companion. Julia moved to the sink to cool down her face with a splash of water and reapply some lip-gloss. She was embarrassed when she realized the ladies were staring at her, but she forced herself to smile at them before she left.

Not ready to return to the ballroom, Julia spied a quiet bench right outside of the powder room and sat down, hoping to be hidden by the potted plants. With acoustics of restrooms being what they are, she caught the conversation of the two young women.

"Can you believe that?" one asked. "That little mouse of a woman thinks she's going to snag Rick Adams? How hilarious is that?"

"I know," the other added. "Who does she think she is? Did you see her dress? Obviously last year's and off the rack." Julia paled as their petty comments reached her.

Melissa had stopped at the coat check to retrieve her wrap. Julia made her way across the lobby.

"I've got to go," she said to Melissa. "Can you tell Sloan?"

"What on earth happened?" Melissa saw Julia's stricken look as she glanced back at the ladies' room.

"Nothing, I need to go home. Now."

Julia fumbled for her coat-check ticket and handed it to the round-eyed attendant. As Melissa followed Julia's gaze, she saw the two young women heading back into the dining hall.

"What did they say?" Melissa was familiar with the two young debutantes and their vicious propensity for snobbishness.

"Nothing." Julia thanked the coat check attendant and slipped her wrap around her shoulders. "Please tell Sloan that I'm okay and I've taken a taxi home." Melissa was torn between staying with Julia and delivering the message to Sloan. Or to Rick.

"Julia, you've got to tell me what they said," Melissa insisted, placing a gentle hand on Julia's arm. "They are mean, nasty gossips and you can't believe anything they say."

"Everything they said was true," Julia said. "I don't belong here. I should never have fooled myself into thinking I could do this. Please, Melissa, just give my message to Sloan."

"Can you call me a cab?" Julia asked the young coatroom attendant who had heard the entire conversation. She nodded and dialed the number quickly.

"One will be out front in two minutes," the young woman said. "Miss, is everything okay?"

"Yes, thank you." Julia said, but the tears in her eyes didn't help convince the girl. Avoiding any further questioning, Julia made her way outside and waited patiently next to the doorman. Within a minute, a taxi pulled up.

In the meantime, Melissa had hurried to the ballroom, deciding to bypass Sloan and delivered the message directly to Rick. As the doorman escorted Julia toward the cab, a livid Rick Adams intercepted them.

"I'll take this from here." Rick reached around the doorman and closed the taxi door. He took out his wallet and threw two ten-dollar bills to the stunned taxi driver through the open window. When the football player turned and slipped his arm around Julia's waist, the doorman watched in disbelief. Julia peeled Rick's arm away and swung to face him.

"Miss?" The doorman took a step closer to Julia. He was not going to let the fame of Mr. Richard Adams prevent him from defending the distraught young woman.

"I can get home on my own, Rick," Julia said, ignoring her crusader for a moment.

"I will take you home."

"That is unnecessary."

"That is your opinion," Rick said. "I disagree." It was obvious he wasn't going to back down. She hesitated.

"Miss?" The doorman was more insistent this time.

"Please." Rick's tone had changed suddenly. She knew she at least owed him an explanation. It was better to get it over with now.

"Thank you, sir." Julia turned to her would-be rescuer and smiled gently. "I'll let Mr. Adams escort me home. He will behave, I promise. There are several people that he would have to answer to if I come to any harm."

She hoped her playful toned alleviated the doorman's fears. She could tell it was doing nothing to calm Rick down. He had tossed his car receipt to the valet parking attendant as he sprinted out the door after her, so the truck was pulling up as she finished thanking the young doorman.

"No problem, miss," he said. "Good night to you. I trust you will both have a safe trip home, Mr. Adams." His nod to Rick held a hint of warning.

27
Quitting the Team

As Rick settled her into the truck and tucked her long dress out of the way, she knew this would be the most unpleasant ride she had taken in a long time.

Before they pulled away, he pounded the steering wheel with a clenched fist, but didn't look at her. Julia turned and stared out her window as Rick drove toward the interstate. His silence was excruciating.

"Rick," Julia finally spoke, not daring to look at him yet.

"Be quiet, Julia. I'm too angry right now to trust what I might say."

The silence was broken with her quiet sobs.

"I'm sorry," she said. "I can't do this. I don't want to hurt you, but I can't do this."

"What part of 'Be quiet' did you not understand?"

She had never seen him so angry, including the time he had to force her to talk about the bonus money. As they drove through the city streets, she pulled her legs up onto the seat and wrapped her arms around her knees. She huddled as far away from him as possible. She thought she heard him growl in frustration. As they drove onto the entrance ramp, he finally broke his silence.

"Julia, I am angry, but I'm not going to hurt you." One slender shoulder lifted in a shrug.

He must have been watching her, because she saw him clutch the steering wheel. Two miles down the highway, he suddenly exited at a rest area. He parked at the far end of the parking lot and turned off the ignition.

"I need to cool down. Stay in the truck and lock the doors." He slammed the door and walked toward the picnic area, away from the lights of the facilities. She watched helplessly as he stomped across the lawn. He picked up a stray branch, swiping at random garbage cans and light poles.

He stopped at the farthest picnic table and sat facing away from her. He buried his head in his hands, his elbows resting on his knees.

He's either praying or trying to think of the best place to hide my body. Julia thought of the possible morning headlines and stifled a giggle. Realizing she was bordering on panic, she leaned her head back and sought strength in a simple prayer.

Lord, please help me out of this terrible situation I've landed myself in. I cannot face being part of the world I saw tonight. I cannot go through the pain of rejection again. I just want to go back to the simple life the kids and I had before Rick Adams appeared. Please, Lord, I don't want to hurt him, but I don't think I can go on like this.

She wiped the tears from her face. *I probably look terrible,* she thought. *As if how I look is the biggest of my worries.* Her hysteria threatened to return.

She checked the clock. Rick had been gone for fifteen minutes. She wanted to go home. If she had her phone, she could call a taxi, but she had foolishly left it at home simply because it hadn't left room in her small clutch purse for makeup.

Julia climbed out of the truck, no small feat in itself. After two steps onto the grass, she realized how foolish spiked heels were right now. She stopped and slipped them off, now having to hold up the hem of her dress as she made her way toward Rick.

Julia saw his bent head and knew he was praying and not plotting her demise. She hated causing him such anguish, but she knew now she had been fooling herself thinking that this relationship was going to work. It was better to get it over with now before either one of them was in any deeper.

Rick raised his head slightly as he heard her stop in front of him. A set of brightly painted purple toenails attached to a pair of tiny feet came slowly into focus. Purple beads around a slender ankle matched the bracelet on his wrist.

"I want to go home now, please. If you'll let me borrow your phone, I'll call a cab." Her shaky voice reached through the cloud of his frustration and sadness.

His stood abruptly and lifted her into his arms. As he carried her back to the truck, she slipped her arms around his neck, partly out of habit and partly out of fear that he would drop her.

When he set her down and then left her to climb into the truck on her own, Julia knew then that he was still angry with her. The slam of the driver's side door confirmed her suspicions.

"Do not *ever* do that to me again." It wasn't a request, but a command. "Seeing you walk out of the lobby was the scariest thing I have ever experienced."

"I'm sorry I frightened you," Julia said. "Please take me home, Rick."

"That's it? You're not going to give me an explanation?"

"Please don't make this any harder than it already is."

They spent the remainder of their ride in almost complete silence. Rick finally flipped on the radio to fill the void with noise. The first song that came on was about a tragic love affair, and he immediately turned it off.

Julia couldn't stop a nervous giggle.

"I'm so glad you find my pain amusing." Rick's harsh tone made Julia retreat against the door again, this time wrapping herself in the short velvet cape.

Even though Malcolm was on duty, Rick didn't stop at the gatehouse but instead punched in the pass code and drove through, barely waiting for the safety arm to clear his truck.

Knowing he couldn't be any angrier than he already was, Julia didn't wait for him to come get her out of the car. She leapt down as soon as the car stopped in the parking space. She was halfway to the door before she heard his door slam behind her.

Sloan had already called Terry to warn her. Mrs. Hampton had stayed with Terry after the kids went to bed to finish a movie marathon they had planned. The two ladies watched silently as the couple stormed into the townhouse, with Julia trying to pretend that nothing was wrong.

"Are they asleep?" she asked. Terry nodded.

"Thanks, then," Julia said. "I'll talk to you tomorrow?" The two Hampton ladies wisely slipped out the door.

Rick had gone straight upstairs. Stopping when he heard the front door close, he called down to Julia.

"I'm going to look in on the kids, if that's all right with you, Your Highness." Sarcasm bitterly dripped from his words.

Julia ignored him and went straight to her room. She heard Rick shush the puppy's whines and hoped he hadn't wakened the kids. As stood in front of her dresser, grasping the edge, her tears returned. Taking a deep breath, she decided to tackle the necklace, remembering the trouble she had putting it on earlier.

Great, she thought, *I'm going to have to sleep in my evening gown and necklace. Lovely.*

As she continued to struggle with the necklace, she was so intent on her task that she jumped in surprise as Rick appeared behind her.

Her eyes, bright from her tears, met his in the mirror. He'd been standing in the doorway watching her battle the clasp of the necklace. The intimacy of her bedroom, her bare shoulders, and the single curl that brushed the top of her bodice mesmerized him.

He moved to stand behind her and gently pushed her hands away from the necklace. Her hands sought the dresser again, trying to keep herself upright. She could feel his breath on her neck as he bent his head, intent on unclasping the necklace. When he located the latch, he raised his eyes to meet hers once again.

He dropped one end of the necklace and let it slide across her skin before he placed it gently on the dresser. Her eyes closed and she swayed towards him as he leaned down and placed a soft kiss on her shoulder. Her emotional armor was slipping. Knowing he was beyond his own willpower, Rick leaned his forehead against the top of her soft curls and prayed for deliverance.

Their rescuer was dressed not in shiny armor, but in superhero pajamas.

"Mommy?" C.J.'s voice came from his bedroom. "Mommy?" The second call was slightly more alarmed. Julia pushed past Rick.

"Mommy's here," Julia said when she reached her son. She stayed longer than necessary beside C.J.'s side, hoping that Rick would take the hint and leave.

Rick was sitting on her bed when she returned. She stopped at the doorway.

"I know you don't want to talk about this tonight, but I want you to at least hear me out." Rick's tone was serious but no longer angry. "First, I'm sorry for what just happened. I should never have put us in such a tempting situation."

Julia turned away and made her way around the bed to stand in front of the dresser once more. Rick stood and moved to the doorway.

"I'm also sorry my angry frightened you. It wasn't directed at you, but I panicked when Melissa told me you had left." He watched as she silently placed the necklace in her jewelry box.

Rick sighed and resumed his plea. "I love you, and I know you love me. I'm not foolish enough to think you'll tell me what happened tonight, but I do know that you're afraid. I don't know why, but I want to find out so I can fix it. There is nothing, and I mean nothing, that I won't do to make this right. If I have to quit my job, give up my lifestyle—whatever it takes—I'm willing to do it." He paused, hoping his words were getting through to her.

"I am convinced that God has orchestrated our relationship," he continued. "I'm willing to trust Him. I need you to be willing to do so, too."

"You're right," Julia said. The simple statement brought him a glimmer of hope, but she squelched it with her next words. "I don't want to talk about this. But you're wrong, too. It *is* over. I can't face this anymore. You need to leave." In the mirror, their gaze locked in silent combat. She was the first to look away.

Battle won, Rick thought. *She is not being completely truthful, with herself or me.* As he watched the defiant figure, he decided to retreat for the evening.

"I'll leave, but this is not over."

28
Talking to the Coach

"Where is she?" Rick leaned over and asked Terry. His favorite five-year-old was sitting next between the young woman and Sloan. Bethany reached for her uncle Rick as he settled into the pew.

"Nursery duty," Terry answered.

"Convenient," Rick mumbled.

As the first notes of the call to worship sounded from the praise band, Rick realized his focus and priorities were sorely out of line. As much as he had talked to Julia about trusting God in their relationship, he needed to practice what he was preaching. Of course, having Julia's daughter in his arms didn't help.

Terry insisted on taking the kids to their classes when they were dismissed for children's church. Sloan agreed.

"Julia would not be happy to see you delivering them to class," Sloan insisted. "You know that. Don't push your luck."

Rick reluctantly released Bethany to Terry and watched them exit the back of the sanctuary.

"You look like a pitiful puppy," Sloan said. "Snap out of it."

"Now who's pushing their luck?" Rick's tone held distinct hints of anger and frustration. "I'd tell you to stay out of this, but I know you too well."

"Plus, you need me." Sloan raised an eyebrow. "From what I hear, she's not taking your calls."

Thankfully, the pastor's sermon started before their conversation reached the point of physical blows. Sloan placed a friendly arm around Rick's shoulders during the pastoral prayer. Rick knew that despite his words, Sloan did sympathize with his heartbreak.

As Rick turned to the notes page in the church bulletin, he saw the Scripture passage for this Sunday's sermon. It was Philippians 4:6-7: *"Do not be anxious about anything, but in everything by prayer and supplication with thanksgiving let your requests be made known to God. And the peace of God, which surpasses all understanding, will guard your hearts and your minds in Christ Jesus."*

Sloan must have seen it about the same time, because he leaned over and commented to Rick.

"Coincidence? I think not." Rick shot him a shaky smile.

"Let's get out of here before Julia comes out," Sloan suggested after the service. "I know you'd like to see her, but trust me, my friend, if she says she needs some time, you'd better give her some time. And space."

"She doesn't want time," Rick said. "Or space. According to her, it's over. Period."

Rick checked the exiting congregation several times as he and Sloan crossed the parking lot. Sloan picked up his pace.

They chose a favorite mom-and-pop diner that Sloan had discovered by accident. The two friends frequented the establishment when Rick first moved to town, but they hadn't been in for several weeks. Ramon and Juanita, the owners, welcomed them like family. Although several patrons recognized Rick, they left him alone. He nodded his thanks to one father who hastily but gently refrained his preteen son, a Wolves fan if his jacket was any indication. Sloan and Rick settled into a booth at the back of the restaurant.

"So, I know from your message last night that things went badly after you left the ballroom. I wish I hadn't been called into work, or I would've called you back." Sloan waited until the chips and salsa arrived before heading into the counseling session. "But now you need to tell me exactly what happened and what you want me to do to fix it."

"After the auction fiasco, apparently Julia overheard someone in the ladies room say something about women who are reaching above their class." Rick stared unseeingly at the chip in his hand as he explained the details he had gotten from Melissa after he left Julia's apartment. In the ballroom he hadn't waited for an explanation, bolting after Julia as soon as Melissa cried, "She's leaving!"

"What did Julia say about it?" Sloan asked.

"According to Her Highness," Rick said, crushing the chip between his fingers, "we're done. It's over." He brushed the crumbs on the table into a pile. "Whatever 'it' was to begin with."

"And you disagree?" Sloan swept the crumbs onto a plate. "You're making a mess."

Rick's raised eyebrow meant he understood Sloan's double meaning.

"She loves me. I know that. She knows that." Rick took another chip, dipped it into the spicy salsa and actually ate this one. "She knows I love her. I don't understand why she won't give us a chance."

"Maybe I can enlighten you a little, but you have to be prepared to listen." Sloan paused. "After your message last night, I thought long and hard about what Julia's been through the last few years. I feel bad now that I've encouraged this relationship as much as I have."

"Excuse me?" Rick started to rise from his chair.

"Calm down, Teddy," Sloan said. "I told you, you'll have to listen. I guess I should have added 'patiently.'"

The two friends paused as Juanita brought out their lunch. The plates full of authentic Mexican comfort food were a welcome break in the tension that was building at the table. Sloan settled immediately into his meal. Rick took a couple bites, and then pushed his plate away. "Continue, please."

"The scars that the Fitzgerald family left on Julia are deeper than I even imagined. That's the only explanation I've come up with for her continued doubts. To fall in love with someone, have that love returned, and then watch him be forced to choose between you and his family must have been a terrible experience."

"But my family doesn't hate her, they love her," Rick insisted. "As a matter of fact, they'd probably pick her over me!" He buried his head in his hands and groaned. "How am I going to tell my mom? She's going to be furious that I've messed this up so quickly."

"I think she'll understand," Sloan said, pushing the plate back towards Rick. "Eat."

"Okay, but explain why the rejection from the Fitzgerald family means she wants nothing to do with me." Rick refocused his thoughts. His mom was the least of his worries at this point.

"I know the high society circles you are sometimes forced into, isn't your family, per se," Sloan explained, "but Julia was out of her element at the auction and yet you seemed so at ease that it probably seemed like you were amongst friends, family— your people—and she was definitely an outsider."

"I hated every minute of it." Rick took several bites of his meal as he relived the distress of the auction. "I hate those events with a passion. She should know that by now."

"Why should she know that?" Sloan pressed the point. "Have you told her? Or have you simply assumed that she knew you well enough to read your mind by now?"

Rick leaned in his head back against the booth. Sloan's shot had landed.

"I would give up my job, my status, and all my money if it would make her believe it all doesn't matter to me," Rick said quietly. "I've told her that."

"Oh, and then expect her to live for the rest of your lives with the guilt of what you've given up for her?" Sloan's voice dripped with sarcasm. "That'll work out just peachy, don't you think?"

Rick sat forward. As Sloan's words soaked in, his brows furrowed.

"She felt guilty about James giving all that up for her?"

"You bet she did." Sloan was revealing a secret that Julia had shared with only him. "James never knew."

"I've been such a jerk." Rick pushed his food away, no longer hungry. "I guess it seemed like such a simple thing to ask: Trade your entire lifestyle, everything you've always known, and come live in my insulated, well-guarded, well-funded kingdom. Like she should thank me for the offer."

"True," Sloan said. "But ouch! I think you're being a tad hard on yourself."

"So there's no hope for me, is there?"

"Well, I wouldn't go that far," Sloan said. "The fact that she and James had a wonderful marriage, despite the guilt she occasionally felt, shows that she's not an utterly lost cause."

Rick raised an eyebrow in subtle threat.

"Sorry," Sloan said. "Maybe 'lost cause' is a poor choice of words. What I mean is, I agree with you. It's clear to me that this relationship has a mysterious, or not-so-mysterious, hand behind its journey. God obviously has something planned for you two, whether this brief interlude is to teach you both something before moving you on or, as you hope, this is the beginning of your adventure."

"You really believe that?"

"Yes, I do." Sloan nodded. "The fun, light-hearted Julia that I grew up with had started to return. Honestly, the affection I've seen her give you...and please don't elaborate on any I *haven't* seen...surprised me, and probably surprised her, too. She seems at ease with you on a level that is amazing." Sloan knew he was dangerously close to giving Rick a green light, when Julia's alarm was probably still blinking yellow, if not red. As much as he wanted to give his friend hope, truth was the best remedy right now. "I think there's more to her concerns, though, Rick."

"I don't know how much more I can take, Sloan." Juanita came to refill their drinks. She patted Rick's hand gently, seeing his distress. Rick was touched by her concern.

"Tough," Sloan said. He fell quiet as he thought about what he was getting ready to tell Rick. The memories of the weeks and months following James's death were as fresh as if it had happened yesterday and not over three years ago. Sloan fought back tears as he shared with Rick the devastation that the loss of his close friend had wrought in Julia, her family, and in everyone that knew him.

"I miss my friend," Sloan said quietly. "He was one of the kindest, coolest guys I ever knew. To look at him, you would think he was a typical nerd, but seeing him on the soccer field or playing with his son or gazing at his wife..." Sloan couldn't continue.

"Do you remember when you got hurt at the game and Julia hid at her parents' house afterward?" Sloan finally collected himself enough to continue. The change of subject puzzled Rick.

"Yes," Rick said. "I never clearly understood what had upset her so much. I talked to her from the training room on a house phone. I thought she understood that I was fine. What does that have to do with her reaction Friday night?"

"It's something her dad mentioned to me at Christmas." Sloan tried to remember Mr. Pearson's exact words. "When Julia didn't come home but went to her parents, it was partly because of the fear and the memories that seeing you hurt probably brought back."

Rick listened intently, but the confusion on his face was evident.

"I think by the time she got back to the bleachers, the trauma of the phone call, and picturing you in the training room, finally hit her. I'm sure it brought back memories of being in the emergency room with James."

"I'm such an idiot!" Rick said. "My conversation with her parents that evening makes so much more sense now. She must hate me."

"I was pleased to see how quickly she got over that. I'm just glad she wasn't actually *in* the locker room with you," Sloan continued, "since I'm sure the trainer's room looks exactly like an emergency room. The last time Julia was in a hospital was when James died. She avoids them like the plague."

Rick stopped him. "The last time she was in a hospital was when James died? What about Bethany? She wasn't born in a hospital?"

"No. Emergency delivery," Sloan said, between bites of his last burrito. "Back of a taxi. By me and Jocelyn." Sloan watched as the import of that statement hit his friend.

"They didn't make her stay in the hospital? Or even go to the emergency room?"

"She was using one of these new-fangled birthing centers. Looked more like a spa. Pretty impressive. Despite the circumstances, mother and daughter came through beautifully. Taxi driver was pretty freaked out, though."

"I'll bet," Rick said. "I see now why she's 'Princess Bethany' to you."

The friends paid their bill, and Rick stopped to greet the young fan who had been so excited to see him come in. As they headed to their cars, Sloan stopped his friend. "You love her, don't you?"

"Dumbest question you've ever asked," Rick answered, leaning his forearms against his car roof.

"Well, I think she loves you too, but she's still so frightened of the whole idea that her natural defense mechanisms are going to take over. I'm not even sure if what I've told you today is all that's going on in that pretty little head," Sloan said, trying to prepare Rick for the work he'd have to do to win her back. "There may be even more to her fears than I've been able to figure out. But I do know she's going to hide from you, from her feelings, from everything."

"From everything?" Rick asked.

"Well, she's not even taking my calls," Sloan said, "and we both know I'm much more charming than you are."

"Funny. Don't quit your day job," Rick said. "What do you propose that I do?"

Sloan leaned against Rick's car, arms folded.

"Rick, you know I love you like a brother, right?" Sloan asked.

"Yes," Rick said. "I sense a 'but.' Go ahead, but remember I've had a terrible weekend." Sloan ignored Rick's comment.

"I think there's something you need to consider." Sloan hesitated.

"I'm not sure I'm going to like this," Rick said.

"I'm sure you won't." Sloan took a deep breath. "I know you say that the money isn't an issue for you, but really, Rick, you're a bit of a snob."

"Excuse me?" Rick pushed away from the car.

"I think you've gotten so comfortable with your lifestyle," Sloan said, holding up a hand to stop the protest that he was sure was coming, "and I know you would probably be willing to give it all up, but I don't think you have any idea how the rest of the world lives. You're part of an elite group, and I think you're a bit out of touch."

"So, although you sympathize with my situation, you're saying I'm a hopeless case? I'm too high and mighty that she could never believe it if I offered to lower myself to her level?" The bitterness was evident in his voice.

Sloan waited. He understood Rick well enough to know that this initial reaction would wear off quickly. He was right.

"Sorry," Rick said a minute later. The friends stood in silence for a few moments, Sloan waiting patiently.

"Out of touch, huh? Probably true. The past few weeks I've been feeling a little guilty. Not about the money—I know that's a gift from God—but more about my comfort. I say I care about other people, and I give a lot of money to worthy causes, but I'm not willing to give up my time or my comfort for anything."

"Rick, I do think that your attitude about money is heartfelt." Sloan tried to encourage him. "I honestly think that if God took it all away from you tomorrow, you would be okay with it."

"Thanks," Rick said. "I think so, too, but I need to find a way to put my heart into action. Any ideas?"

"Not off the top of my head," Sloan said, "but I'll think about it. In my spare time."

Rick groaned.

"Oh, Sloan! I forgot all about the wedding! Like you had time to listen to me gripe and moan. There are probably a thousand things Jocelyn needed you to do today. I'm so sorry!"

"No, you're safe from the wrath of the bride-to-be!" Sloan tried to calm Rick's alarm. "I drove over there last weekend and packed up most of her apartment and brought it back. She won't be in town until tomorrow. You will be at the wedding, right?"

"Wouldn't miss it," Rick paused. "She knows I will be there, right?"

"Yes," Sloan said, "although I think Julia would be thrilled if I told her you had decided to suddenly go on an around-the-world excursion instead."

"Fat chance," Rick said. "Knowing I get to see her at the wedding will be the one thing that'll get me through the next several days!"

Later that day, Sloan called Jocelyn for help. He knew there was some missing piece to this puzzle.

"I think she's afraid to be in love with Rick," Jocelyn said.

"Afraid?" Sloan was confused.

"I think she's afraid of losing him," Jocelyn said. "She is shocked, and I think confused, by her reaction to him. She felt instantly comfortable with him, despite her objections."

"And?" Sloan asked. "Why is that a problem?"

"The closer they get—the more she depends on him, trusts him, lets him in—the more frightened she gets thinking of having to face life without him. She lost James, a tragedy she still seems to deny at times, so maybe she's decided to end it with Rick before she gets hurt again."

"And how do we get her past that?" Sloan asked.

"Hey, I figured out what was wrong." She threw up her hands. "I'll leave it up to you to fix it."

29

Opposing Teams

"Are you nervous?" Rick asked Sloan when he called to deliver his news three days later.

"No, of course not," Sloan answered. "It's not like I'm about to make the most important commitment of my lifetime or anything. Why on earth should I be nervous?"

"Sarcasm, huh? That's a good sign." Rick said. "Would it help to know I'm incredibly jealous?"

"No," Sloan said. "You've reminded me that two of my closest friends are locked in a seemingly hopeless morass of misunderstanding. Thanks so much, Rick. Now I'm depressed on top of nervous."

"Sorry," Rick said. "Now I'm depressed too. Maybe I should hang up and start over."

"Hello, Rick." Sloan pretended to answer the call again. "What's up?" Rick laughed.

"I've got some big news, Sloan," he said.

"News?" Sloan was leery. He had finally gotten Julia to answer his calls yesterday, and then it was only because she knew Jocelyn was with him. Being one of the bridesmaids and the mother of the flower girl meant Julia couldn't keep ignoring him.

"You remember your idea that I take a world tour?"

"Vaguely," Sloan said. "Does this mean you're not coming to the wedding?" The anxious groom-to-be was counting on all the moral support he could get.

"No, I'll be there, but I've decided what I'm going to do to get over my pouting," Rick said.

"You're not giving up, are you?"

"No, but I am going to give her the space she wants," Rick said. "I contacted the missions pastor at church. He was able to pull some strings, and I'll be joining the team in Uganda on Tuesday. I'll be there for ten days, then I'm going to stop and see my sister in London. After that I'll meet up with the Jamaica team for another week."

"You sound excited," Sloan said.

"I am. You were right. I may say I'm willing to give up everything, but until I see the heartache and tough times that the rest of the world experiences, I don't think I will truly appreciate the blessings I have, and the responsibilities that come with them."

"Wow." Sloan thought he'd never hear Rick get to this point. "Have you told Julia?"

"That's one of the reasons I called. I don't want her to think that I'm doing this merely to impress her, although our situation, and your eloquent indictment, showed me the depth of my selfishness. What do you think about me not telling her until after I leave?"

"You still haven't talked to her, have you?"

"No," Rick said. Giving her the time and space everyone advised had been one of the hardest things he had ever done. He hadn't called, texted, or even sent a message through Stephen or Sloan. He hoped she appreciated the effort.

"No, but according to a not-so-subtle message, delivered through Terry and poor Stephen, she implied I should keep my distance at the wedding. Stupid picture almost ruined everything."

The day after the auction, social media sites featured a picture of Lady Tiffany clutching Rick's tuxedo lapel as he playfully tweaked her finely sculptured nose. The caption read, 'Star Quarterback Rick Adams shares an affectionate moment with Lady Tiffany after she won his favors in the Bachelor's Charity Auction.'

Although Julia had seen the couples posing for pictures after each bid closed, she had missed that particular interlude, most likely while she was suffering through her humiliation outside the ladies' room. Had she seen it, she wouldn't have agreed to let Rick take her home that evening.

"How was your date, by the way?" Sloan asked. He hadn't brought up the issue, knowing it would be a sore spot with Rick.

"Fantastic, actually," Rick said.

"Excuse me?"

"Haven't you heard? My former agent Morris and Lady Tiffany are an item now," Rick said. Sloan demanded an explanation.

The picture in the paper had been snapped at the charity event, right after Rick had reminded the chic Ms. Tiffany that she should read the fine print in any document she signed. All bidders at the auction had to agree to a chaperoned date, should the bachelor so choose. Rick had insisted that Morris go along on the date. The agent was accompanied by his sister, who was also his boss at the public relations firm. Rick had spent the first part of the night fending off Tiffany's wandering hands until she transferred her attention to the noticeably beguiled Morris.

"Does Julia know?" Sloan asked. "It would probably make your life a little easier, you know."

"Nope." Rick said. "A little jealousy will be good for her."

"Well, it's your call. You don't sound too concerned that she's adamant that it's all over between you two," Sloan said, surprised at how calm Rick sounded.

"I'm not worried. She'll be so wowed by how gorgeous I look at the wedding that she won't be able to resist me," Rick said.

"Keep telling yourself that." Sloan raised an eyebrow. "I've seen the bridesmaid dresses. I'm betting that it's you we'll be mopping off the floor, not Julia."

"You're a cruel, cruel man, Sloan Mackenzie. Does your future wife know?" As he spoke the playful words, guilt over the way he had acted the night of the auction resurfaced. He had spent time on his knees but the shame over his anger and fear of how close he had come to giving into temptation was still real.

"I'll see you on Saturday, Rick," Sloan said as he got into his car. "Pray for me as I face my last days of freedom."

The object of their conversation was at the same time helping the bride-to-be with last-minute decorations. Julia's children were attempting to help. Fortunately, filling jars with chocolate candies was a task even an almost three-year-old could handle. They had barricaded the dog in the other room to prevent him from cleaning up the candies that didn't make it into the jars.

"You know, if you weren't the closest thing I have to a sister, I wouldn't be going on Saturday," Julia said to Jocelyn.

"I know, I know." Jocelyn said. "I'm sorry I've put you in this position. Maybe Mr. Richard Adams will come down with some rare wedding-day virus and won't show up."

"Not likely," Julia grumbled.

"I'm glad now that we stuck with family for the bridal party. Otherwise, Rick would probably be a groomsman," Jocelyn said. "That would be awkward!"

Julia dreaded facing Rick. Her resolve to break off their relationship wavered every time she pictured him with the kids. Or with the puppy. Or in his library. Or standing in her bedroom.

"This is not over," he had said.

"Yes, it is," she said.

"Yes, what is?" Jocelyn asked. Julia didn't realize she had spoken aloud.

"Sorry," Julia said, sheepishly. "Daydreaming."

"Any chance a tall, handsome quarterback is part of that dream?" Her cousin's teasing was good-natured, but it hit a little too close to home.

"I'll be fine." Julia tried to convince herself as well as Jocelyn. "Don't let my stupid problems worry you. Sloan would never forgive me if his bride was too worried about her lovesick cousin to enjoy her big day."

"Mommy said 'stupid,'" C.J. informed his sister.

"Stupid," Bethany parroted.

"Mommy should not have said that word." Julia reprimanded herself, trying to restore order to the chaos a spilled bag of candy had just created.

"My other concern is offspring one and two." Julia used carefully selected words so her children wouldn't know they were being discussed. "You-know-who is a favorite, and I'm not sure how to prevent any interaction."

"Then don't," her cousin suggested. "There will be enough going on, and other offspring their age will be there, so maybe his attention or inattention won't be a big deal."

"Again," Julia said, "not likely."

"Your optimism knows no bounds, does it?" Jocelyn asked.

"I can still add Terry and Stephen to the guest list if it would help to have them to protect you." Jocelyn said.

"Yeah, like Stephen would be on my side."

"Your parents will be there, so that should help, right?" Jocelyn was trying to help, but her comment served to remind Julia that Rick's parents would be at the wedding, too. He and Sloan had been close in college and had spent many holidays and school breaks together.

I should be able to avoid them if I work at it. She kept this last thought to herself, not wanting to add to Jocelyn's pre-wedding nerves.

"I'm done complaining. Promise," Julia said, with resolve in her voice. Jocelyn realized that this situation was more serious than Sloan had led her to believe. This wasn't a simple lover's quarrel. Julia was serious about ending their relationship—almost as serious as Rick was about continuing it, if Sloan's information was correct.

"Mommy, will Uncle Rick be at the wedding?" Her eldest child expertly sabotaged the resolve Julia had just regained. For some reason, Jocelyn thought the innocent question was hilarious. Julia threw a chocolate candy at her, thankfully without the kids seeing her.

30
Choosing Sides

This must be what ESP feels like, Julia thought. Without a glance, she knew that Rick had slipped into the back of the sanctuary. The bride and bridesmaids were having their pictures taken before the ceremony. Julia had grown increasingly nervous over the last few minutes, and now she knew why. They were wrapping up their last shots as Rick settled into one of the back pews. *He knows he's not supposed to be in here yet,* Julia thought. *He's doing this to annoy me.*

Glimpsing toward the back, she covered her curiosity by pretending to adjust Jocelyn's dress. Remembering the need to distract Bethany before she saw him, Julia wished the photographer would say they were done.

"One last picture with the flower girl, her mom, and the bride," the annoying man said. "Quite a lovely trio you all make!" As he arranged the three ladies, Julia heard the sanctuary door slamming. She forced herself to turn off her Rick Adams radar and concentrated on Jocelyn.

***

Rick realized sneaking into the sanctuary was a terrible idea. How was he ever going to make it through today? Seeing Julia for the first time since she pushed him out of her life was bittersweet agony.

The light green gowns and bouquets of deep-red roses lent the sanctuary a holiday feel. Bethany was concentrating of being still and listening to her mother, a point Rick could tell from the adorable, furrowed brow. He wanted to stand and wave to her, but he knew Julia would go ballistic if he did. Not that a little emotion from her wouldn't be welcome. *Too bad I promised Sloan I wouldn't cause a scene,* he thought.

Seeing Sloan's dad come out of one of the back rooms let Rick know he had found the groom's hideout. He quietly left the sanctuary.

"Rick!" Mr. Mackenzie called down the hallway. "Come on in, son. Join the party!"

"Thank you, sir." Rick shook the older man's hand. He had always enjoyed his time at Sloan's house during breaks from college. "How's the groom? Nervous?"

"More excited and ready to get the ceremony over with, I think," Sloan's dad explained. "Did you notice if the girls were done with their pictures yet?"

"Yes, I noticed," Rick said. "They were finishing up as I came in."

"Good, good." The father of the groom nodded, turning to head down the hall. "Go on in, I'm going to go tell the ushers that they can begin seating people. Ceremony's thirty minutes away!"

"Rick, my man!" Sloan greeted his friend. "Remind me again why I didn't try to talk Jocelyn into eloping?"

"You're a romantic sap, that's why," Rick reminded him. "I, on the other hand, would rather kidnap the girl and escape into the sunset."

"Not tonight, you won't." Sloan threw Rick a warning glance. "You promised."

"Just kidding." Rick said. "Wanted to make sure you were paying attention."

Sloan introduced Rick to Jocelyn's brother, Andrew, who was the other groomsman. Sloan's dad was best man. Jocelyn's older sister Heather was the matron of honor, and her son, Bobby, was the ring bearer.

"How are you doing?" Sloan asked. "Have you seen her?"

"Fine," Rick said, "and, yes, I have."

"Still fine?"

"Okay," Rick conceded. "Not so fine. I'm thinking this was not one of my most brilliant ideas."

"Her parents are here, your parents will be here, and my parents are probably torn by the whole mess, so it looks like the troops are fairly evenly divided."

"Your battle analogy is appropriate," Rick said, as he handed Sloan his tie.

"Just warning you," Sloan said. "You promised not to make a scene, but I'll back you all the way if you find it is absolutely necessary."

"Really?" Rick rubbed his hands together. "Let me see...."

"Whoa! Just make sure it's after the ceremony," Sloan added. "I want to be good and married before all you-know-what breaks loose."

"Don't you trust that I can get her to talk to me without mayhem breaking out?" Rick asked. "I'm deeply offended!"

Sloan's mom appeared moments later, barely waiting for an all-clear sign after her brief knock.

"Do you need help with anything? Oh, hello, Rick!" She gave him a quick kiss and pat on the cheek. Rick remembered her vivaciousness from the times he visited with Sloan during college. She seemed to be in constant motion, but she was still always aware of everything going on around her.

"Hello, Mrs. Mackenzie," Rick replied obediently. "You look lovely today."

"Sloan, I don't want to worry Jocelyn, but we missed a little detail. With your dad being best man, I will need someone else to seat me. You and your dad will be coming in with the pastor, and Andrew will be seating his mom."

"I can do it," Rick offered without thinking.

"Oh, that would be perfect!" Mrs. Mackenzie gave him an enthusiastic hug. "See, we took care of it and no one will have to know it wasn't planned like this from the beginning! I'm going to go let the wedding coordinator know. Ten minutes, Sloan, and you'll need to be in the lobby!"

"Are you sure about this Rick?" Sloan lowered his voice as he adjusted the cuff links his mom had hooked on during her rambling explanation. "It will mean you're in the lobby with you-know-who." He didn't know how much Andrew knew about the situation and didn't have time to explain it.

"You seem to forget that I'm not the one that is avoiding you-know-who," Rick pointed out. "It happens to be the other way around. So, you-know-who will just have to deal with it, now won't she?"

"I know that you're talking about Julia, guys," Andrew piped in. "I'm not an idiot. Jocelyn told me everything."

Rick and Sloan both laughed.

"So much for our covert skills," Rick said.

"But, honestly, Rick, I think you need to make her talk to you. Why don't you ask her to dance? Or even better, I can get her on the dance floor and you can cut in."

"I wouldn't put it past her to find a way out of dancing with you, me, or anyone," Rick said.

"No, I'm sure she won't refuse," Sloan said. "It would draw attention, and we both know how she feels about that."

"That seems unfair to use that against her," Rick said.

"Do you want to talk to her or not?" Sloan pressed. "I'm about ready to give up on you two!"

The signal came from the wedding coordinator, and the men made their way into the lobby. Sloan and his dad walked down the hallway and waited outside the side entrance. Andrew would sprint around to join them as soon as he finished seating his mom.

As the music began, the bridesmaids appeared from their dressing room. Rick's breath caught as he saw Julia. She immediately stooped down to caution her daughter.

Rick hadn't thought about Bethany being the one to make a scene. Rick quickly picked up the little girl and whispered to her, "Hello, Princess. Give me a kiss and then get ready to be the best flower girl ever, okay?" The blonde head bobbed excitedly. She gave him a resounding kiss and then squirmed to be put down.

"Thank you," Julia said.

Rick simply nodded.

As he escorted Mrs. Mackenzie, Rick winked at C.J., where he was sitting with Julia's parents. The little boy beamed. Sloan's mom safely delivered to her seat, Rick slipped into the back pew, not trusting himself to sit any closer. It was going to be torture enough sitting through the ceremony as it was.

Bethany waved to him as she passed, and he blew her a kiss. Julia didn't even meet his gaze. *Stubborn woman,* thought Rick. *You've met your match, my dear.* Rick was ready for this battle, still convinced this relationship was right and good.

The ceremony was mercifully short. Rick drank in every word, more convinced than ever that these feelings for Julia were not a fleeting flirtation, but were deep and true. He winked at her when he saw her glance his way as the vows were spoken. She looked away quickly.

He was poised and ready to retrieve Mrs. Mackenzie as soon as Jocelyn's parents made their way behind the attendants. The pastor then informed the guests that appetizers were already ready for them while the wedding party took a few pictures.

Rick found his parents and they made their way into the reception hall.

"Uncle Rick!" C.J.'s voice cut through the noise of the exodus. Rick swung the young boy up and onto his back in one fluid movement.

"Hey, what's this growth I have on my back?" Rick asked his mom. "It's awfully wiggly!"

Julia's parents had seen the reunion and made their way over to Rick. He made the introductions, aware that all four parents knew the reality of the situation.

"How are you, Rick?" Mrs. Pearson was the first to break the awkwardness.

"Not so great, but thank you for asking. Of course, seeing this monkey helps." Rick swung C.J. back down and plopped him on a stool.

"Are you hungry, big guy? I'm starving," Rick said. He bent down so he was eye-to-eye with the young man. "I came thinking I could just sit around and eat and enjoy myself, and did you see that they put me to work?! I had to walk all the way down the aisle! Twice!" All the parents joined C.J.'s delighted giggles.

"You're silly, Uncle Rick," C.J. informed him. "Mommy says so, too." Rick's smile disappeared. The young boy had completely deflated the mood with his simple statement.

"I'll go get us something to eat," Rick's dad offered.

"I'll help." Mr. Pearson quickly followed. "C'mon, C.J., you can help us get the yummy stuff."

Rick sat on the chair vacated by C.J., flanked by both moms.

"Oh, I'm fine," he said, propping his elbows on the table. "Just peachy." He fiddled with the set of silverware in front of him, forming various shapes, until his mom finally scooped the utensils up and placed them out of his reach.

"I hope to talk to her," Rick glared playfully at his mom, "but if I don't, it's not the end of the world. And, no," he said, correctly interpreting the look of concern he saw pass between the two ladies, "I haven't given up. I still love her. She still loves me, despite her denial, and we will work this out. Satisfied?"

"Just making sure," his mom said. "How do you and Julia's dad feel about the whole situation, Joyce?"

"We think she is being unfair to Rick, but we know she's afraid," Julia's mom explained. "We were hoping a few days apart would help her see things more clearly, but I'm not sure there's been much movement yet. Her fears are a lot deeper than we thought."

Rick remembered what Sloan had told him at the restaurant. Knowing that she still carried a deep-seated guilt made it easier for him to give her the space she needed. On the other hand, knowing that he was going out of the country for several weeks made getting the chance to talk to her more pressing.

After the wedding party finished their formal photographs, the emcee announced their arrival to the dining hall.

"Mrs. Julia and Miss Bethany Fitzgerald, escorted by Andrew Pearson."

Bethany abandoned her mom as soon as they came through the door and she spotted Rick. The little girl's "Unka Rick! Unka Rick!" echoed across the hall. Julia started to reach for Bethany but let her go when she saw her parents. Her slight frown was not missed by Rick, or Julia's mom.

"She feels betrayed," Joyce said.

"You saw that, too?" Rick asked, as he settled Bethany on his lap.

Had anyone asked him for a description of the evening's festivities, he would be at a loss. The one thing he remembered clearly was watching Julia intently all evening. Despite her attempts to avoid him, they crossed paths more times than she wanted and less than he had hoped. Each time she smiled sweetly, then quickly found an excuse to move away.

From what he had observed, she hadn't sat down long enough to eat anything, and she looked a little pale for his liking. She had left the buffet line abruptly when he joined it, taking the chance to check in with her parents while he was away from their table.

Both Sloan and Jocelyn's parents had joined the others and hugged Julia warmly. Rick watched her hide behind a façade of joviality, her laugh a little too loud and giddy. He filled his plate with her favorites, hoping she would stay after he returned to the table with it.

She was helping Bethany with her cake when he rejoined the party.

"Julia," he said, placing the plate in front of her.

"Mr. Adams," she said, glancing at the plate. "Thank you, but I wouldn't dream of taking from your bounty." She grimaced slightly as she turned to look up at him. Her comment had brought looks of concern from most of the parents at the table and the threat of a reprimand from hers. Mrs. Pearson patted her husband's arms to prevent him from intervening.

"No problem," Rick proceeded to reach around her and grab one of the small sandwiches, and then stuffed the entire thing in his mouth. "Delectable," he said, staring pointedly at Julia. She opened her mouth to respond, but simply shook her head. The motion brought another grimace.

"Are you okay?" Rick asked as she slipped a bit clumsily from the stool.

"Yes, of course. I'll leave you to your fun." She turned to her mother. "Let me know if the children become unruly."

From the raised dais, Jocelyn watched Rick watch Julia walk away. She too was concerned with how her cousin was acting.

"Honey, I think something's wrong with Julia," the new bride whispered to her groom during their first dance.

"You mean besides Rick Adams?"

"Very funny." She leaned back and insisted he help. "I'm serious. Look at her."

"I'd rather look at you." Sloan pulled her close and tried to nibble her ear.

"Stop it!" Jocelyn pushed him away playfully. Sloan twirled her around slowly so he could see Julia.

"You're right, she does look a little shaky." agreed with her assessment. "She's obviously trying to put on a brave front. Tell you what, after I dance with Mom, I'll grab Julia. I'm sure Rick will remember his cue and cut in on us. I promised to help him get her alone to talk, so now is as good a time as any."

As Sloan led Julia onto the dance floor, he realized she wasn't very steady on her feet.

"Are you feeling okay?" he asked.

"I haven't gotten a chance to eat yet," she said. "I'm a little light-headed." She swayed noticeably.

"May I cut in?" As Rick formally tapped Sloan on the shoulder, the look on Julia's face would have been funny had it not been so truly terrified.

"Relax, Julia." Rick took her hand from Sloan. "I just want to talk to you. I won't bite." The dance was a slow, romantic classic, and he tried to concentrate on what he needed to say. Having her in his arms once again made thinking difficult. She was silent, and as he leaned back slightly to look at her, he realized how pale she was.

"Julia, have you eaten anything?" Rick asked. For some reason, she seemed to find this funny. She playfully patted him on the cheek.

"No, Officer Adams of the Food Patrol." She giggled again. "I've had some punch, so I should be fine. There's no danger that I'll expire at your feet. That would inconvenience you, I'm sure."

He slowed their movement as he realized what was wrong.

"Which punch have you been drinking, Julia?" His voice was full of concern now. If his suspicions were correct, based on the symptoms she was showing, he would have to move quickly or she would be thoroughly embarrassed quite soon.

"That one." She waved to the bowl being faithfully manned by one of the wait staff. The bowl next to the dessert table was self-service. Rick realized she had been sampling the champagne punch, not the family-friendly version.

Rick swirled her as quickly as he dared toward the edge of the dance floor, given her lack of balance that was shakier by the minute. Wrapping his arm tightly around her waist, he pushed her into the hallway.

"What are you doing?"

"You, my dear, are drunk!"

31

Pulled from the Game

Rick's voice held no humor. He had never found it particularly funny to see tipsy women portrayed as adorable innocents on television or in film, and he didn't find it amusing in real life—and absolutely not with this woman in particular.

"What? That's ridiculous," Julia cried. "I'm fine!"

Having watched their offspring dancing, the two sets of parents remaining at the table were aware something was wrong. Both dads came quickly to Rick's side as they saw his desperate signal.

"I've got to take her home. Now. She's been accidently drinking the wrong punch. I need you to take care of the kids. Tell Sloan, and have Mom or Joyce meet me at the car with Julia's bag."

The leadership Rick exhibited on the field was evident in his no-nonsense orders. Within seconds, Julia's rescue was underway. Rick pulled Julia around the corner into more privacy before unceremoniously lifting her into his arms.

"Put me down! I'm fine!" She pounded his chest with weak fists. "Plus, I'm dizzy and I don't like heights." She found her own comment irresistibly funny, if her chuckles were any indication.

Rick settled her into his truck as Joyce arrived with Julia's purse and coat. His mom arrived at the same time, with a sandwich and a bottle of water.

"I'll call you when I get her settled," he said. "Make sure the kids don't worry."

As they pulled out of the church's parking lot, Rick urged her to try to eat something. "Take small bites and try to drink a little bit of water."

"I don't feel so good." Julia's stomach was objecting to the rough treatment it perceived she had received over the last few minutes.

"You'll probably get sick before this is all over. Just give me warning so I can pull over, okay?" He didn't care about his truck, but he knew she would be devastated and embarrassed by the situation.

"Now would be a good time," she said weakly. He pulled over quickly and held her as she leaned into the bushes. He settled her back in the truck and wiped her face with the paper towels her mom had thoughtfully provided. He made her take small sips of water before getting back into the driver's seat.

"I'm going to die," she said. "Please, shoot me now and put me out of my misery." Rick had taken his tuxedo jacket off, rolled it up, and placed it on the seat between them.

"Come here." He pulled her down on to the makeshift pillow. "Close your eyes. Here's the water if you want any more." As he pulled back onto the road, he offered up a quick prayer. He knew she wasn't over the worst part, but he hoped her suffering would be short-lived.

As they drove, he gently rubbed the back of her neck. He felt her relax, but he tried not to be too optimistic. After all, she wasn't in complete control of herself right now. While they were still ten minutes out, he pressed the phone button on his steering wheel.

"Call Terry Hampton."

"You're talking to your car." Julia giggled again.

"Hello?" Terry had stared at her phone as it identified the caller as Rick Adams.

"Terry, this is Rick. Julia became ill at the wedding and I'm bringing her home. Can you meet me at her door?"

"What happened?" Terry was on her way out the door almost before he finished his statement.

"I'll explain when we get there," he said. "I need you to help her get changed into something more comfortable than the bridesmaid's dress she's in right now."

"Okay." Rick could tell Terry was concerned and curious.

"She's going to be fine," he tried to assure her. "We'll be there in five minutes."

Julia's townhouse door opened, and Rick carried her straight up to the bathroom. She was still shaky, but no longer queasy.

"I've got this," Terry insisted and pulled him out of the bathroom. Julia's mom had called right after Rick did, so Terry knew what had happened.

Rick suppressed his impatience and occupied himself by taking Bouncer outside. Unfortunately, that chore only took a few minutes, so Rick was pacing the living room when he heard the ladies come out of the bathroom ten minutes later. He knew Julia was still weak, so he met them at the top of the stairs and scooped her into his arms. He took the stairs slowly, knowing she was probably still dizzy.

She instinctively clung to him, nestling her head into his neck.

"You smell good," she breathed against his neck. Rick almost dropped her. He gritted his teeth and deposited her on the couch.

"Drink," he insisted as he handed her a large glass of ice water. "Do you feel like you could eat something?" She nodded, and then winced. He had a plateful of crackers ready and offered her one at a time, watching her intensely.

"We're good here," he told Terry who was still hovering watchfully from the kitchen. "I promise I'll call if I need anything. I want to get something into her stomach right now. Apparently, she didn't eat much lunch and nothing to speak of at the reception."

"Stop talking about me like I'm not here," Julia chimed in.

"See?" Rick smiled. "She's already feeling better. Back to her ornery self."

Terry's look was more relaxed as she left, but she insisted on telling Julia to call her if she needed anything.

Julia's shakiness was subsiding, and she was suddenly sleepy. Rick propped a pillow next to him and pulled her gently down onto it. Bouncer snuggled protectively at her feet.

"Try to sleep." He brushed the hair away from her face. "I'll be here when you wake up." A restful half hour later, Julia stirred.

"I'm starving," she grumbled.

"Sit still and I'll get you a couple pieces of toast." Rick went to the kitchen, with one eye on her as she stretched and tried to stand.

"I said to sit still," he commanded.

She obeyed, but not before she made a childish face at him.

"I saw that," he said. She had forgotten that he could see her reflection in the sliding glass door.

"Thank you," she finally said after eating the toast slowly. "Am I going to live?" Rick turned her so that he could lightly rub her shoulders, hoping it would help her relax and sleep.

"Yes." He continued to rub her shoulders. She knew she would regret allowing this intimacy considering her resolve to end their relationship, but her weakened state, both physical and mental, meant she couldn't resist the comfort.

"I'm sorry for ruining your evening," she said quietly. "I'm sorry to be such a problem."

"You didn't ruin my evening," he said. "You are not a problem, except that you seem to keep forgetting that I love you. Sickness or health."

"Subtle, Rick," she said. "Did you want to add 'better' and 'worse'?"

"Don't play games, Julia," Rick said. "You know I love you. You're the one that has a problem with this."

"Especially the 'richer'" or 'poorer' part," she muttered.

He sat in silence for a few moments. Sloan's reprimands about his selfishness came to mind, and he sighed.

"Am I boring you?" she asked.

He ignored her question. "Julia, we need to talk," he said, his tone serious. "About us."

"There is no 'us.' I thought I made myself clear." She turned to stare at him, hoping her gaze was convincing.

"Are you trying to convince me or yourself?"

Her eyes dropped.

"All right, I'll make this quick. I love you, you know that," he began. "That is not going to change. I think you love me, too. It's evident to everyone that knows and cares for us. I will wait as long as it takes for you to admit that you love me enough to work this out."

Her stance remained unresponsive. As her sobriety returned, so did her fear—and resolve.

"Sloan set me straight on some issues, and I've realized that I have indeed turned into quite a selfish person. I was unwilling to admit it until last weekend. Call it an epiphany."

"I'm so glad you have seen the light. Congratulations. Feel free to leave now." Julia weakly waved her hand toward the door.

"I'm almost done," Rick continued. He grabbed both her hands in his own and pulled her around to face him. "I'm going away for several weeks. I know you don't want to hear from me and wish I'd fall off the edge of the earth, but that's not going to happen. I'm hoping this trip will help me work out the issues that Sloan so painfully brought to my attention. As much as I'm going to miss you, I'm actually looking forward to the adventure."

"Where are you going?" She tried to pull her hands away, but he didn't let them go.

"I'm not going to tell you yet," he said, "but I need you to know that I'm not doing this to win your approval or regain your trust. I'm doing this because I need to for me, for my spiritual well-being. Understand?"

She pulled away. "Have a safe trip, wherever you're going. How long will you be gone?" She stood and calmly folded the blanket he had covered placed over her. Rick realized she was retreating again and decided to change the subject.

"Are you ready for something more substantial to eat?" he asked, ignoring her question.

His own stomach was growling, since he hadn't eaten much at the reception, having spent most of his time watching her.

"I guess so." She knew she needed to eat, but she just wanted to crawl into bed and forget about everything. He whipped up some scrambled eggs, more toast, and a pot of coffee. He hoped the coffee wouldn't prevent her from sleeping, but he knew the aroma would help snap her out of her depression.

By the end of their meal, her eyes were drooping. As he picked her up and carried her back to the sofa, she protested.

"I can walk to the living room. I am not a child," she stubbornly insisted. "You seem to have a propensity for picking me up and carrying me around."

"Let's call it practice," Rick mumbled. Julia chose not to respond to his obvious reference. He unfolded the blanket and tucked it in as he sat on the edge of the couch. The puppy protested as Rick placed him on the floor. Julia pulled the covers up and turned her back towards him. He knew she wasn't asleep and waited, knowing they still had things to discuss, but her silence concerned him. Her next words confirmed his fears.

"Being here and taking care of me hasn't changed my mind, Rick."

"I love you, Julia," he said. He moved across the room and settled in the recliner. Several minutes later, he thought she was asleep, until she turned over to face him.

"It hurts, Rick," she said quietly.

"Hurts? What hurts?" Rick started to move back to her side.

"No," she stopped him. "Stay there."

"What hurts?" he asked again.

"Loving you." Her simple words stunned him. "I can't do it anymore." She was giving up. Rick searched for words to change her mind.

"Can't?" he asked. "Or won't?"

"Does it matter?" Julia turned back towards the cushions. Rick left as soon as Julia's parents arrived.

32
A New Play Book

"He's where?" Terry asked as Julia reluctantly admitted that she had heard from Rick.

"Uganda."

"Uganda? With the church group?" Terry asked.

"Yes, they apparently fit him into the itinerary at the last minute. He has an up-to-date passport since his brother-in-law is often stationed overseas, plus his former team played in London three years ago."

"I remember that," Terry said. "Who would've ever thought that a soccer-crazy country like England could pack out a stadium for American football?"

What Julia didn't tell Terry was that Rick e-mailed her almost daily, filling her in on the details of his experience. She remembered the depression she felt the day after the wedding, partly because of the punch, but mainly over having sent Rick away. His message had simply stated that he wouldn't be using his phone except in an emergency but would be e-mailing her whenever he could. Whether she read them or deleted them was up to her. Julia could have no idea how painful it had been for Rick to compose and send that first message.

This is fascinating, Julia remembered thinking when she read his next e-mail, his first journal-like entry. *He's an excellent writer.*

"Don't you miss him, even a little bit?" Terry's question brought Julia rudely back to the present.

"Truthfully? I miss him more than a little bit," Julia said. "But that doesn't make any difference in our situation." Julia would never own up to missing Rick to anyone but Terry. Jocelyn was still on her honeymoon, and Julia hesitated to confide in her anyway, now that she was married to one of Rick's best friends. Never mind that Sloan was also one of Julia's best friends.

"You know my feelings on the matter, so I won't beat a dead horse, as they say." The two friends had discussed this so many times, Terry felt that she had done all she could.

Later that night, Julia reread Rick's e-mail. She had copied it into a document and printed it out, always leery of her old computer's ability to preserve important documents. It was a fascinating exposé about the strangeness of the landscape, the warmth of the people, and their contentment despite their harsh circumstances.

A Bible verse came to mind as she read his words, and she jotted it down on the bottom of the document, along with some thoughts that his musings had planted. As she carefully put the pages into a binder and hid it under a stack on her desk, a beep indicated she had a new message. It was from Rick.

Dear Julia:

I don't know if you got my e-mail yesterday, but I thought I should explain. It's only been four days, but my experiences here so far have been so overwhelming that I had to share them. Simply writing them down has helped, though, so I want you to know that if you don't want to read them, that's okay. Of course, if you're not reading my mail, then you won't even get this, which is kind of ironic.

Julia could almost hear him mocking himself with the irony. She read on.

This will be the only personal note I include, but I need you to know what's really going on with me. Our friend Sloan should consider opening a marriage counseling service.

"Marriage counseling? You're getting a little ahead of yourself, Rick," Julia said, apparently aloud as her son called out, "Who are you talking to, Mommy?"

"No one, honey." Julia glanced into the dining room where the two kids were coloring pictures for Sloan and Jocelyn, who were due back from their honeymoon tomorrow.

Julia turned back to Rick's letter. What on earth did Sloan tell Rick?

He pointed out some hard truths to me that I must say I didn't take well initially. The first day I was here, one of the local missionaries shared something that almost knocked me over. His words let me know that Sloan couldn't have been more correct.

The missionary told me that poverty has a way of bringing out great wisdom. Many people think that the impoverished of the world have great envy for the wealth of the West. Because they realize it's not riches that bring happiness, they pity the wealthy in many ways.

Of course, this was something I had heard before, but his next words cut like a knife. He told me that what surprised him most was that the villagers knew it was not wealth that made rich people unhappy. It was selfishness.

Amazing how the Lord of Creation can drag me halfway around the world to wake me up with the simple wisdom of my African spiritual brothers and sisters.

In a nutshell, I am arrogant and selfish. "I," "I," "I." It's all about me. Since we met, I've been all about what I want. It's been about me, not about what's best for you, what God wants for you, or even what God wants for me.

How many times have you heard me say, "I'm not letting this go," "I am going to convince you," "I know this is right"? Me, me, me.

I didn't realize how used to getting my own way I had become. What a fool. How you ever put up with me for as long as you did is amazing.

Now for the bad news. None of my new self-awareness has changed the fact that I love you. I want to be part of your life. I want to spend the rest of my life on this journey with you. But even as I write this, I hear my selfishness...but, at least I am now willing to give the relationship over to God's will. As painful as it will be, I am finally willing to let you go if that's what He asks me to do. Do you have any idea how hard that is for me?

We both know God has caused our paths to cross, and what I want now more than anything, is for you to see Him in your life, see you grow closer to Him, with or without me. If that means I must step out of the way, then I will. I won't be happy about it, but I'll do it.

Kiss the kids for me, and the eternal optimist in me would like you to tell Bouncer to keep my spot on the couch warm while I'm away.

I'll send you updates when I can get to town. If you are reading them, thank you. I couldn't think of anyone else I wanted to entrust them to. Whatever happens, I know you care about this spiritual journey.

Julia, I know you don't want to hear it but, I will say it once more: I love you.

~Rick.

Julia hadn't heard her son come up behind her chair.

"Mommy, why are you crying?"

She simply hugged him close, taking comfort in his simple concern. The days and weeks ahead stretched before her like an unwelcome journey.

33
Tackled

Today is the day, Julia thought several days later. Thinking that this year would be different, she was disappointed to find that she not only was dreading this day as always, but somehow this year, her sadness seemed worse than ever.

Here she was, facing the anniversary of her husband's death once again alone. Of course, her parents, Terry, and the newlyweds Sloan and Jocelyn had all offered to come over.

"No," Julia insisted to each as they called. "I'm okay, I promise. At least C.J. is still young enough to not completely understand, so I don't want to make a big deal of it."

I've handled this fine for the last four years. I can do this. She kept telling herself. *Why then do I just want to crawl under the covers and hide?*

It was a regular school day, so that took up most of the morning. She had begged off her tutoring appointments, telling Monica that she was behind with some grading. It wasn't a lie, but it wasn't technically the real reason she didn't want to go out, either.

"You sure everything is okay?" Monica had asked. Sloan had asked Rick to keep as much of Julia's story quiet as possible, knowing she would be uncomfortable with unwanted sympathy.

"Yes, I just need to take a break this week," Julia said, hoping her tone didn't betray her. "Could you let Coach know, too?" Julia had continued to tutor Gary, and at Monica's recommendation, she was helping the assistant coach's high school senior with calculus once a week.

After school, Julia treated the kids to lunch at their favorite fast-food restaurant, and she planned to fill the afternoon with movies or crafts. She considered letting them build a fort with all the blankets and pillows, too. At least that would keep them occupied for most of the afternoon. It would also keep her busy cleaning up that evening.

A pizza dinner was Julia's one concession to outright melancholy, since it had been a weekly tradition for her and James. After she tucked her kids into bed, she fought the desire to pull out the family photo albums and sit in misery. Instead, she forced herself to work on the papers that she had told Monica she needed to grade.

By nine o'clock, she had completed the schoolwork and restarted her computer to enter the grades into the school's bookkeeping system. She had lost count of how many times she had checked her inbox during the day. Rick had continued to send almost daily e-mails, but none were personal in any way, as he promised. Today, and yesterday for that matter, there had been nothing. *He really has let me go,* she thought.

She waited patiently for her ancient computer to cycle on. Finally, she saw the "unread mail" symbol flashing at her. It was from Rick.

Dear Julia,

I know I promised no more personal notes after the first one. Forgive me. I know I have no right to intrude on your life, especially today, but I wanted you to know that I am praying for you. You're not alone. Psalm 23.

~Rick

The last of her self-control crumbled.

***

"Uncle Sloan?" the scared young voice came through the phone. Sloan shot off the coach, nearly knocking his new wife on the floor.

"C.J.? Anything wrong, buddy?" Sloan was grabbing his keys and wallet as he spoke. Jocelyn slipped on her shoes and turned off the movie they had been watching.

"It's Mommy," C.J. said. "She can't stop crying. I'm scared, Uncle Sloan."

"You're being so brave, big guy," Sloan said. "Aunt Jocelyn and I are on our way. I'm going to give the phone to her while I drive. Just tell her everything that you can. It's going to be okay, I promise."

Jocelyn calmed the boy down and was able to get the story. He had found Julia downstairs curled up the sofa when she hadn't come to his room to tuck him in.

"You were very smart to call Uncle Sloan, C.J.," she told him. "I'm glad you knew how to use her phone." Sloan and Julia had taught him how to call for help in an emergency after watching a news story about a grandfather who had suffered a heart and survived due to his quick-thinking young grandson.

Sloan and Jocelyn found Julia just as C.J. described. Jocelyn scooted C.J. upstairs, reassuring him the whole way. Sloan gathered Julia in his arms. She was no longer sobbing, but silent tears still streamed down her cheeks.

"Finally," he said. "I really had hoped it wouldn't take this long, though."

"What do you mean?" Julia whispered weakly.

218

"It has taken four years, but I think you are finally mourning the death of your husband."

He heard her sharp intake of breath.

"What?" She pushed out of his hold. "What makes you think I haven't grieved over James? How cold do you think I am? I have done perfectly well, thank you. I don't need you to tell me how to mourn my loss!"

Sloan let her rant. Jocelyn had come back downstairs and joined the pair on the sofa, sitting on Julia's other side.

"You don't think I'm a cold, unfeeling shrew, too, do you?" Julia asked Jocelyn.

"No, Julia," Jocelyn said as she gently rubbed her back. "But if you'll look at the situation objectively, which I know you can do, you will see our point." Julia relaxed as Jocelyn's calm words began to sink in.

"You had a young son and were very pregnant when your husband died suddenly. When did you ever have time to grieve?" Sloan spoke the truth he and Julia's parents had been discussing for months. "It's okay, dear. You don't have to be strong all the time. It's okay to let people know you need help."

Julia pulled her legs up onto the sofa and rested crossed arms on her knees.

"Why now?" she asked. "I've been doing everything right, haven't I?"

"Oh, Julia," Jocelyn laughed. "We are not saying you've done anything wrong. But recently those of us who love you realized that you were doing a little too well. Or at least you appeared to be doing well."

"Recently? What do you mean? Have you all been conspiring behind my back?" Sloan moved to the coffee table in front of her. She squeezed her eyes shut. It reminded her of the times Rick had sat in the same spot.

"Julia, look at me," Sloan said, prying her arms off her knees.

"No. I get your point. I'll be fine now. I need to cry over my loss and move on. There, I get it. You can go."

"Now you're just being a brat," he said.

"Sloan!" Jocelyn punched his arm. "Stop. I know you want to get to the real point, but give her a chance."

"The real point?" Julia asked. "You mean there's more? Please, go ahead. Let's get this over with." She stood and caught her breath. "I need some coffee. Anyone else want some?"

Sloan buried his head in his hands. "This is not going well," he said to his wife.

"So glad you realized that, dear," Jocelyn replied and followed Julia into the kitchen. She took three mugs out of the cabinet and pulled out the creamer and sugar jar. As the coffee started brewing, Julia moved to sit at the dining room table.

"Am I a bad person?" she asked Jocelyn.

"Why do you ask?"

"Was it wrong to begin a relationship with Rick?" Julia whispered. If she had looked up, she would have seen a triumphant smile on her cousin's face.

"I think your relationship with Rick is what got you to this point," Jocelyn said. "Letting someone into your life means you're finally willing to be vulnerable."

A watery smile met the broader one. "I suppose you're going to make me talk about all this now, aren't you?" Jocelyn nodded.

The trio talked about James through two pots of coffee and a batch of brownies that Sloan hilariously prepared 'all by myself,' which in reality meant with the constant input from the ladies.

Jocelyn and Sloan made their way home in the early hours of the morning. "I think that went well," Jocelyn said.

"For the most part." Sloan pulled her close as they settled in bed. "I think she's still in denial about Rick."

"She told me it was over," Jocelyn said, "which she's been saying since the charity fiasco, but somehow this is different. I think she really believes it now."

"Well, at least she's dealing with her sorrow over James more appropriately now." Sloan yawned broadly. "I'll deal with my boy Rick when he gets back if he's messed this up for good."

"Yes, dear." Jocelyn kissed him and turned off the light.

34
Reading the Defense

Three weeks later, Julia had twelve chapters of a book printed and bound on her desk. Rick's writing was poignant and inspirational. She had added Scripture and thoughts of her own, along with experiences from other friends and family, to each of his posts.

Since her breakdown with Jocelyn and Sloan, Julia had gained clarity about her feelings for Rick. The clarity brought little comfort. *How ironic. Just as I know my heart, I've ruined my chances. What a fool I am!*

My Journey by Rick Adams was a private treasure she knew would never see print. She kept it tucked under files on her desk and had managed so far to hide its existence. A couple of times she'd been working on it when Terry had stopped by unexpectedly. Julia knew Terry had watched her with curiosity as she frantically hid papers and switched off the computer screen. That secret had remained hidden. So had the secret of her misery and hopelessness. To the casual observer, all was well with Ms. Julia Fitzgerald.

Spring had arrived in full force, and C.J.'s allergies had decided to celebrate his birthday with several nasty days of torment. Today was the first Saturday in a couple of weeks that he was sneeze-free, so Garrett and Monica planned a picnic at the zoo.

Julia planned to tell them that next week would be the last time she could meet to tutor Gary. It was too painful, but she treasured the friendship with Monica. She decided that when Rick returned, she'd have to stop.

The Stahls had refused to let Julia continue her work without pay, so Garrett had set up a fund for C.J. and Bethany's school expenses. C.J. would be in full-day kindergarten next year and would need uniforms. Julia also wanted him to play soccer, and Monica insisted that she use the tutoring money wherever was necessary.

"We can't tell Garrett or Rick that you're using it for the 'S' word!" The two friends laughed at the continued snobbery of American footballers. What Julia didn't share was that the star quarterback of the Wolves had spent much of the last few weeks playing soccer, both in a small village in Africa and now in Jamaica.

Julia remembered the humility of his comment in one of the early chapters of his saga: "And since I'm so well known for my fancy footwork, this soccer thing has come naturally to me. Of course, my new coaches, who are all nine or ten years old, find my attempts hilarious."

"When's Rick due back?" Monica asked, seemingly out of the blue. The insightful woman had seen the look on Julia's face when Rick was mentioned.

"How should I know?" She hurriedly moved away to catch up with Garrett and the kids. She thought she heard Monica laugh.

Julia didn't know exactly when he was due back. His last post was from Jamaica. He had left Uganda and spent a couple days with his sister in London, before heading to join the church's team at the Christian Deaf School. One brief message was all she received from London.

"What a culture shock," he had written. "Not sure I'm ready to get back to civilization."

Wishing she had paid more attention to the mission team announcements before they left, Julia thought the group was returning in a week, but she wasn't sure if Rick was officially traveling with them or was meeting up with them as he did in Uganda.

From his writings, Julia could tell that the conditions at the deaf school weren't as primitive as the village in Africa, but the children were just as friendly and welcoming. He had done some reading while he was in London, so he wasn't surprised that it took several days before he was awarded a name sign.

A sign-language name sign was not something you could choose for yourself. It had to be given to you by a deaf or hearing-impaired person.

Rick had worn a Wolves T-shirt on the first few days he was there, and one of the teachers had explained to the students about American football and their team mascots. Combine that with the fact that he had let his hair and beard grow over the last three weeks, and his sign was almost a given. Since the sign for 'wolf' was similar to the sign for 'sleep,' his early attempts earned lots of laughter. He became known as Sleepy Wolf.

Monica's mention of Rick brought all Julia's doubts, frustrations, and longings back to the surface. The last weeks had been spent alternately denying her feelings and wallowing in self-pity. That her Heavenly Father had a sense of humor, she had no doubt, as she caught up to her children and Garrett as they approached the wolf family's compound. As she arrived, she heard her son share his vast knowledge of American Sign Language. Or at least the part that applied to his uncle Rick.

"Mommy says Uncle Rick's name means 'sleepy wolf,' and it looks like this." The intense young instructor made the hand motion of a wolf's snout.

"Sleepy Wolf, huh?" Garrett asked, looking pointedly at Julia. "Interesting. I wonder how your mother knows about Uncle Rick's sign-language name."

"Oh, she reads his e-mails every night," her traitorous son announced.

"That's enough information, C.J." Julia intervened before any more damage could be done. "I'm sure Uncle Garrett isn't interested in what I read each night. Let's go look at the giraffes. The nice zookeeper told me they have a new baby."

There was no doubt that Julia heard laughter this time. She was sure Garrett was explaining the situation to his wife as she joined them.

The Stahls treated everyone to ice cream on the way home from their outing.

"So, does Rick know?" Garrett asked Julia as they sat at the ice-cream shop's picnic tables.

"Know what?" She pretended ignorance.

"That you read his e-mails? That you still love him?" His straightforward approach earned him a kick under the table from his wife.

"The e-mails to which my overzealous son referred are not personal nor are they written to me specifically. He's just journaling about his trip." Julia said over her shoulder as she rescued Bethany's ice cream from where it teetered precariously on the end of her kid-sized cone.

"Is that so?" Garrett moved his leg in time to miss his wife's second kick. "What about the other part?"

"What's done is done, Garrett," Julia said. "I told him there was no chance, and he took me at my word." She met the lineman's gaze steadily. Tears gathered in her eyes. Garrett looked quickly to his wife for help.

"Julia?" Monica asked. "What has Rick said that makes you think he has changed his mind?"

"It's not what he's said," Julia answered quietly. "It's what he's not saying. At least not anymore."

"Oh," Garrett said. "Let me get this straight. You don't want him to be in love with you, but now you're upset because he's not saying he loves you?"

"Yes," Julia said.

"Makes perfect sense to me," Monica said. The two ladies nodded in agreement.

"Oh, brother!" Garrett said, throwing up his hands.

On the way home, Julia watched her two exhausted kids, grateful that they would sleep well tonight. She was still concerned about C.J. and hoped that the long day, the blooming shrubs, the hay, and animals didn't aggravate his allergies.

The doctor had said there was a fine line between exposing him to things he may be allergic to so he could develop a natural immunity and protecting him when his system wasn't ready for the overload. Julia hoped she hadn't pushed him too far today. At midnight, she had her answer.

35
The Touchdown

Having trouble sleeping even six weeks after the auction fiasco, Julia was still awake, flipping through old movies on the television. She had changed into her most comfortable stretch jeans and, as if to punish herself, one of Rick's jerseys. He had given it to her for Christmas, although the gift tag technically said it was from C.J. and Bethany.

With the acute hearing of a mother, her son's labored breathing caught Julia's attention almost immediately. His fevered skin wasn't as concerning as the apparent struggle he was having with each breath. The allergist had mentioned the possibility that his allergic reaction may progress to a more severe level, but she was surprised at how quickly these symptoms had developed. A week ago, he had been sneezing and nothing more.

Instincts taking over, she didn't panic, knowing that she was on her own, so losing control wasn't an option. The hospital was twenty minutes away. Deciding not to risk C.J.'s condition worsening without intervention during the drive, she called 911.

The emergency response operator dispatched an ambulance immediately and patched her through to the EMT. The kind voice on the other end thanked her for remaining calm and assured her that they would be there shortly.

"Do you have any other children in the house?" the first responder asked.

"Yes, my daughter. She's almost three, but the neighbor can be here in minutes. Is it okay if I put you on hold and call her?" Julia asked, hoping she was making sense.

"Yes, we'll stay on the line to keep tabs on his condition or if you have any questions. The ambulance is three minutes away."

She woke Terry with her call. "I'm so sorry, Terry. I need to take C.J. to the hospital. The ambulance is on its way. Can you come? I have to call Malcolm to open the gate."

"On my way." Terry was amazed at Julia's calmness. *Must be a mom thing,* she thought.

Malcolm was watching for the emergency lights, and Julia saw the gate open as the ambulance approached.

"Are you sure you're going to be okay?" Terry asked her friend, trying to figure a way to take care of Bethany and be there for Julia.

"I don't have a choice, do I?" Julia busied herself with gathering her insurance information, and a couple of books, knowing she was in for a long night.

"I miss Rick, I need him here, but I was too stupid to see that and I sent him away." Julia's voice was still calm and controlled. "So other than that, and the fact that I'm on the way to the hospital with my son, I'm fine."

"Call me when you know what's going on, okay?" Terry knew it was the emotions of the ordeal causing Julia's sarcasm, so she ignored Julia's tone. As the paramedics bundled C.J. onto a stretcher, Julia asked Terry for one more favor.

"Could you text Sloan for me? I don't want to wake him, but if he's on call tonight, he'll check his messages." Sloan met the ambulance at the emergency entrance.

"Jocelyn said she can take care of Bethany if Terry needs to go to class or anything." Sloan helped Julia out of the ambulance. The emergency-room pediatric specialist was already tending to C.J. The ambulance workers had started oxygen, and the pediatrician ordered medication as he walked the stretcher down the hall. "Are you okay?" Sloan asked as she stopped at the registration desk to get the stack of paperwork that would need to be filled out. This was one of the rare times the Fitzgerald clan came to mind in a non-negative way. They continued to pay for the children's medical insurance. She hated to think that it was simply to save face.

"Take your time," the nurse said as she handed Julia a clipboard. "Go be with your son." The Sloan's popularity among the hospital staff held meant his friend would be treated with special care. Julia smiled her thanks.

"Nice pajamas," Sloan teased as they stood outside the room, watching the nurses transfer her son to a regular bed. His breathing was already less labored, and the bluish tint was gone from his lips. His blue eyes were still wide with fear. Sloan winked at him and then made a silly face. C.J. waved weakly.

Julia looked down at her outfit. She remembered Rick's smug look on Christmas day when she had opened the present that was supposedly from her kids. Rick knew she would have refused the jersey if it had come from him.

"These are not pajamas," she said, pointing to her jeans. "Plus, everything else was dirty."

"Yeah, right." Sloan grinned.

Sloan looked at his watch. It was almost two in the morning. Rick was heading to the Miami airport by now. His plane was due to land here at six that morning. Rick had finally contacted Sloan from Jamaica a couple days ago but asked him not to tell Julia. "I don't want her to feel any pressure to see me when I get back."

"Do you need to go?" Julia asked, knowing he was still on call.

"I need to make a quick call and then I'll be right back. Do you want me to call Terry and let her know how he's doing? I can find out if she needs Jocelyn, too."

"That'd be good." Julia was intent on watching her son and didn't want to leave him to make a phone call. Sloan's call to Terry included additional instructions for Stephen, who was scheduled to pick up Rick at the airport.

"Sloan," Terry said hesitantly, after they settled all the details. "You'll never believe what I found on her desk." Terry had uncovered the manuscript Julia had created from Rick's journals while looking for Sloan's phone number. She described the packet.

"That little stinker!" Sloan laughed. "I knew she still loved him."

"It's pretty obvious," Terry said. "Even without the note on the last page that says, 'What was I thinking? I love this man.'"

"Send it with Stephen. Rick needs to know before he gets to the hospital."

A thousand miles away, the Wolves' star quarterback was boarding a plane for the last leg of his trip. His longer hair and beard made it easier for him to travel unnoticed by all but the most rabid fans. So far, today's trip had been uneventful, probably because it began in the wee hours of the morning. As his time on this journey was ending, Rick knew he had decisions to make.

Only Stephen and Sloan knew exactly when he was arriving. Since he was returning a day before the church team, he would need someone to pick him up at the airport. He resisted the longing to see Julia right away. *Patience.*

Traveling light meant he could bypass baggage claim. He left most of his clothes in Uganda, and the rest in Jamaica for the school's administrator to distribute to the neediest of the students. He had souvenirs, bracelets made by the villagers in Uganda, and necklaces made by the students in Montego Bay. Other than that, he carried his Bible, journal, and phone in his backpack. It was almost a visual picture of the change in his spiritual perspective.

Four hours later, right on time, Rick Adams walked through the customs checkpoint and saw Stephen push away from the column he had been leaning against. He seemed anxious.

"Please tell me you don't have any bags to pick up." The younger man's abrupt statement was delivered as he grabbed Rick's backpack and headed for the exit.

"Nice to see you, Rick. We've missed you. How was your trip?" Rick's sarcasm was lost on Stephen as he broke into a trot.

"C.J.'s in the hospital," Stephen called over his shoulder. Rick passed him at a full-out run.

36
The Red Zone

"Truck's on the second level," Stephen said as he caught up to Rick. "I'll drive." Rick ignored the offer and started to open the driver's side door. Stephen stopped him.

"No," he insisted. "There's something you need to read on the way." Stephen explained the situation with C.J. as they drove out of the parking garage. Rick took time to call his mom before looking at the folder that Stephen had handed him.

"Mom, how quickly can you be at the house?" Rick asked. "I need you to watch Bethany and probably Bouncer, too, and get a room ready for C.J. and Julia. He's in the hospital and I just landed."

Rick knew his mother would be able to follow his somewhat convoluted instructions.

"Welcome home, son," Mrs. Adams said. "I'll be there in an hour. Is Terry with Bethany now?" Stephen nodded, having overheard the question.

"Yes," Rick said. "Thanks, Mom. I'll call when I know more."

Rick sent Sloan a message, hoping to be able to meet him at the emergency-room door. Rick didn't like pulling strings, but he wasn't willing to wait for permission or make the necessary explanations in order to see C.J. and be with Julia.

Sloan didn't immediately answer, so Rick turned his attention to the folder. "So, what's this that I need to read?" Rick finally asked, opening the folder. His shock registered on his face.

"Yep, thought you might find that interesting," Stephen had thumbed through the manuscript while he waited impatiently for Rick's plane.

"Did you all know about this, and no one bothered to tell me? Do you know the agony I've been through, not knowing if she was even getting my messages?"

"Slow down there, buddy," Stephen said. "Terry found it a few hours ago."

As he read the first few additions Julia had made to his writings, he fell silent. Then he saw her note on the back page.

"Oh, thank you, Lord," Rick said, leaning his head back against the seat. As they neared the hospital, Stephen interrupted the silence.

"Terry packed some clothes and stuff for Julia," he said. "She left the house pretty quickly."

Rick's phone rang as Sloan finally called.

"We're about five minutes away," Rick said. "Where is Julia?"

"Well, they're in the process of moving C.J. up to the children's floor. She'll be filling out paperwork for a while. If you want to meet me at the emergency room entrance, you can see him before they take him upstairs."

"Where is Julia?" Rick repeated his question.

"She'll be upstairs by the time you get here, but if you want to see C.J. right away, you need to meet me downstairs. They'll have him sequestered while they run vitals on him after they take him upstairs."

"I'll meet you wherever it will get me upstairs the fastest. I want to see Julia first."

"But—" Sloan started to repeat his suggestion.

"Sloan." Rick was rapidly losing patience. "Switch Jocelyn for Julia and you for me. Where would you want to be?"

"You're right." Sloan acquiesced. "Upstairs it is. I'll meet you in the front lobby." When Rick walked through the hospital doors, Sloan greeted Rick with a huge bear hug.

"Missed you, brother" he said. They made their way to the elevator. Before Rick could press the button, Sloan grabbed his arm.

"Would you like to keep that hand?" Rick asked.

"There's something I need to tell you before we go upstairs," Sloan said. He released Rick's arm, but still blocked his access to the elevator controls. "Julia had a bit of a breakdown while you were gone."

Rick grabbed Sloan by the lapel.

"Excuse me? She had a breakdown, and no one called me? What on earth do you think the paper titled *Emergency Contacts* was for?"

"Relax, Rick!" Sloan pried the athlete's hand off his lab coat. "Maybe breakdown was a poor choice of words. It was more like a breakthrough. I'll explain on the way up."

As succinctly as possible, Sloan described the crisis Julia had finally faced and overcome. Rick listened without interrupting. When they reached the pediatric floor, they paused outside the elevator doors.

"The other thing you need to know is that Julia thinks you've given up on your relationship," Sloan said. Rick's look of disbelief confirmed Sloan's suspicions. "We think the probability of losing you was the proverbial last straw."

Rick hesitated. Sloan pushed him toward the reception desk. The nurses confirmed that Julia was indeed inside the lounge, resting.

"We told her the paperwork could wait. She's exhausted," the young nurse said, trying not to gawk at the man with Dr. Mackenzie. He looked remarkably like Wolves quarterback Rick Adams. "They called from downstairs, and her son will be up within a half an hour."

Sloan pulled his friend toward the small waiting room that the hospital provided solely for parents of the patients on the children's ward. It had recliners that were more comfortable, provided free Internet access, and several other amenities that made the overnight stays more bearable.

Through the half-glass door, they could see Julia curled up on one of the recliners. Although the wear of the day could be seen in her face, she looked to be asleep.

"I don't want to wake her if she's finally getting some rest." Rick backed away from the door.

"Liar," Sloan said. "You want to wake her up, sling her over your shoulder, and march her down to the chapel, after kidnapping an unsuspecting chaplain along the way." Sloan's teasing brought a tentative smile to Rick's face.

"Go," Sloan said. "I'm going to wait here for C.J. and get him settled. Even Julia won't be able to go in his room until they get him all checked in. Hospital policy."

"Okay," Rick said. "Pray for us, please."

"Haven't stopped since Thanksgiving," Sloan said to himself as Rick disappeared into the waiting room.

Facing away from the door in the semi-dark room, Julia wasn't asleep, but she didn't hear Rick's approach. The mantra that had been running through her mind all day was keeping her awake.

Where are you, Rick? How can you not know I need you right now? What was I thinking to send you away? She would shake herself out of the self-indulgent pity party occasionally and pray.

Lord, I think I've made a big mistake. Please let me know if You want me to be open to Rick's offer of a relationship. I'm no longer afraid of his money or position, but now I'm afraid of losing him. Please help me see Your hand in this and trust You whether or not Rick is a part of my life.

"Where are you?" she asked quietly. Rick heard her deep sigh as he knelt next to the recliner.

"Julia?" he said softly, not wanting to startle her.

Deep blue eyes blinked at him as she turned toward his voice.

"Rick?" She reached out a shaky hand and gently touched his cheek. "You're here?"

"Yes, I'm here. Where else would I be?" Rick smiled at her bemused look. The reality of his presence penetrated her hazy thoughts, and she suddenly burst into tears. Rick stood and gathered her into his arms. As he settled into the recliner, she sobbed into his chest, alternately clutching his jacket lapels and softly pounding him with her fists.

"I needed you and you weren't here!"

"I'm here now," he assured her. "And I will never, ever, spend that much time away from you again. It was torture."

As these words sunk in, Julia's sobs quieted. She relaxed in his arms, her head tucked under his chin. Minutes later, she was asleep.

37
Returning to the Game

C.J.'s transfer had gone quicker than expected, and Sloan returned within fifteen minutes. He stopped in the waiting room to check on Rick and Julia. Sloan grinned as Rick shrugged his shoulders and pointed questioningly toward the woman in his arms.

Sloan quietly explained, hoping their conversation wouldn't wake Julia.

"I should have warned you," he said. "Parents in Julia's position often seem calm and in control because they have no choice. When the person they depend on shows up, they let go of everything. She's releasing the burden that she wanted to share with you all along. She needs you, but couldn't admit it until she knew you were going to be there for her."

"You should have been a psychiatrist," Rick said. "And, yes, knowing that ahead of time would've helped. It was scary having her railing at me one minute and sound asleep the next."

"You can go in and see C.J. now," Sloan said, not wanting to interrupt their reunion. "He's pretty sleepy, though. Do you want me to wake her up?"

"No." Rick shook his head. "I'll do it." He pulled Julia closer.

Sloan left to go tell C.J. that his mom would be in soon. Julia's parents were on their way too, and he let the nurses know to watch for them and to be prepared for an onslaught of visitors.

"Hopefully the team doesn't find out or this place will be a zoo," he told the head nurse.

Back in the waiting room, Rick brushed the hair back from Julia's face and kissed her forehead softly.

"It's time to wake up. They've got C.J. settled in his room. We can go see him now."

"I'm not asleep," Julia said from the comfort of Rick's embrace. "I woke up when Sloan so rudely interrupted my nap." She stretched and slipped her arms around his neck.

"You're here," she said.

"You're repeating yourself, woman," Rick teased. "Kiss me so we can go see our boy."

She obliged. As she brushed her fingers through his longer hair, and along his neatly trimmed beard, his arms tightened around her. He deepened their kiss.

In the corner of his consciousness, Rick heard the doctor at the nursing station, asking for C.J.'s mom. Thankfully, the doctor's approach gave Rick the chance to break off the embrace before he lost his faltering self-control.

"Mrs. Fitzgerald?" The doctor's face registered surprise as he stepped into the room. He hadn't expected to see Rick Adams with his arm around the waist of his patient's mother.

Rick introduced himself, although it was clearly unnecessary. "Rick Adams," he said. "I'm Julia's soon-to-be fiancé."

The doctor's questioning look turned to a grin as he saw the glare Julia sent Rick's way. "I see."

"We're still in the convincing mode," Rick answered with a grin of his own. Julia recovered, quickly switching into mommy mode.

"How is he?" she asked.

"He's going to be fine. The respiration therapist will be back in an hour to run one more test, but I think then the oxygen mask can come off. I'd like to keep him overnight, just to be sure. We'll plan for his discharge by midmorning tomorrow."

"Thank you so much, Doctor," she said. Rick could feel her relax.

"You need to get some rest, too," he instructed. "Looks like you have backup now, so I'd suggest going home, getting something to eat, and taking a nap. But as much as I prescribe that," he continued, "I don't ever seem to get the moms to agree to it. There are shower facilities down the hall, though, and the recliner in the room turns into a bed."

"'Soon-to-be fiancé'?" Julia turned on Rick as soon as the doctor left. Rick shrugged and playfully ducked as she threw a pillow at him.

C.J. was thrilled to see Rick, but the doctor had cautioned against too much excitement, so their usual antics would have to wait. It was hard to remember that laughter was not the best medicine when recovering from a bout of asthma, so Rick worked at being more serious than usual.

Julia's parents arrived about the same time as Jocelyn and, after greeting their grandson and making sure of his recovery, Joyce accompanied her daughter to the family lounge so she could shower and change clothes. When they returned to the room, Rick insisted that Julia go downstairs for breakfast with Jocelyn and her parents. He planned to read quietly to C.J. and pointed to the stack of children's books the nurses had provided.

Before the group could head downstairs, Rick pulled Julia aside.

"I preferred your other outfit," he said, quietly enough so only she could hear. She was now wearing a button-up top and khakis. Gone was his old jersey.

"What on earth did he say to make you blush like a schoolgirl?" Her mom asked as they walked to the elevator.

"Nothing, Mother." Julia punched the elevator down button several times.

Sloan went home to get some sleep as soon as his wife arrived mid-afternoon. She had picked up Bethany and Bouncer and taken them to Rick's house before coming to the hospital.

"Bethany is fine," Jocelyn assured a concerned Julia. "Bouncer has the run of Rick's house, and Bethany is looking forward to seeing Granny and Grandpa. She did ask about Uncle Rick, though, wondering why they were at his house and he was not."

Rick made a trip home to check on Bethany and fulfill C.J.'s request that he also check on Bouncer. He was gone less than an hour and returned with a book for Julia and himself, informing her clearly that he was staying put for the night.

"I'm much bigger than you," he reminded her, "and you may beat me with your wimpy little fists all you want, but I'm staying."

C.J. was asleep and Rick took the opportunity to pull Julia into his arms. She wrapped her arms around his waist and relaxed against his chest.

"Thank you, Rick." It was obvious she was sleepy again, so he pushed her gently into the large convertible chair next to C.J.'s bed. The nurses had already set it up as a bed, complete with a pillow and blanket for her.

"Try to sleep, sweetheart," Rick said. "I'll be here when you wake up."

38
Home Field Advantage

Shortly after midnight, C.J. was roused by a short coughing spell. Julia shot out of the bed and was by his side in seconds. As she brushed the hair back from his forehead, he relaxed. A movement on the other side of the bed caught her eye. She blinked in surprise.

"Rick?" she asked, uncertainty obvious in her face. "Rick. You're here."

"Yes, my dear," Rick said, now standing across from her. Their whispers were quiet enough to not wake C.J. who had settled quickly back to sleep.

"I thought I was dreaming," her gaze softened.

"Julia," Rick's voice pleaded. "Don't do that to me."

"Do what?"

"Make me want to leap over this bed and make up for not being able to touch you for the last six weeks."

"Oh," she could feel the warmth in her cheeks and decided to change the subject. "Have you been awake this whole time?"

"Still struggling a little with jet lag, even though being in Jamaica helped some," he said, now holding one of her hands across the bed. "Plus, I was distracted."

"Distracted?" she asked, one eyebrow raised.

"Stop that," Rick warned. "Or we will be in danger of putting on a public display of affection that I'm sure C.J., or the nurses for that matter, would not appreciate."

"What's a play of 'fection?" The quiet question came from the young patient. Julia stifled a laugh.

241

"That's something your mom will have to explain, big guy," Rick said after quickly dropping Julia's hands.

"Oh, no, Uncle Rick," Julia said, as she made her way to the door, "I wouldn't rob you of the privilege. I'm going to check in with the nurses. You explain what a 'play of 'fection' is!"

Julia paused right outside the door, which she left slightly ajar. She held up a finger to warn the nurse that had been ready to come in to check on C.J. Julia and the nurse both listened as Rick stumbled through his explanation.

"Well, C.J.," he started, "a *display* of *affection* is when a mommy and a daddy love each other very much and like to show that by hugging and kissing and stuff like that."

The nurse gave Julia a 'thumbs up' sign. "He's a keeper," she whispered, not noticing that Julia had gulped at the 'mommy and daddy' comment.

Back inside the room, C.J. yawned. "Oh," the little boy said, "I thought it was a football thing."

"You go back to sleep, buddy," Rick said.

"I'm glad you're back, Uncle Rick," the young boy's eyes filled with tears. "I missed you."

"I know, C.J." Rick leaned over and kissed the top of the boy's head. "I missed you guys, too." He wiped the tears from the boy's cheeks, as he felt the tears on his own.

"Uncle Sloan says it's okay for boys to cry," C.J. defended his emotional display. "He says you know that for sure."

"I am sure he did," Rick laughed.

The nurse handed Julia a tissue. The tenderness she felt for him at that moment almost evaporated the next morning.

"We're going where?" She asked as he bundled C.J. into the backseat of his truck.

What Rick hadn't told Julia yet was that he had made plans for her to go to his house when C.J. was released. Rooms were already made up for her and the kids in the guest wing of his house. He even insisted that Julia's parents stay there also, knowing that Julia would need her rest.

Although the house was large enough for all of them, he didn't want any hint of indiscretion, so he was crashing at Monica and Garrett's house for several days. Both moms would be there to help care for C.J. until Rick was sure Julia had recovered her equilibrium.

Of course, Rick's design was that she would need several days, if not a week, to recover, but his mom knew that they would be lucky to get Julia to agree to stay more than one night.

True to the prediction, three days later, Julia made her escape. Her parents had left for home that morning, with Mr. Pearson having a work project that needed his attention and Joyce knowing that Julia was anxious to get back to normalcy.

"I couldn't have done this without you, but we need to get back home and back to our routine." Julia hugged Rick's mom and thanked her profusely for all the help.

"My son won't be happy with me for letting you go." Mrs. Adams watched Julia put their bags in the taxi. "Have pity on me!"

"I've got to go back to work tomorrow, and the doctor has cleared C.J. to go to school, too."

"You need to call and tell Rick you're leaving," the older lady tried to convince Julia.

"I know, but I'm a bigger chicken than you are," she said. "Plus, you're his mom. I'm sure he's more afraid of you than you are of him."

Elaine Adams laughed at the probable truth of the statement, but she knew Rick was going to be unhappy no matter what. Unhappy was an understatement.

Julia's phone rang a few minutes after she and the kids got home.

"You better be glad I have mini-camp this week, or I would be pounding on your door and hauling you back to the house, young lady!" Rick's call was short and pointed. He tried to sound more upset than he was. He was disappointed, but not mad. He knew that her staying with him long-term wasn't an option, so he put aside his sulking.

"We have some serious talking to do, you know," he said that evening as he cleaned up the dessert dishes. Even though she wasn't at his house he wasn't willing to go without seeing her every day.

"I need to get back to work and back to normal." Julia deflected the topic.

"You missed two days of work," Rick reminded her. "As brilliant as your students are, mainly because you're their teacher, I think they'll be fine."

Julia ignored his blatant flattery and finished putting away the dishes. He was sitting at the dining room table, reading their book through one more time. He had let Morris ask around to see if there was any interest among his literary friends.

"You have another early day tomorrow, too," she said. "I know we need to talk, but I need to get back on my feet. The last few days have been unsettling."

"Unsettling like a super fun amusement park ride or unsettling like a tornado?" Rick grabbed the tail of her long t-shirt and pulled her around to face him.

"A little of both." She laced her fingers around his neck. The fully recovered C.J. interrupted their kiss.

"Ew!" the boy said as he came bounding into the kitchen, chasing Bouncer.

"Aren't you supposed to be sick, little man?" Rick leaned around Julia and glared playfully at C.J. "Go away while I kiss your mother."

"Bethany's asleep and you promised to tuck us in." C.J. ignored Rick's request.

"Okay, okay." Rick said, stole another quick kiss, and then followed C.J. upstairs.

"We'll talk tomorrow, understand?" Rick tempered his demand with a kiss before he left a few minutes later.

39
Contract Negotiations

"What?" Dr. Mackenzie bellowed into the phone. He quickly realized the insurance coordinator at the hospital didn't deserve his wrath and quickly apologized. "Sorry," he said, "tell me again." Sloan had insisted that Julia put him down as a contact on all her medical forms. He knew from watching many patients and families struggle that the morass of hospital forms, bills, and regulations could be daunting. The insurance office had wisely called him first.

"The policy that Mrs. Fitzgerald listed on her forms has been cancelled. We called to confirm, and even resubmitted the forms. They tell us the policy is no longer in effect."

"You haven't called Mrs. Fitzgerald yet, have you?" Sloan asked, hoping they had not. Julia didn't need to know yet.

"No, we called you first, thinking that you may know if there was some sort of mix-up," the young office worker said, trying nervously to not upset the pleasant, yet somewhat hotheaded, Dr. Mackenzie. He was known for his mild-mannered rants, which were usually aimed at perceived or real injustices.

"Good. Let me handle this, please," Sloan said. "I will get back to you by the end of the day with new payment information, okay?"

"What's up?" Jocelyn asked. They were sitting in his office, sharing a large salad from the hospital cafeteria.

"Those rats! Julia's former in-laws cancelled the kids' medical insurance and didn't bother to tell Julia," he said, pacing the small office—if you could call two steps and a turn "pacing."

"Sit down, dear," Jocelyn said. "You're making me dizzy."

"Rick is going to be furious," Sloan said. "He'll probably march down here and pay the amount in full, and then Julia will be furious. Great. The proverbial rock and hard place!"

"Call Rick," Jocelyn said. "Let him take care of it and let him tell Julia. You and I both know they'll probably be married within a few weeks, and if this is one more hurdle they need to get over, then they better to do it now."

"You're right." Sloan gave his wife an appreciative kiss. "Smartest move I ever made was to marry you."

"You're so right," she said, returning his kiss.

Sloan had left a message for Rick right away. When Rick got the news, he was furious. After he finally calmed down, he called the business office to arrange for his accountant to pay the hospital bill. He also gave instructions for the accountant to either get them added to his policy or open a separate one for them.

Unfortunately, the message that Dr. Mackenzie was handling the situation did not reach the entire office. Julia received a call that afternoon telling her the insurance had been denied. By the time Rick arrived for dinner, she was beyond distraught, but she tried to hide it from him.

Julia's forced smiles didn't fool him.

"Talk to me, Julia," he insisted. "I know something's bothering you. Would it surprise you or make you mad if I told you I know what it is?"

He watched her process his admission. Confusion turned to frustration, then anger.

"Sloan," she said. "They must have called him first."

"Yes," Rick said, pulling her down onto the couch next to him. The kids were watching their favorite cartoon, the one regular show their mom allowed.

"He had no business telling you." Julia tried to scoot away from Rick.

"No business?" Rick hauled her back to him. "Are you saying it doesn't matter that I love you and that we both know where this relationship is going? I think that makes it my business!"

Julia didn't resist the closeness but remained silent. Rick leaned over so the kids wouldn't hear their discussion.

"Even though I've honored your obvious wishes and not brought up the topic yet, you know my intentions."

"Yes," Julia relented. She scooted closer to him on the couch and put his arm around her.

"Don't scare me like that, woman," he said. "We still need to talk, you know."

"I know." She draped her legs across his lap.

"Is Terry free right now?" Rick asked.

"She's done so much, Rick," Julia said. "I hate to keep bugging her."

As she pulled herself closer, enjoying the warmth of his arms, the doorbell rang. Rick burst out laughing at the look on Julia's face when she opened the door. It was Terry and Stephen.

"Who wants ice cream?" they asked as they unloaded a bag of groceries on the kitchen counter.

"Me! Me!" the cries came from the smallest of the ice-cream lovers in the room.

Rick filled Stephen in on their great timing, grabbed Bouncer's leash, and then pulled Julia out to the beautifully landscaped and softly lit path that wound through the complex.

"Perfect." He pulled her into a quick hug as they walked the Yorkie slowly around the small lake. "You can't say that wasn't a sign from above."

"True," Julia agreed.

Rick stopped at one of the wooden swings along the trail. Bouncer, tired from the exercise, plopped down underneath a bush.

"So, let's talk," Rick said. "I love you. You love me."

"If you break into song, I'm going back inside," Julia threatened. "You sound like that annoying children's television jingle."

They sat quietly, Rick trying to put his thoughts into the perfect words to convince her that this relationship was a good thing.

"I love you, Rick," Julia spoke first, surprising him and thrilling him at the same time. "Yes, I'm still nervous about this huge leap that you want me to take. I appreciate your patience."

Rick kissed her gently, then tucked her hair behind her ear and ran his finger along her jaw. She snuggled closer.

"Julia, I have not decided exactly when, but I am going to propose officially. Soon. I'll expect an answer right then. If I give you too much time, I'm afraid you're going to think of all the reasons why this won't work instead of concentrating on all the reasons it will."

"You know that I still struggle with the idea of being part of the world you live in, but I realized something while you were gone. I have been on my own for so long that I didn't recognize it at first."

"Go on." He kissed her forehead gently. "You have my full attention."

"You settled into my life so quickly, I was shocked, and frightened, with how comfortable I was. It took me a while to figure out why I was so afraid." She sensed that he was going to interrupt her. "Let me finish."

"When you got hurt," she continued, "I panicked. And then when you had me talk about James," Julia's voice trailed off. "My reaction to you"—she blushed at the memory of her behavior—"was so unexpected that I had to figure out why I acted like that."

"It's simple," Rick offered. "I'm irresistible."

"Hush." She elbowed him. "That's true, but it's not the entire reason. You brought out a vulnerability in me that was so unexpected, it frightened me. I found myself crying more than I have in my entire life." She tugged him down and peered at him nose to nose. "Do you know how frustrating that is, mister?"

He grinned. "I'd say I'm sorry but that would be a lie," he said. "A little vulnerability has been good for you, Miss I'm-in-Control and Life-is-just-fine. So, explain exactly what you learned while I was suffering in exile."

"I know Sloan told you about the night he and Jocelyn had to rescue me. The patience that everyone had shown me for all these years is overwhelming."

"Julia, you're being too hard on yourself. You lost your husband. You had a small child and then weeks later, a newborn. It's not surprising that you never set aside time to mourn." He captured a quick kiss before letting her continue.

"You're biased, but thank you," she said. "Sloan and Jocelyn wisely let me figure out the issues behind my reaction to you, and how it led me to finally letting myself grieve for James."

"This is the part I've been curious about," Rick admitted. "As willing as I am to play my part, exactly what did I do, or not do, to get you to that point?"

"The fear of being in a relationship turned quickly to the fear of *not* being in a relationship." Julia wrapped her arms around his waist and leaned her head on his chest. His strong arms encircled her. "When you stopped saying, 'I love you,' in your emails, I felt lost. I realized that depending on you, wanting you in my life, wanting to be part of your life, were all now important to me. Finally having the freedom from my pain and guilt to be with someone made the thought of losing you devastating."

"I stopped ending my letters with that because I didn't think you wanted to hear it anymore," Rick said, resting his chin on her head.

"I know. Garrett explained how convoluted my logic was." Bouncer interrupted their lingering kiss with a plea for attention.

"Go away, dog," Rick said, as he lifted the pup onto his lap.

"So, that's it?" he asked as Julia nestled closer. "Where does that leave us?"

"It's clear to me now that God has indeed brought you to me, so I've decided to be brave." She saw his grin and knew he would be gloating, so she sighed in resignation. "As much as I'm still not thrilled with the idea, I know God is in this. I guess I'll have to give in."

"You are a cruel, cruel woman." His passionate kiss proved he didn't believe his own words.

40

The Interception

Spring meetings continued for the next several days. Rick's duties as team captain meant he missed the next couple of nights of dinner with Julia and the kids. His late-night calls had to suffice.

Julia planned to avoid being alone with him for some weeks to come, knowing his proposal would be coming soon, but every time he called, she got more accustomed to the idea.

The next Saturday, Monica called to invite them to a park she had recently found in a nearby neighborhood. She wanted to check it out and rounded up the crew wives and kids to come along. Julia knew getting out of the house would be good for the kids. For the past week, they had only been out of the house to go to school.

"Garrett usually watches the kids on Saturdays, but with the coach calling a team meeting, I'll have to entertain them today. I think the rain that the weatherman predicted yesterday will hold off, and maybe the threat of bad weather will mean we'll have the park to ourselves," Monica said hopefully.

Monica, Carolyn Burns, and Becky Michaels, along with all their kids, were already at the park when Julia arrived.

"Is C.J. okay to play?" Carolyn asked. They all knew about the visit to the hospital.

"Yes, as long as I keep an eye on him," Julia said. "The doctor said that in the long run, lots of exercise is actually good. It helps strengthen his lungs. Of course, that means soccer will be better for him than football."

"That's going to go over well," Monica said with a laugh.

Shortly after their picnic lunch, Julia looked up to the sound of several trucks pulling into the playground's gravel parking lot.

"They didn't!" Monica laughed. "Julia, you'd better run. That's Rick and the rest of them. Apparently, he's run out of patience. You need to make him work for the honor a little bit!"

Julia knew it was foolish to think she could outrun even the slowest professional football player, but instinct took over. She bolted across the playground, dodging between the swings and around the slide. It didn't help that she was laughing, either.

Garrett, Zeke, and Tyson hit the ground running. As if they had diagrammed the play in the locker room, they cut off her retreat with precision. Bouncer yipped noisily at the excitement, his barks getting more frantic when he spotted Rick.

Rick calmly walked to the far picnic table, away from the sight of the stunned ladies and curious children. He sat facing the spectacle of his minions chasing down his girlfriend. It was quite funny.

Garrett reached her first. With his back to Rick, he made sure Julia was a willing participant. "Are you okay with this spectacle, Julia?" She laughed and nodded. He grinned in return. "We'll have to make this look convincing, so try to struggle a little."

He scooped her up and slung her gently over his shoulder. She pounded his broad back, kicking and wiggling fruitlessly.

"Put me down, you big bully!" she yelled.

"I will, in a second," Garrett said, calmly walking toward Rick.

"Your lady, my lord." Garrett stood regally before his team captain. The other two, whose feet were all Julia could see, apparently found this hilarious.

"Traitors!" she said, lifting up as best she could to glare at them.

"Thank you, Sir Garrett," Rick said. "You may leave her here and join your ladies. We won't be but a minute, I'm sure."

Garrett unceremoniously plopped Julia in front of Rick, her back toward the seated quarterback, and steadied her before grinning at her crossed arms and furious face.

"My lady," the huge linebacker bowed.

"Traitor," Julia repeated, but she smiled as he bowed over her hand. As soon as Garret started to walk away, Julia moved to follow him. Rick had hooked a finger through her back belt loop. She wasn't going anywhere.

"My lady," Rick said, "we have unfinished business." Rick tugged her closer until her back rested against his chest. She sighed. His arms came around her, and she leaned her head back onto his shoulder.

"I think this belongs to you," Rick said, opening his hand. A gold band with a simple diamond sat in his palm.

She gasped.

"Marry me, Julia," Rick said. His words were more like a command than a question.

"Yes, Rick," Julia said, as she slipped the ring onto her finger. As he turned her around, she added, "If I must."

Rick laughed and rewarded her acquiescence with a kiss. Sounds of cheers echoed from across the playground.

Epilogue
Once Upon a Victory

"What do you want for your birthday?"

"Cake, ice cream, balloons." Julia snuggled with her husband in their family-sized hammock. "No clowns, though."

"Darn," Rick said. "Remind me to call and cancel the clowns."

"Ha, ha." Julia poked him. "Very funny."

The family was enjoying the quiet lazy Sunday afternoon. Preseason started in a week, and this would be their last reprieve for several months.

"Honestly, though, what do you want?" Rick asked again. "I'll never be able to top your gift to me, but I'd like to do something special."

"I still think you wanted to get married on your birthday so that you'd be less likely to forget our anniversary," Julia teased her husband. "I know you gave us all some line about it being the only weekend open, but I still think that was just an excuse."

"I'll never admit such nefarious motivation," Rick said.

"Well, I could use some new clothes." Julia sighed.

"Yeah, right," Rick said. "Like that will ever happen." It was a constant struggle to get his new wife to spend any money on herself.

"I'm serious about the clothes." She wiggled closer to his warmth, listening to the sounds of C.J. and Bethany playing next to them on the deck. "But since you think I'm so hard to buy for, how about I give you a gift instead?"

"C'mon, Julia," Rick said. "You've got to help me out here. You can't give me something for your birthday. At least give me some ideas."

"Sorry, but I've already got a gift for you, big guy." Julia tried to keep her voice calm.

"Is that so?" Rick pulled her closer. "Tell me."

"Next to the marvelous privilege of spending the rest of your life with me"—she paused to let him assure her that indeed he relished the privilege—"what is something that would make you happy?"

"Oh, I don't know." Rick was distracted as she walked her fingers across his chest. "What could possibly make me any happier?"

"Think, Rick." She waited for her words to sink in. Moments later, she felt him tense.

"Julia," he murmured her name. His voice was quiet, almost reverent. "Are you telling me what I think you're telling me?"

"I don't know." She leaned back, pulled his chin around, and kissed him. "What do you think I'm telling you?"

"Are you... Are we...?" Rick was almost incoherent.

"Say it, Rick." Julia watched his dawning excitement.

"A baby?" His words were part question, part eager plea.

"Yes, dear," Julia said. Rick gathered his wife in his arms.

"I love you," he said.

"I know," she said. "And that, my dear husband, is the best birthday gift I could ever receive."

"Mommy, is Daddy Rick crying or laughing?" A voice from the edge of the hammock interrupted their embrace.

"Both, sweetheart, because he's happy," Julia said to the blonde curls that were all she could see of her daughter.

"Why?" Bethany asked. Rick groaned. The three-year-old's favorite word for the last month had been 'why'. Rick had counted ten in a row one night.

"Come here, Princess." Rick pulled the little girl up into the hammock. "You too, big guy," he said to C.J., who was playing with Bouncer below them.

When they were all settled in, Rick shared their news.

"I'm going to tell you a story," he said. "Once upon a time, there lived a beautiful grown-up mommy princess named Julia. Princess Julia had a handsome son named Prince Curtis and a lovely daughter named Princess Elizabeth Ann."

"That's us," C.J. explained to Bethany in his best big-brother tone.

"One day Princess Julia met a lonely prince, named Prince Richard...."

~A note from the author~

Thank you so much for taking the time to read Rick and Julia's story. I hope you enjoyed it.

My prayer is that you found encouragement, a few laughs, and a good dose of romance.

I'd love to hear from you. Words of encouragement are good for everyone, and for me, are needed as I sometimes wonder if others love my characters as much as I do!

You can find me on Facebook (Lyn Ellerbe Books) and my website (Lynellerbebooks.com)

And above all these put on love, which binds
everything together in perfect harmony.
Colossians 3:14

Lyn